WARRIORS OF THE WASTELAND

I.Y. WADE

Limits of Liability and Disclaimer of Warranty
The author and publisher shall not be liable for your misuse of this material. This book is strictly for entertainment purposes.

Warning – Disclaimer
This is a work of fiction. Names, characters, business, places, events, and incidents are either the products of the author's imagination or used in a fictitious manner. Any resemblance to actual persons, living or dead or actual events is purely coincidental.

Cover Design: O'niel De La Cruz – Designs on the Fly
Interior Design: Shavonna Bush – All Write Editing
Editor: Shavonna Bush – All Write Editing

I.Y. Wade
166publishing@gmail.com
166publishing.com

Printed in the United States of America
First Printing, 2018
ISBN 978-1-5136-3425-8

WARRIORS OF THE WASTELAND

Acknowledgments

I'd like to give thanks to our Father who art in Heaven and to Christ the Messiah, for through them all things are possible.

To my family, friends, and the readers who have supported me and given me the encouragement to continue, thank you, thank you, and thank you!

Finally, to my son; the wind beneath my wings, you make me a better man. I love you more than life!

I.Y. Wade

WARRIORS OF THE WASTELAND

Preface

The beginning of the end of the age of innocence! That's how I would describe my life growing up in the Bronx in the 70's. The Civil Rights Movement was in America's rearview mirror, and the Viet Nam war would come to an end in 1975; Life was indeed carefree, but a change would come and come quickly. As a young boy, I would be exposed to violence, sex, and drugs all before the age of ten. This account is a journal of those shortcomings.

Some will find the words that I have written on these pages offensive. I understand, but what I have written is true. Well, at least 75% of it is. The other 25% is me taking a bit of literary licensing to make an otherwise intriguing story even more captivating. Names have been changed to protect the identity of family, friends, and associates, but I've still been as honest as possible, and I pray you enjoy the story.

Prologue

I had gone over this moment at least a hundred times in my head, but here I was having a hard time finding the words to get my point across. I didn't want to come off as preachy or arrogant with a know it all demeanor, but the truth is, I had unknowingly been preparing for this moment my entire life since that day in 1977, watching Alex Haley's "Roots" on television as a youth, even up until this point as an adult, realizing that Blacks in America are still second-class citizens angered me. Now if I could only get my crew to see our plight. Wasn't no time like the present. I had to seize the moment. The truth is our future looked bleak.

"Tell me what it takes to make y'all niggas' hungry?" I asked talking to my right-hand man Pap and my two lieutenants Ya-ya and Stan.

"I mean look at us, we ain't got shit!"

They could see I was upset.

"Don't y'all see? At a glance, this neighborhood is at least 50% Black, right? Except for the few barber shops and beauty salons, how many of the businesses are Black huh? None that's how many, none! No bodegas, no supermarkets, no clothin' stores, no restaurants, nothin'! All we fuckin' eat is Spanish food, Chinese food, and Jamaican food almost every day. We have to go at least ten or fifteen blocks to get some fuckin' soul food and then if we lucky, that restaurant may stay open two years tops.

"It ain't no different on the streets! Puerto Ricans got the dope game locked, Dominicans got the coke game locked, and Jamaicans is makin' a killin' wit' the weed. The Arabs got all the smoke shops, delis, and chicken places. They sending all that money home to support their cause, and a Black man can't get a business loan to save his life. Now here come the Africans bringin' in heroin and coke. Plus, they openin' up shippin' businesses, African markets and becomin' our landlords.

"What I'm sayin' is this, I'm not in this shit for sneakers, jewelry or fuckin' cars. I want businesses, real estate, restaurants, clubs, clothing stores and anything else a nigga' can make a dollar from. If y'all ain't serious about this, then leave! I'm tired of being on the bottom; we already know the outcome. Nine times outta' ten, we gon' end up in jail, the grave, or worse than the grave, poor! If we gon' do this shit then les' do it right.

"Anybody, and I mean anybody who's not with this organization is gon' have to pay. You understand? If we don't eat-nobody eats. I on't give a fuck. If you ain't givin' back to the hood and makin' sure niggas' know where to git' it, then you gon' pay one way or another. That goes for any of them motherfuckin' cats that's gittin' it, and I ain't just talkin' bout' givin' out turkeys on Thanksgivin'. Athletes, rappers, actors, doctors, lawyers, and entrepreneurs from all walks of life are gon' hafta' pay! Not only that, we gon' be equal opportunity extortionist. We gon' touch the unions, boxing, and gambling. We gon' make motherfuckas' let us in Hollywood, the radio, and the newspaper business.

"This is where we at; I say we take this shit to a new level. We gon' change the way the world looks at the Black man in America. If a motherfucka' wanna' sell oranges in the hood, we better be gittin' a cut. Our people got the highest rate of AIDS, highest rate of incarceration, the highest percentage of children in the foster care system, highest percentage of unemployment, and to top it all off, motherfuckas' is barely gittin' an education. I swear to God Black America is lost! But this is a new era, a new agenda," I said smacking my hands together for emphasis.

"We gon' do whatever it takes to git' niggas' on the right track. We gon' do what Malcolm-X and the Black Panthers failed to do, we gon' galvanize Black America. We gon' change the face of America and the world over, or we gon' maim and murder til' we do!"

Psalms 9:12
For, when looking for bloodshed,
God will certainly remember those very ones;
He is sure not to forget outcry of the afflicted ones!

Although the recession officially ended more than a year ago, 2010 saw the largest increase in poverty following an economic downturn in the United States since 1981. Nowhere is poverty more apparent today than in the Bronx. Specifically, the South Bronx. One in three (30.2%) Bronx residents live below the poverty level, less than $18,310 per year for a family of three, and nearly one in seven (13.4%) experience severe poverty (earning less than 50% of the federal poverty level), both of which are twice the state and national rates (see table 1). The situation is even more dire in the South Bronx, which constitutes Congressional District 16, the poorest congressional district in the country, where the poverty rate is 36.9%, and the severe poverty rate is 16.6%.

High rates of poverty, combined with overcrowding, rent burdens, and low vacancy levels—push families out of stable housing and into homelessness. While many Bronx residents live in poverty, Black and Hispanic families are most at risk of becoming homeless. Nearly one-third (28.3%) of Blacks in the Bronx are poor. In 2010, more than half of New York City's homeless family shelter applicants were Black (52.8%).

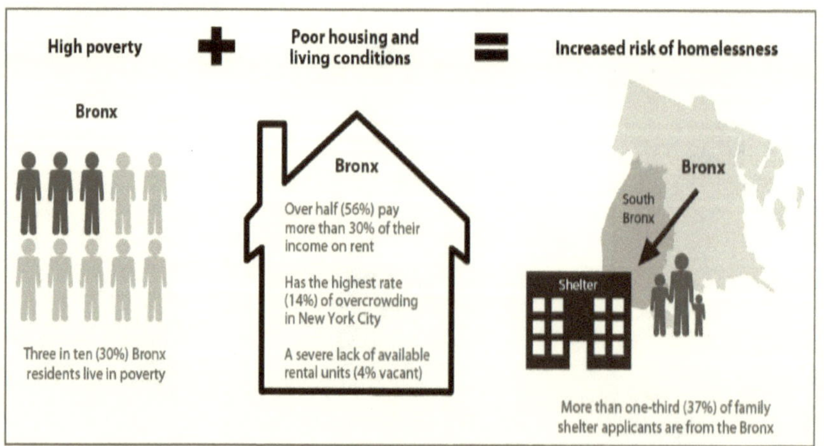

Chapter 1
GENESIS: In the Beginning

"Mommy, Llord is crying."

That was the voice of my cousin Asia telling my Aunt Pat that I was lying in bed crying again. That was my earliest childhood memory. Why was I crying? Well, because I missed my mother, Zenobia. She had been in federal prison for quite some time now. I didn't remember how long, but as a young boy, it seemed like forever to me.

I really had no reason to cry. My aunt was good to me and my younger sister Yvonne or "Vonnie" as she was known. Vonnie was the one who started calling me Llord because she had a hard time pronouncing my name. You know how young kids are with names, so the name Llord stuck with me. My real name is Lloyd, Lloyd Atkins.

Vonnie and I lived with my aunt while our mother was away doing time for bank robbery and attempted murder. My aunt treated us just like she treated her two daughters, my younger cousin Asia and my older cousin Karen. At the time, I was five, Vonnie was three, Asia was four, and Karen was seven.

We all lived at 2158 Mapes Ave. in apartment 1D. That's where the make-up of my character was formed without me realizing it. We would play games of the ghetto, like ring-a-levio, manhunt, run-catch, and kiss, and hot peas and butter. Hot peas and butter is a game you play with an old belt. The object of the game is to hide the belt and guide the other kids playing in the vicinity of the belt by saying hot if they're getting near or cold if they stray too far. Once a person finds the belt, they wail on the person closest to them. It sounds sadistic, but trust me, it was fun like a motherfucker.

We would spend our summer days outside in the courtyard eating egg sandwiches and drinking Kool-Aid. I remember one sunny afternoon a UPS truck pulled up in front of the building. A White delivery man jumped out of the truck and entered the courtyard to drop off a package. He only got a couple of steps when these two brothers ran in behind him. One of the dudes pulled out a switchblade and put it to his neck while the other nigga' went in his pockets. The poor bastard only had a lousy five dollar bill, but they snatched that and took off running. The delivery man's face was beet red as he ran out of the courtyard. I don't have to tell you it would be a long time before we saw UPS on our block again.

Some days we would just eat our sandwiches out back on the fire escape. That's what Karen and I were doing that day I saw a toy gun down in the backyard.

"Karen look!" I said excitedly.

"Look at what?" she asked.

"Down in the yard," I said, pointing down in the backyard. "A toy gun."

Her eyes lit up. "Hurry up; go git' it," she said.

I ran downstairs and picked it up. Being young I didn't notice how heavy it was. I ran into the kitchen and back out onto the fire escape and handed it to her. When I passed it to her, she didn't notice the weight of the gun either. She pointed the gun directly at my face and pulled the trigger. *Blam!* Yes, it was a real thirty-eight revolver.

When she pulled the trigger I ducked. Karen's hands were shaking as she tried to squeeze the gun through the fire escape bars. I ran back into the house through the window to tell my Aunt Pat, but having heard the shot, she was already running into the kitchen screaming.

"What the hell was that noise?"

We showed her the gun and told her what happened. She called the police and gave them the gun. They took her statement and left. Finding a discarded gun in the hood is nothing unusual, especially in the seventies, but the thing that stands out in my mind as I tell this story is what made me duck? As a child, I believed the gun to be a toy, so was I psychic? Were angels watching over me, or had God Almighty himself come off of his throne to intervene in my young life?

My Aunt Pat would take us to our great-grandmother and grandmother's church over on Hoe Avenue. It was one of those old-school churches where all the kids had to join the choir. I remember the color of the robes; they were a midnight navy blue color that stood out against my white button-up shirt.

I didn't pay much attention to the sermon. I only went to church and sang in the choir because I had to. My great-grandmother didn't play. At the time, I suppose she was in her mid to late eighties. She had beautiful silver hair that was as fine as silk. Her name was June badger, a name that reflected her Black and Sioux Indian heritage. I recall her telling us tales of how as a child her parents and some of her older siblings who were sharecroppers told her stories of the slavery they were born into. At the time we as children didn't understand the significance of our lineage having been free for a mere three generations.

After the service, the congregation would go downstairs for some southern style cookin' wit' all the fixings. Turkey wings, potato salad, rice and gravy, with black-eyed peas, string beans and a variety of other soul foods. My favorite part of the day.

On some occasions, the upstairs neighbor Ms. Audrey and her daughter Barbara would go to church with us. After church, my cousins, my sister, Barbara and I were at my aunt's house playing in the living room. I'm not sure where my Aunt Pat and Ms. Audrey were, but me and Barbara, who I think was the same age as me, ended up under the covers humping. All while Karen, Asia, and even little Vonnie watched, which really wasn't a big deal because me and my cousins were humping too. We didn't know any better at the time, but I guess most young kids experiment with their siblings. Although at the time, we as Blacks tried to act like it was a just a Hispanic thing.

Barbara and I pulled our pants down. I recollect trying to put my penis in her vagina. I also vividly remember the warmth and tightness of her vagina as I tried to insert my manhood, well boyhood into her. She told me she couldn't feel anything, so I pushed until I felt a pop. I know now that it was her hymen or "cherry" as we call it in the hood. She said it hurt and started crying, so we stopped, pulled our pants up and went on playing games like nothing happened. I guess you could call that my first sexual experience, I was six at the time.

My Aunt Pat would drink a lot: She would spend all day on the weekends and sometimes all night down the block at this place called the "Mapes Bar." I would go down the block to the bar and buy peanuts from the little red vending machines. You know the ones, where you put a quarter in, turn the slot and a handful of candy or whatever comes out. In those days it was only a nickel.

We kids would often go down to the bar and get my aunt. As a child, I didn't understand alcoholism, but unfortunately, that's what my aunt was an alcoholic. One night she threw a house party, and some people from the bar came over. Everyone was drinking and partying, having a good time until around one o'clock in the morning, but this one guy hung around after the party. When everyone left, he pulled out a knife and told my aunt to go into the bathroom. He must have told her to be quiet because we couldn't hear anything. But inside the bathroom, he was raping her. When they came out, my aunt had a deep cut on her hand. Her rapist didn't say a word, he just looked at us, zipped his pants up and headed out the door.

After about fifteen minutes my aunt called the police. They came and asked my aunt some questions, gave her their cards and told her to call if she saw him in the neighborhood again. In those days there wasn't much the police could do. There weren't any forensics or DNA to speak of, so consequently, her rapist was never caught.

As for Barbara and her mother Ms. Audrey, who happened to be a close friend of my aunt, she was found dead in her apartment. She would often come downstairs to talk with my Aunt Pat from time to time. Ms. Audrey was gorgeous, and although I was young, I was old enough to know what fine was, and Ms. Audrey was fine. She was a beautiful woman with legs like a thoroughbred, but she wasn't into men, she was a lesbian who went out with this butch type of chick. I don't remember her lover's name, but that's not important. What stuck with me is the circumstances surrounding her death.

I heard she was diabetic and one day she had a fatal diabetic seizure. We overheard my aunt and the adults talking about what happened. They said Ms. Audrey's lover found her dead in the house. Her face was covered in the blood that she had vomited up as a result of the seizure. She walked into the house, saw Ms. Audrey's lifeless body on the floor, and pried a ring that Ms. Audrey's deceased mother had given her from her bloody fingers and left her there.

As a child, consciously things like that don't immediately affect you, but perhaps on a subconscious level as you mature it makes you cynical. After Ms. Audrey's funeral, Barbara went to live with her grandmother. That would be the last time I saw her.

The great thing about being young in the Bronx was that there were so many things going on, both good and bad. Across the street was the Bronx Zoo and at least twice a week in the summertime we would sneak into the zoo without paying. A couple of blocks away there was Little Italy, and at that time Little Italy was just that! The adults called it "Ginny Town". There were no Blacks, no Puerto Ricans, no Jews, no one but Italians, and maybe the Irish.

As a boy, I called Little Italy "Ginny Town," because that's what I heard the adults refer to it as. I didn't understand the racist connotations that it had. In fact, I wouldn't become aware of what racism was, or what it meant until a few years later in my life. In most parts of the Bronx in those times we had gangs. The Black gangs that I knew of were the Black Falcons, the Black Spades, and the Peacemakers. The Puerto Ricans had the Flying Dutchmen, the Ching-a-Lings, the Savage Skulls, and the Crazy Homicides. The Italians had the "Golden Ginnies". The Golden Ginnies protected their neighborhood like it was a bank, but still, a group of us from our block would go to Ginny Town to steal. We would take petty shit like soda, potato chips, and things of that nature.

It was always a bunch of us. Some of the older kids would lead the pack; Jimmy, who was about twelve, and Peter, who was also around twelve. My main man Steve, my other partners Eddie, Kevin, his little brother Anthony and even a couple of the girls who used to hang out with the boys would tag along. We went into this deli where there was this old Italian man was working behind the counter. There were a few other people in the store standing around socializing, but we didn't pay much attention to them. We were focused on the chips and the sodas. I slid around the back to the soda refrigerator and stuck a bottle of Pepsi in my shorts. The Pepsi was sticking out from here to Mississippi but pops just looked me dead in the face and didn't say a word. Mission accomplished, or so we thought! Those old geezers were setting us up. We got a block away, and the fucking Golden Ginnies started chasing us. We were out, hauling ass back to the neighborhood, but they caught Peter.

It wasn't enough that they beat him, but those crazy motherfuckers shot him up with heroin. Somehow when he made it back to the block, he was tore up. He looked sick. His eyes were rolling back in his head. When his mother saw him, she started screaming hysterically. His father came running down the block, saw his boy overdosing on the ground, scooped him up and rushed him to the hospital.

It didn't end there. The Black Falcons found out what happened, and from what the streets said they had an ongoing beef with the Golden Ginnies. They went up to Little Italy and started putting their foot deep in some Italian ass. By nightfall, there was a full-blown race riot! Before it was all over a Black Falcon named "Big George" was dead, stores in Little Italy were looted and burned, and the whole crew of kids, myself included, got the worse ass whipping of our lives.

It would be almost two decades before I would step foot in Little Italy again, and though still mostly Italian, it's now a mixed neighborhood of Blacks, Hispanics and any other nationality that can afford to live there. It's funny how time will change things that men won't. What was amazing about growing up in that era was that everything still felt relatively new as far as drugs and violence were concerned in the Black neighborhoods. The Italians, Irish, and the Jews had their gang wars during prohibition and the battle for organized labor, but after Vietnam, it was the niggas and Hispanics turn.

My first exposure to the drug war happened right across the street. A Spanish man was standing outside his building in a white tee-shirt. Three cars came speeding down the block, a red Corvette, a black Corvette, and a bright yellow Corvette. There was a Black man driving each one. All I heard was *pow*! It was a single shot. The Spanish man standing across the street fell to the ground; a red spot began to spread in the middle of his tee-shirt. All the kids stood there and watched as his family drug him into the house. I was too young to understand why he got shot. I knew nothing about drugs, but all too soon I would learn.

I didn't have much of a father figure in my life at that point except my Uncle Darryl. Now he wasn't my real uncle, just my Aunt Pat's boyfriend. Karen and Asia used to call him daddy, but he wasn't their real father either. Like many of the kids in the ghetto we all had different fathers. Karen's real father's name was Clarence. I think Asia's father's name was Jerry, but I never saw Clarence or Jerry at my Aunt Pat's house. Vonnie's father's name was Trevor and as for me, not only did I not know who my father was, I didn't even know his name. Me and Asia's last name was Atkins, Karen was named after her father whose last name was Johnson, and Vonnie's last name was Patterson. In the sixties, everyone was into some "Make love not war," peace and whatever, but it left many Black children without fathers. I guess all that free love wasn't free after all; it came with a terrible price. As I grew older, I often wondered how a man could just up and leave his children and not give a second thought about their welfare.

Uncle Darryl was one of those old school niggas, clean as hell. His hair was fried, dyed and laid to the side, but between you and me, that niggas feet used to stink. He would take his shoes off, and the whole room would be lit the fuck up. He would pop in and out of my Aunt Pat's life from time to time, never really helping her out with any of the bills. You know how niggas come over when they want some pussy. He cared enough to be a father figure in our lives for many, many years, but never cared enough to make sure Karen and Asia had a decent Christmas. Some twenty years later when I would See Uncle Darryl again, he looked like a homeless crackhead, but as a child, he was the only male role model I had to identify with.

He helped to make our house a home, and in some ways because of him, my cousins and I are like brothers and sisters whose life was pretty much that of your average adolescents, but every once in a while something would happen to shake things up like the time I was molested by my babysitter Michelle.

Michelle was this pretty fourteen-year-old neighbor who would babysit us from time to time. One day we were playing hide and seek in the house, and Michelle was "It." Well, when she caught me, she took me to the bedroom and pulled my pants down and tried to sit on my penis. It didn't even occur to me that I was being molested when my penis slid into her vagina. Before she could get into a rhythm, my seventeen-year-old cousin Mickey who was visiting, burst into the room, saw what was happening and said, "I'm tellin' auntie." Later that night my aunt, Michelle's mother, Michelle, Mickey and I were all in the kitchen.

My aunt was telling me "Don't worry baby you didn't do nothin."

I didn't do nothing! Damn, right I didn't do anything. I was about to do something before Mickey, and her big mouth came bursting into the room. No, seriously I'm bullshitting. I was still too young to understand sex despite my experimentation. Nothing happened to me, but Michelle was put on punishment and forbidden to step foot in our house. It wasn't a big deal to me, the only thing that bothered me was when Karen and her girlfriends would try to pull my pants down in the courtyard so they could see my penis. I didn't realize that I had a big penis or what the big deal was (no pun intended.), but I would come to understand the power that a man possesses if he is well endowed. A large penis is just as important as a master's degree, (especially if you know how to use it) at least in a young man's mind. As I matured, I realized that there are many more qualities that attract women, intelligence, power, self-confidence to name a few, but a big dick don't hurt either.

Not long after the incident with Michelle, my cousin Mickey would let me watch her use the bathroom. I can recall the pre-cum on the lips of her vagina, go figure, she told on Michelle and turned around and did the same thing. In many ways, I think it has contributed to my fascination with the female genitalia, specifically my oral fetish.

Chapter 2
Zenobia Comes Home

Out of the blue, Zenobia was back. It wasn't like it was a big event or anything; on the contrary, it was as though she never left. One day we looked up, and there she was, Zenobia Atkins. When she finished her prison stint, she came to Aunt Pat's house, packed Vonnie and me up, and we went to stay at our grandmother's house until she got on her feet. The three of us would sleep on the floor. Every once in a while my mother would sleep with no underwear on. I can remember the scent of her womanhood under the covers while Vonnie and I would play games at the bottom of her feet. Maybe that's where I also developed my love for the smell of pussy. I know it's sick, but take into consideration what I had already been exposed to.

My mother must have been home a month when she met this motherfucker named Jake Bryson. He seemed cool. They dated for a while, and before you know it, my mother had us moving upstairs to his house. He lived in the next building across from my Aunt Pat, so it wasn't too traumatic for Vonnie and me. We still went to the same school and had the same friends. Shit started out smooth like it always does when a nigga is trying to make a good impression on a woman by being really nice to her children. But before you know it Prince Charming turns into a motherfucking monster.

I remember the night Vonnie and I got together and decided we were going to call Jake daddy. We got out of the tub that night and put our PJ's on. At that time I was eight and Vonnie was six. We strolled into the living room which was also my mother and Jake's bedroom, and said, "Goodnight mommy! Goodnight daddy!" We ran off into our bedroom feeling as though we had re-invented the wheel. But that feeling of euphoria wouldn't last very long. The next day Jake sat us down and told us that he wasn't our father and we shouldn't call him daddy. Now that shit hurt, and to tell the truth, it had a lasting effect on my sister and me. As we got older, we refused to call Jake daddy, even when he asked us to.

Life outside on Mapes Ave. was still great, but things upstairs were miserable for us. Jake had just come home from Vietnam, and he brought home a lot of peculiarities with him. Sometimes Vonnie and I would be playing in our room with the door open, and when we would look up, Jake would be standing there watching us from in between the crack of the door. After we caught him spying on us a couple of times we started closing the door when we were playing. That was just one of the head trips he would subject us to.

It escapes me when the physical abuse started, but when it did, it seemed as though it was interminable. I have always been an A-type personality, always up and about, talkative, and ambitious with my own ideas on how I feel things should be done. Those traits are great when you're an adult, but when you're eight or nine years old it's categorized as "hyperactivity" or "bad behavior" and that's a problem. I mean, maybe I was physically abused, or maybe I wasn't, but Jake would beat the shit out of Vonnie and me. He would walk into the room and give us a speech on whatever it was that we did wrong; tell us to take off all of our clothes and strip down naked. He would then talk to us a little longer, and then he would tell us to bend over and grab onto the bedpost. He would take the belt out of his bathrobe pocket and start whipping us. *Wap, Wap, Wap*. He beat us over and over again. We would have welts all over our tiny bodies. It didn't hurt me physically as much as it hurt me seeing my younger sister naked and covered in welts.

I heard stories about abuse where children are beaten with broomsticks and extension cords, but I never thought that we were abused. My best friend Eddie would come to school with black eyes and a busted lip, so my ass whippings were minor to me. But as I said, I was hyper in school so my mother and Jake would tell the teacher to sign the back of my notebook every day to see if I was bad or good that day in school. Well, this particular morning before I left school Jake told me that if I get one more bad report, he was going to have "something special" for me when I got home. All that day in my young mind I believed I was behaving well, but at the end of the day when it was time to get my notebook signed by the teacher, she thought differently. I'll never forget her name. Mrs. Rubberbarrell. It's pronounced just like it's spelled {R-u-b-b-e-r-b-a-r-r-e-l-l}. Neither she nor I had any idea what I was headed home to.

When I got home, Jake opened up my notebook, took a look inside and saw that Mrs. Rubberbarrell had written that I had been misbehaving all day. He looked at me and told me to go into the room and take off my shirt and undershirt. He stood about six foot three, and I was about four foot nine, maybe fifty-five pounds. I was small and frail for my age. When Jake called me into the kitchen, he was standing by the stove with a butter knife on the front burner. The butter knife was orange it was so fucking hot. He grabbed me by my arm and pulled me over his knee. I heard my flesh searing before I felt it burning. I started screaming and pleading like all children do, swearing I would never misbehave again. It felt like he had it on my skin forever. When he finished, he told me that the next time I took my little ass to school and acted up, he would have the iron plugged in and waiting for me. (Yes, just like that episode of *Good Times* when Penny's mother burned her with an iron). As you can see, he picked up a lot of sick habits over in "Nam." For the next few years, there would be more incidents like that one.

Once I was outside playing stickball, and I told a friend to "Hurry up and throw the fuckin' ball."

Well, you know who walked by. He didn't say a word. He just looked at me and kept walking. When I got upstairs Jake had a large piece of Ivory Soap waiting for me to chew. When I began to chew it, it felt like razors were cutting into my gums. I learned my lesson. After that, I watched what I said when I was in my neighborhood. Another time, Jake was going over my homework with me. I think it was math. I was having a difficult time understanding the work; Jake picked me up and threw me across the living room where I landed square on a nail. He never asked if I was okay, he simply told me to go into the room and shut the door. Some thirty years later I still have that scar on my leg. I hated Jake as much as I feared him. The thought never crossed my mind to tell my mother; I don't know why, I guess I thought this abusive behavior was normal.

The common thread in my life has been a combination of these circumstances at one time or another, sex, violence, drugs, racism and God and not necessarily in that order, sometimes separate, sometimes entwined. I have been exposed to all of these things throughout my life. Some of them at a very young age. I was only nine when my parents called my sister and me into the living room and passed us a joint. We couldn't stop laughing and falling on the floor. Everything was hysterical, but the true irony is that it wasn't funny at all. It was actually very tragic.

From that first time, I was hooked, and my life would never be the same. Unbelievably there were a lot of other kids my age already smoking weed, too. Steve, Eddie, and I would put our pocket change together and buy loose joints for a dollar. Back in those days loose joints would be the size of a baseball bat and have exotic names like *Cess*, *Buddha*, and *Thai stick*. I'm now an adult, and while I take full responsibilities for my life and actions, I still hold my mother and Jake somewhat responsible for the years of drug selling, drug abuse, and a lot of other bad decisions.

WARRIORS OF THE WASTELAND

Around that same time, I got involved in the neighborhood gang. Down the block, there was this large family named the Lamays. Altogether, there were sixteen of them, eight boys and eight girls. The boys from the family and other boys from the block formed a gang called the Baby Peacemakers. They were a younger version of an older set. Initiation was simple; you had to be jumped in. Not like today where gangs go out and slash or shoot some innocent victim. No, in those days you had to run (emphasis on run) through a line of guys that were already in the gang and get your ass pummeled. We didn't do much, just hang around, smoke weed, play stickball, and bullshit.

I remember the day that my man Joe Lamay was teasing my sister Vonnie. He was about eleven. He wasn't doing anything serious. All he did was turn up his eyelids to scare Vonnie, but that was enough for me to pick up a stick and crack him in the head with it. Unfortunately or luckily, depending on your point of view, the stick had a nail in it and went right into his skull. I didn't know it at the time but that incident helped me earn a reputation for being crazy, plus we used to slap box, and I was nice with my hands. In the ghetto, being violent is equivalent to being powerful, and power is what you need to make it in the streets. Sort of like survival of the fittest, but being the fittest doesn't necessarily mean being the biggest or the strongest. You can be smart, or you can be a wild motherfucker. You can weigh a hundred pounds soaking wet and still get it on.

Back in our parent's day I suppose violence had a purpose, you know, a crime of passion, or perhaps money related. Growing up, my generation didn't wear a lot of gold and diamonds. Shit was simple, but things were changing. First came the gold-plated glasses named Cazals, then came the sheepskin coats. That was the first time I ever heard of a nigga' getting robbed and killed for some insignificant shit like clothing. What was insane is that you had niggas' killing motherfuckers for something that cost as little as a hundred and fifty dollars, and a year later it went out of style.

Maybe it was drugs, or maybe it was TV, but we were the right now generation. Everything that our parents worked their whole lives for, we wanted by the time we were sixteen or seventeen and we were just getting started. Crack and the nine- millimeter hadn't made its way to the ghetto yet. As I've gotten older, violence has become second nature or innate to me if you will. In my life, I have seen it all. Sometimes I have experienced it first hand, other times I have been a witness to it. Some of it is necessary, some of it senseless.

For example, there was this family named the Calloways who used to live downstairs in the basement apartment of our building. Mr. Calloway was Black, his wife was White, and of course their son Butch was bi-racial. He looked to be about nineteen, tall and slender. His parents looked to be in their fifties, an unusually older couple to have a teenage son. Another unusual thing that struck me was how the mother looked much more worn out than the father. You could say that the Calloways were the epitome of a dysfunctional family. The son and the father would beat the mother mercilessly. I can't imagine the agony she must have felt being abused by her husband and then her own child.

That was just the tip of the iceberg of Butch's psychopathic behavior. This nigga' had two German Shepherds that would tremble at the sound of his voice. One afternoon outside in front of the building he castrated one of the dogs with all of the kids from the neighborhood standing there watching. The sound of the dog's howls and the sight of blood spewing everywhere made this young girl named Shakina throw up whatever she had for lunch. The rest of us took off running. The next morning someone found the dog's carcass in a garbage can in the alleyway. People just looked the other way, and Butch continued to walk around like nothing happened, but I knew not to fuck with him. I recall another day he was across the street practicing archery in an empty lot. That's right, archery. He asked me to pick up the arrows that missed the target and told me he would pay me a dollar to retrieve them for him, but I was smart and scared enough to lie and tell him I was going with my mother.

In the Bible, fear is described as wisdom, and it is that wisdom that would carry me through life. As much as the sex, violence and the drugs have affected me, I understand that God's grace and wisdom have been there with me also. If at that age I didn't have the forethought to say, "No" and walk away from the money, who knows what might have happened. It would have been nothing for Butch to shoot me with an arrow and say it was an accident. As a matter of fact, criminologist have noted that many serial killers start out abusing animals.

The next few years were pretty much a blur. My mother got a job at a Wall Street firm, and Jake started working at a group home which was good for me and Vonnie because he was hardly ever home. Although one of the things that I must give Jake credit for is his being adamant about our education. He would bring books home from Fordham University and make Vonnie and I complete the reading and comprehension. By the time I was in the sixth grade, I was reading at a college level. So the only thing that kept me from excelling in school was my behavior, and me being a pothead.

The late 70's were a turning point in inner-city America, or at least for the Bronx and my life. There was the big blackout of 77', and new music called rap exploded on the urban scene. That year my grandmother died, we moved away from Mapes Ave, the Vietnam War had been over for two years, and the "Son of Sam" had been arrested.

I remember the night my mother came in the house and put Kurtis Blow's, "Christmas Rapping" on. It was a 33-inch vinyl disc. The record went, "He was roly, he was poly, and I said holy-moly, you got a lot of hairs on your chinny- chin- chin." That was that shit! Then I heard the Sugar Hill Gang's "Rappers Delight." I mean I'm not sure which really came first, but "Rappers Delight." is the first rap record to go multi-platinum. Yes, times were changing.

During the Blackout, everyone in my family headed up to Tremont Ave. to loot. My older cousins were coming down the block with TVs and all kinds of shit. In those days that's what people did. I watched, and I learned. Was it wrong? Yes, without a doubt, but that's how we survived. Right and wrong was a matter of opinion and opportunity.

When Momma passed away (My Grandmother), Vonnie and I were at our grandfather's house. His name was Isaac. We called him Granddaddy. He was a smooth, educated older gentleman but he was also a street nigga' with little respect for women, and a drinking problem to match a violent temper and an obnoxious mouth. My mother used to tell us stories about him when he was a young hustler. Stories about his days selling heroin, and some of his violent exploits. One of her more memorable tales was about how he stabbed this one nigga' in the neck with a chicken bone he was gnawing on. I wanted to be just like him when I got older.

He called us into the room and sat us down and told us that "Momma" had died.

"Stop playing," I said.

"Granddaddy, that's not funny."

My mother never told us that Momma was dying from cancer, so when she passed, it kicked me square in the chest. Shit is just like on TV where your grandmother is the glue that holds the family together. I broke down crying.

Momma was the one who got me hooked on chocolate chip cookies. Her house was the family's home away from home. Vonnie didn't cry so my cousins and I interpreted that to mean she didn't love our grandmother as much as we did, so we bullied her until she finally bawled relentlessly. We were kids what did we know? My family was devastated, but the one who felt it the most was my eighteen-year-old cousin Dwayne. Momma had raised him since he was a child. I heard the story of how he came to Momma's house with some of his mother's boyfriend's shoes on his small feet. A pair of pants and a jacket that was all three sizes too big for him when he knocked on her door. My Aunt Clarissa, who was mildly retarded, was Dwayne's mother. She had about seventeen or eighteen kids, and I believe almost all of them were in foster homes. Dwayne fell on the floor in front of Momma's coffin and laid there and cried as though his world had ended. In a sense it did.

It's odd in some way that I can't explain, but our family would never be the same, and as time passed we grew apart. For some strange reason, Karen didn't come to the funeral. I don't know what the fuck she was thinking about, but when our great-grandmother left the church, she went straight to the nearest tree and got a nice long switch off that motherfucker. I've never seen that old lady move so fast in my life. Karen had the nerve to be in the courtyard playing. Great-grandma didn't say a word she just got on her job and got to whipping that ass right there on the spot. Enough said.

It wouldn't be long after that before we moved from Mapes Ave. Three or four times a month our building was being set on fire. That was the landlord's way of getting the tenants to move out. I was going to miss Mapes Ave. All of my friends and all of my earliest childhood memories were there. I saw and learned so much on that block. It's where I had my first piece of pussy if you can call it that.

It's where I developed my hand skills slap boxing with my homeboys, smoked my first joint, and learned about courage and wisdom all before puberty.

Chapter 3
Hello, Rosedale Ave.

Moving to Rosedale Ave. was a step up. We now had a security patrolled building with the front and back door monitored by closed-circuit TV. The tenants had access to it by turning to channels three and six on their home televisions. There was a pool on the side of the building, a park, and a football/baseball field across the street.

As we moved up, my weed smoking escalated, and so did the stealing. The only difference was I was now hanging with middle-class kids, and instead of going to Ginny Town to steal, we would go downtown to Macy's on 34th street or the Macy's in Parkchester. The Macy's on 34th street is where I would have my first encounter with law enforcement at the tender age of eleven. I had juvenile shit like "Archie" comic books and other nonsense. While we didn't go to jail and the store security didn't call our parents, they did take our names and ages before letting us go. I now believe that did me more harm than good. It wasn't even a wake-up call for me, so I continued on a downward spiral.

Again, the next two or three years were pretty much uneventful. There was a situation or two that stood out, but not much else. A new gang or organization popped up called, The Mighty Zulu Nation. They were into both the rap music scene and the Black movement and if you said you were in the Zulu Nation, a nigga' would faint; he'd be so scared. I was one of the motherfuckers that was shook. Growing up on Mapes Ave. was a cocooned like environment. When I moved across town to a new school and new neighborhood I had to earn my stripes all over again. The only problem was that I was a lot smaller than my peers physically because of all of the years of drug use. Imagine that, at thirteen I already had years of drug abuse under my belt.

I attended Castle Hill Junior High 127 for the seventh and eighth grade. This would be my first introduction into the racial melting pot with kids from all walks of life. The Italian kids from Archer Ave, Blacks and Hispanics from the Parkchester area, and my neighborhood. There were also the kids from the Bronx River Projects who grew up on the proverbial wrong side of the tracks. That was where Simone was from. Who's Simone? Simone was the first motherfucker to beat my ass. I weighed about ninety-five pounds and Simone weighed about one sixty to one seventy-five solid and in the seventh grade no less. I was in the lunchroom talking shit.

"Wait til' three after school. It's gon' be on."

I'll be honest, I had forgotten all about 3 o'clock and Simone. As I was walking out of the front door running my mouth with my boys, out of nowhere this big bitch literally snatched me up, punched me in the face, and swung me around like a rag-doll. I didn't get one lick in. Oh, the humility! The agony! Simone beat my ass in front of the whole school. Welcome to junior high.

Entering junior high, I was in class 7-E2, the fourth highest class in the entire seventh grade, but my behavior would get me put back two classes. So, a quarter into the school year, I landed in a class a bit more immature, which was right up my alley. In those days schools weren't as protective of its students as they are now. As young boys, we would walk through the school halls feeling girls' asses. My nickname was "The Glove," and my man, Tommy Gant's nickname, was "The Finger." I got my moniker because I could walk around school feeling asses all day without getting caught. It was like I had a magic glove on. Tommy lived up to his nickname also. One day we were all standing in the schoolyard talking, and this Puerto Rican chick named Athena came strolling by. As she walked past us, Tommy stuck his middle finger up the crack of her ass, through her pants and all. Fwoop! It slid right in. Athena gasped and started crying. She walked off saying she was going to tell the principal but nothing happened. In those days being sexually harassed was par for the course.

Nowadays in the wake of Columbine and numerous incidents that have occurred such as students being raped on school grounds or having sex voluntarily in stairwells and bathrooms, some as young as eight or nine years old, there is a zero-tolerance policy. As a result, children in elementary schools are subject to intense scrutiny. If a child points a finger at another child and says, "Bang!" he or she is expelled, and the police may be called in to investigate. In some cases charges of terroristic threats are brought up. Times have really changed.

Anyway, we lived on Rosedale for three years, and not many incidents stood out in my mind. That is except what happened to a fourteen-year-old friend of mine named Doris. She and some of the older kids from the building skipped school and had a hooky party at this guy named Tony Green's house. From the rumors floating around the building, I heard Tony was playing with his father's gun twirling it on his index finger like he was a cowboy. The other kids at the hooky party said the gun went off and shot Doris behind her left ear which was terrible in itself, but the tragedy was compounded when Tony drug her body out in the stairwell where she bled to death. It was believed that if Tony had called 911, she would have lived. I heard that Doris's father, who was supposed to be some big time dude selling weed, put a hit out on Tony, so his family had to send him to Atlanta until shit blew over.

The second was the birth of my youngest sister Charmane. I can remember changing her diapers, taking her to the penny candy store, and promising to take her to Hawaii when we got older. Regrettably, as she grew up, she would become devious and deceitful, much like Zenobia and Jake, for no good reason at all. Or, maybe she too, like me, was a product of her environment.

The last incident was embarrassing. It was an indicator of the underlying effects of Jake and Zenobia's drug abuse. I was thirteen-years old and in the 8th grade when my parents pulled up in Jakes old hooptie.

Jake told me to, "Git' in the car."

"No, that's okay I'ma walk home with my friends," I responded.

He gave me a look that said I better get my ass in the car. I later found out that we had been evicted, and the marshals had thrown all of our belongings out on the street. However, more embarrassing than that, I had to continue going to school with the kids who lived in my building and had seen my family's things out on the street.

We lived from relative to relative for a while, until once again we moved up to a better neighborhood. This time it was Mount Vernon, a suburb of New York. The difference was like night and day from the Bronx. I finished out the eighth grade in Castle Hill 127 and then I went to Mount Vernon High. In Mount Vernon, everyone had the latest fashions on, well, everyone except me. I had become more aware of styles and trends and now realized that amongst my peers, I was the fashion misfit. While other kids had on Jordache and Sergio Valente jeans, my parents bought Vonnie and me some knock-off brand shit that turned purple when you washed them. Other kids were wearing Pumas and British Walkers, and I was still rocking Pro-Keds and Converse. They would buy me and Vonnie clothes twice a year. Two pairs of pants and two shirts at the beginning of the school year and maybe an outfit or two at Easter. Now that I'm grown I understand that clothes are not as important as the necessities, but when you're a teenager in a new school and a new hood' those things tend to matter. It's because of Easter outfits that I hate corduroys to this day. One Easter I got corduroy pants, and when the summer came I had to cut them into shorts. Since that summer I refuse to wear corduroy.

In our home, for a long time when we were growing up we always had a beautiful Christmas, but somehow things weren't what they seemed. Something wasn't right. Jake started a new job as a correction officer (Vonnie and I used to pray that a prisoner would kill his ass.) working on Rikers Island, but we never had much food in our house or decent furniture. I had seen Jake and my mother sniffing cocaine, but at that age, I couldn't put two and two together. This nigga' would steal or take food from Rikers Island and bring it home for us to eat. He and my mother would rarely go food shopping. We were some Rikers Island, Hamburger Helper eating motherfuckers. I remember this new dude moved into our building and saw these black boots Jake had brought me. He asked me if I had ever done a bid. Come to find out; Jake had taken a pair of prison boots and given them to me to wear for the winter.

I was always the kid who was begging for a bite of everyone's pizza and chips after school. On top of that, my weed habit was full-blown, and all of us little niggas' were smoking heavily. On the weekends we would all go to different Te-Amo and Optimo cigar and tobacco stores and steal cartons of Newports to support our habits. That's right, there wasn't any crack, and we were stealing on a regular. A motherfucker can't tell me shit about weed being a harmless drug. Meanwhile, I was devoid of any moral fiber. Vonnie and I started having sex when I was thirteen and continued up until experienced my first orgasm. Ain't that something, experiencing my first orgasm with my own sister.

When I turned fourteen, shit really started moving. My Aunt Pat moved downtown further into the South Bronx to east 138th

Street, Millbrook projects. That's where I would start hanging hard. Me and Vonnie couldn't wait to get away from Jakes annoying ass. Yeah, as we got older the beatings stopped, but the mental bullshit just kept on rolling. Millbrook was an oasis for me. I met some kids who would become my homeboys. One dude named Chase, another kid who was a deaf-mute named Tyler and a couple of other niggas. We would hang out into the wee hours of the morning, breaking night, drinking brews, and getting high. I would dread going back home on Sunday night. That year flew by, and before I knew it, it was the summer.

I was fifteen working my first summer job as a youth counselor; I would cash my check, give my mother twenty- five dollars and leave for the weekend. I spent the whole summer downtown hanging out, smoking weed, and I was now sniffing coke. It was a natural transition for me graduating from one drug to the next. Oh, and before I forget, I was also smoking dust. I was out of control, plus I was doing grimy shit on the side. Like the time this young kid named Justin, who was one of the kids in my summer camp group who lived in my building on the fourth floor, lost his house keys, and I found them. I waited until him and his family went out one day. I went and got my man Q-boy who lived on my floor. We went in this little niggas' house and stole everything that wasn't nailed down. We took their TVs, phones, stereo equipment, and anything electronic. Plus, I took his older sister Marilyn's leather bomber.

Now to put things in perspective, these were my neighbors, and at fifteen, I was robbing them blind with Justin's lost keys. When we went up to their apartment a second time, yes, a second time, they had changed the bottom lock, but that didn't stop us. We opened the top lock, broke the bottom one, and robbed they ass again. We also left them a little keepsake that we had heard about in an urban myth.

We took pictures (with their camera) with their toothbrushes in the cracks of our asses and left the camera so whenever they got the film developed, they would see it and realize they had been brushing their teeth all that time with those shitty toothbrushes. Now that's funny!

When the summer ended, I had most of my school clothes, a leather bomber and I still had one check coming, but things didn't turn out the way I thought they would. I returned home at the end of the summer to find things had started to sour between Jake and my mother. I walked into the house, and before I could even get settled in, my mother told me she and Jake were having some problems, and she wanted me to give her my last summer youth check to buy my sisters some school clothes.

"But ma,' I was goin' to git' the last of my school clothes wit' this money," I said.

Zenobia didn't say a word. She snatched the money out of my hand and raked her fingernails down my face like I was someone on the street. I left and went back down to my aunt's house. That set up a pattern between myself and Zenobia. She didn't give a fuck, just have that money. She didn't care how you got it or where it came from. I went back to my aunt's house. I told her what happened, and although she didn't want to come between my mother and me, she did say that I could stay until my mother and I worked things out. I spent the next three months doing absolutely nothing but getting into trouble. My friends and I would walk the train platform in the middle of the night looking for people to rob, man or woman; it didn't matter. We were a bunch of hungry young wolves.

One evening we caught this old man on the stairwell in my man Tyler's building. Our homie Donnie put him in the dope fiend yoke. The old man looked to be in his sixties. When Donnie choked him, he went out like a light. Donnie let him drop to the floor. His head hit the concrete with a thud. We were all going through his pockets. He had about thirty dollars, and since there were five of us, that was only six dollars apiece. While we were counting the old man was still out on the floor. Suddenly he started convulsing.

Donnie said, "Oh shit, I'm out."

One of our friends, this kid named Blaze smacked the old timer in his face a couple of times until he came around. Before he could start yelling for the police, we bounced.

I would spend the next few weeks wilding, smoking weed, and sniffing coke. In all of my years of drug dealing, I would never sell to kids too young, pregnant women, motherfuckers too old, anyone too sick, or who had just come out of the hospital. But reality is, niggas don't care what your situation is. So at fifteen, we were going down to 137th and Brooke Ave. to buy dime bags of coke. In those days, coke was sold in glassine bags and was identified with different colored tape. So all up and down the block you would hear niggas shouting, "Green tape, yellow tape, red tape, cop and go."

In mid-November, my Uncle Stratford, my mother's half-brother on my grandfather's side, called me at my Aunt Pat's house. From what I understood Uncle Stratford didn't get along with granddaddy. I heard it was because granddaddy told him that his mother wasn't nothing but a one night stand, and he was an accident. Uncle Stratford called me at my aunt's house to speak to me on the phone and told me, and I quote "When I get downtown you better be on your way home." Looking back, I guess he saved my life, but truthfully I was already gone, at least as far as the drugs and criminal behavior were concerned. As I headed home I thought about all the days I missed in school. I was reassigned to a night school program four days a week, but it was fruitless, I still didn't go. At the age of fifteen, I was done with school.

In the midst of everything else, I was starting to notice girls. In particular, Kia Liston. She was an upstairs neighbor who I had my first crush on. She had dirty brown hair, green eyes, and a shape that could melt ice cream. She would come to my house and sit in my room for hours. I remember feeling her up and humping whenever we could since my parents made me keep my bedroom door open. Technically, I was still a virgin because I had never had intercourse with anyone but Vonnie. I would follow Kia everywhere like a little puppy dog. We were in my room sitting on my bed, and I was trying to pull the panties off of that fat brown ass, but I didn't want to fuck her I just wanted to eat her pussy. I think I was different from boys my age back then. When me and the fellas' would be looking at dirty magazines and someone said, "I would love to fuck that." I would say, "Me too," but in my mind, I was thinking how I would love to put my face in it. Again, a sign of the times due to all the sex thrown in our children's faces, via TV, music, and the media in general. You now have young kids, boys, and girls, doing it all.

I never got a chance to fuck Kia or taste that sweet smelling pussy, and yes, pussy does smell sweet, although not all pussy. (Y'all bitches know who you are). I would get my first piece of pussy down in the Mill. Shantel was black and beautiful, and while her face wasn't what you would consider pretty in the conventional sense, her dark skin made her stunning. My first episode wasn't nothing to write home about, it was just that it was my first piece of real ass, and I was happy as hell to finally be getting some. We went to the roof of her building better known as "Pebble Beach." Thinking back, I can recall how wet her vagina was, and how she sat down on my dick and rode it like she had been fucking all her life. After that, Shantel would always want me to hang out with her in her house, or want me to go back up to Pebble Beach with her, but you know how it is, "Boys jus' wanna' have fun."

During the week I would hang out with my friends in Mount Vernon, continuing to steal and get high. It came to a head when I got caught shoplifting in a Waldbaums supermarket. This time, the store security did take action. When I was walking out the front door with a couple of steaks, the manager approached me and reached out to grab my arm. I was only 5'4," but I was strong for my size. Another thing I credit Jake for was getting me interested in weightlifting. So when the manager grabbed me, I shook him loose and was out the door. The reason I got caught was a customer who was shopping at the supermarket saw the incident and ran to the manager's aid. He did a hall of fame tackle and bowled me over. When the police arrived, he had his chest poked out, walking with a "John Wayne" like swagger. He told the police he was glad to help, and wouldn't hesitate to do it again. The year was 1982, and this would be my first time of three being put on probation in my lifetime, and lest I forget, the first of my fourteen or so arrest.

I would spend the next year and a half doing the same thing I had always done which was get high and commit crimes. On top of that, I was now blowing off probation. But somewhere at the beginning of the summer of 84' I would have a coherent train of thought and join the US Army. When I came home with the recruiter, Zenobia was in shock. She didn't want me to join up, but Jake convinced her to let me go. He told her it would make a man out of me.

The morning the recruiter came to pick me up at my home, Jake, my mother, and my youngest sister Charmane were all in Virginia at a department of corrections sponsored basketball game. My sister Vonnie was in school, so that left no one there to see me off to Fort Sill Oklahoma. I took fifty cents off of my parent's dresser and was out the door. My induction station was Ft. Hamilton in Brooklyn, NY. That night we had a layover in Texas, and while Uncle Sam had fed me all that day, that evening I was on my own. So for dinner, I had a bag of M&M's. Uncle Sam was also responsible for my third trip to the doctor thus far in my life. Up to that point, neither Vonnie nor I had ever gone to the doctor for regular checkups, and I had never been to a dentist in seventeen years. Nevertheless, I don't blame my parents; I realize now that many minorities don't have medical coverage or even life insurance for that matter. Although Jake and Charmane were covered by the city, my mother, Vonnie and I wasn't covered because after ten years they still weren't married, but I digress.

Okay, where was I... Oh, yeah, from my second week in basic training until my last few months in the military, I was a fuck up, always in trouble. In basic training, everyone pulls a duty called fireguard. You walk through the barracks making sure all the exits are secure, everyone is in their bunks, and all the lights are out. In the morning everyone has to be up, and out of bed, with their feet on the floor at 4 am sharp. Well it was my turn. Early that morning I was going through the barracks turning on the lights hollering, "Rise and shine, rise and shine." You could say that the position had gone to my head. This one recruit refused to get out of bed, and all of that New York City bravado came flowing out of my mouth. I was seventeen and had never been exposed to any other environment except the Bronx and Mount Vernon. In my naivety, I believed that New Yorkers were unbeatable, especially Black New Yorkers. Now while the recruit was scared, his bunkmate, this stocky White boy from Alabama wasn't having it.

He said, "Shut yo' mouth and git' outta' here boy."

He didn't have to say it twice. Trust me when I say, I didn't want any part of that cock-strong looking redneck. I ran upstairs and got one of the recruits from Brooklyn; my man was diesel. When the White boy saw him, he backed down, but that didn't stop him from giving me dirty looks whenever he saw me alone. Believe it or not, you still have niggas who think all White people can't fight. You see, young niggas like me had never heard of Rocky Marciano or had any idea that you have Jews from Israel or Irish motherfuckers that will stand up and box your ass to death.

Four weeks later I got a chance to call home. Despite all the abuse I had suffered at his hands, both physical and psychological, the first person I wanted to speak to was Jake. I told him that I appreciated his trying to keep me on the straight and narrow and that I loved him for it. It has always been in my nature to forgive and forget. As I have gotten older, while I may still forgive, I sometimes don't forget as easily.

Looking back, while I have many fond memories of Mount Vernon and Millbrook projects, I haven't kept any ties to many of my childhood friends. I came to realize that the common bond that brought us together was the same bond that kept me from getting close to many of them, with the exception of those I call family, and that bond was drugs. Our use of drugs united and divided us in one fell swoop. I've used narcotics and smoked weed long enough to see the two-faced shit that goes on when one of your so-called friends don't want to put you down on the "git high." When you're always the friend without money, you'll find your friends are hard to keep up with, literally. When niggas would see me coming, they would take off running. I'm ashamed to admit, the first couple of times I would chase after them, but after awhile I said fuck them. Later on in life when I started getting money those same niggas that used to dip and leave me, would be hanging on my every word.

I made new friends in the military. I learned what it was like to belong to a unit that depended on you to do the right thing, and if you didn't the drill sergeant would punish your whole platoon. If you kept fucking up, the platoon would give you a "Blanket Party." That's when a blanket is thrown over the head of the misfit, and they beat him to a bloody pulp. Now while I never got a blanket party, I did get sent to a psychiatrist for drinking soda of all things. I also got sent to a conduct correctional facility for telling another soldier to suck my dick. In between all of that, I managed to put on twenty-six pounds and stay out of trouble long enough to graduate from basic training.

After basic training, I was sent to Fort Lee Virginia. That's where I began my AIT, Advanced Individual Training. Mine was 94Bravo, in other words, I was a cook. When I signed my enlistment contract, the recruiter told me that he would enlist me as a 94Bravo, and after I finished basic training, I would be able to transfer over to the infantry. He lied. I now understand the government will lie, say, and do whatever it wants, and there is very little that uneducated, poor minorities and Whites can do about it. In school, I now had a lot more freedom, so it wasn't long before me, and a few of the other guys were smoking weed, again. I finished AIT and went home for a month's leave before I was to ship out to Germany.

When I returned home, I was the same kid who left four months earlier, but the adults who watched me hanging out as a young pothead, now looked at me differently. Even my peers looked at me with admiration and respect, but on the inside, I was still the same fucked up individual; I just looked respectable. I was like a sack of shit in pretty Christmas wrapping. When I returned home from Virginia, once again Jake and my mother had split up. Zenobia asked me for some money to get some things for the house. I gladly gave her seventy- five dollars and everything was hunky-dory. For some reason, she had stopped working, but I never asked why, I was just happy to be back on the block. I hung out with my peoples for the next month doing what I always did, you know, "git high."

Before long, it was time to pack up and report to my next duty station, Fulda Germany. I packed up my duffel bag said my goodbyes and was headed out the door. As I was leaving, Zenobia asked me for some more money. I didn't have a problem with that, but I wasn't sure when I would receive my next check.

I said, "Ma I don't know when I'll be gittin' paid again, but as soon as I get overseas and get some money, I'll send you something."

That wasn't good enough for her. She looked me in the face with a look that I had seen before and said, "Don't come back here again, you don't have a place to come home to anymore."

Truth be told, I wasn't even fazed. I simply picked up my bags and said, "Alright ma', goodbye."

That would be the last words we spoke for the next year and a half. One of my friends came to see me off, my man Sean. He rode with me all the way down to Grand Central Station from Mount Vernon. He was the last face I would see from home for almost two years.

Chapter 4
Germany, {the Deutschland}

In my life up to that point, I had not been exposed to much of anything outside of my self-imposed circumference. Like many Blacks who live in the ghetto, we live our lives going to and from work, every once in a while going to a club on the weekend. Some of us will go down south to visit our relatives in the summer. A few of us as we get older and come into our own may even travel to the Caribbean or Mexico, but I have known only a few Blacks who have been to Europe, Asia, the Middle East or Africa.

My second week in the country I met a pretty German girl named Silvia Dietrich. I was sitting in a bar having a drink. She came and sat down beside me and introduced herself. She was beautiful with blonde hair and blue eyes. Hitler would be ecstatic as well as enraged; ecstatic because he had his "Master Race" genetically aesthetic and enraged because German women couldn't get enough of Black American men. So much for no race mixing and keeping that Aryan blood pure! Right from the start, we hit it off.

The next night we got together, and she took me to her house. It was a little room up the block from her family's home. In Germany, housing is different from the states. You'll have a three bedroom apartment, and two of the rooms will be up the block, or a couple of doors down. This was my first relationship. We would make love every chance we got. I was now eighteen, and she was sixteen. Her mother was an older woman who never said a word about me sleeping with her young daughter every night. Silvia had a younger thirteen-year-old sister named Simona, and an older sister named Heiga. From the first day, I started taking care of Silvia, giving her money when I got paid. I would leave my dirty laundry at her house and go to the base for duty when I got back the next day, my clothes would be washed and folded. When her mother would cook dinner for the family, she would set out a plate for me, along with a glass of coke with a shot of sherry on the side, and two cigarettes. My God, I was in heaven.

In the meantime, I was getting my fill of that young German pussy. Eating it, fucking it, and experimenting. Doing crazy shit, like sticking candles in her young vagina like a dildo. One morning their mother was in the kitchen making breakfast, and Heiga asked Silvia about the size of my penis. Silvia grabbed the Heinz ketchup bottle on the table and said, "It's big like this." Heiga looked at me smiled. For the entire year and a half that I was in Germany, I partied like it was 1999, smoking hash, drinking, hanging in the club four or five nights a week and beating that pussy up. I didn't even take the time to get my GED or driver's license. I was fucking and partying. Somehow I managed to get promoted to the rank of E-4, Army specialist. Now that's a miracle if I've ever seen one!

Silvia couldn't stand when I began smoking hash. She said that it changed my personality and made me more subdued and less upbeat when I was high, but that didn't stop me; I would go into town and cop from the African or Turkish dealers. What was odd, is although the Germans accepted Black Americans and thought nothing of Africans, they were staunch racist against the Turkish. Over in Germany, the Turkish were the niggas. I would hear Germans talk about the Turkish like they were dirt. Even my Silvia was a racist; I often heard her making crude remarks about Turkish people.

Meanwhile my whole tour of duty I stayed high. Some of the other cooks and I would go down into the basement of the mess hall and blow a few bowls of hash, go upstairs and serve on the chow line. My eyes would be bloodshot red, so it wasn't long before I got called in for a piss test. I remember it like it was yesterday. I had just finished smoking the night before. When I got up for duty the next morning, there was yelling in the barrack halls.

"Piss test boys and girls, line up for formation."

Fuck! This was it. Those fucking drugs and bad choices I always seemed to make caught up with me again. Consequently, I got busted down a rank to E-3, private first class. But it wasn't only me, some of the other guys in the unit as well as a sergeant or two, but once more that didn't slow me down, as usual per my m.o., I got worse. Shortly after that, I was stealing again to maintain my habit.

One of my closest friends in Germany made two mistakes, one was trusting me, and the other was leaving twenty dollars in his open locker while he showered. His name was Specialist Byrd, a brother from Chicago who considered himself to be just that, my brother. To say it hurt him is an extreme understatement. He couldn't prove that I took it, but he knew it was me, and our friendship would never be the same. I can't say that I blamed him.

I also stole from another soldier named Newton. I stole his protective mask while we were serving on the East and West German border. He also never said anything. Looking back, I was a real rat turd. You know what they say, the apple doesn't fall far from the tree. In the interim, time was rapidly slipping by, and I had two options for Silvia and me to continue to stay together. I could marry her, or I could try and obtain an extension of my tour of duty in the country. Well, I was too immature to get married, and I procrastinated until it was too late to get an extension, so I was issued my papers to go stateside. When I told Silvia I couldn't stay she was crushed. From that day on, she started preparing herself for me to leave, until finally, she told me that she didn't want to see me anymore. She broke my heart. I was depressed for days on end. It felt like I was physically sick.

When I got over the pain, it didn't take long for me to get back in the groove. At a local club one evening, this rap song came on. It went something like this, "Manhattan makin', Brooklyn takin' somethin', somethin', Queens is whack, blah, blah, blah, blah, blah, blah, and the Bronx is buggin' out on crack." Me being a Bronx native, "I'm like Crack! What the fuck is crack?" God help me when I found out. That same night the girl who I was dancing with took me to her house. When she took off her clothes, she had her feet hidden behind her, but I could smell the stench coming from them, which should have been reason enough for me to get dressed and leave, but not my horny ass. And though this chick also had green discharge coming out of her vagina, I went ahead and fucked her anyway, without a condom no less. Can you say dirty dick!

Three days later my dick was burning, and I had the drips. When I went to the medics, they informed me that I had gonorrhea. Also, I was now their new source of amusement, so whenever the medics came through the chow line, they were calling me G-man or less creatively V.D-man. What was crazy is that the military still allowed me to cook with an infectious disease. That experience with "ol' stinky" led me to make up a catchy jingle, "If a bitch got stink feet don't fuck her wit' your meat!"

In Germany, I was exposed to many things, Mercedes-Benz cabs, beautiful cobblestone streets, the Red Light District where prostitution is legal, the Autobahn where there is no speed limit, and a European cold so brutal it feels as though you could snap your ears off. I learned to speak German, and I fell in love, my first love. In the twenty-plus years since I left Germany I have never forgotten Silvia, "Meine Deutsche Freundin."

When I returned home, it was the same as when I left. No one had any idea that I was coming home for leave. I knocked on the door and found that my mother no longer lived in Mount Vernon.

She took my sisters and moved back to the Bronx. That's another issue her and Jake had. She often complained that Mount Vernon was too quiet for her. When Jake opened up the door, I was surprised. Seeing him was indescribable, but if I had to describe it in a word, I would have to say it was awkward. Not happy, just awkward. I dropped my things off and went to look for my peoples. I bumped into my man Fats.

"Yo' nigga what up?" I asked Fats hugging him. "Where that nigga Sean at?"

Fats gave me a crazy look.

He asked me, "You ain't hear?"

I was puzzled.

"Hear what?" I asked.

Fats began to tell me the story of how Sean got dusted and killed himself.

"What! How that shit happen?" I asked in shock.

He told me that when Sean's mother walked into his room, he was sitting on the window ledge. Fats said he heard that when she called his name, Sean looked back at her, turned around and jumped from the fifteenth floor. Unbelievably, they also said that when he hit the grass, he had so much PCP in his system that he was still alive when he was put into the ambulance. Fats said after that, everyone made a pact not to smoke dust anymore. We talked for a little while longer catching up on old times. Then I asked him the question that would change my life.

"Yo' Fats, what the fuck is crack?"

He told me to come on. He took me up to Third Street. In Mount Vernon, any drug you wanted you could go to Third Street and get it. We copped a small clear plastic bottle with two little white rocks in it for ten dollars. We walked up the block and got a bag of weed. Yeah, niggas made a pact not to smoke dust, but they were doing every other drug in the book. We headed back down to our side of town and went into the stairwell of my building. Fats pulled out a pack of EZ Wider, a dollar bill, and dumped the rocks into the bill and crushed them up. Then he put some weed in the rolling paper and sprinkled the crack over that. He rolled it up, passed it to me and said, "Spark it up."

In retrospect, if Fats was really my man, he would have told me what I told everyone who asked me about crack when it was an epidemic which is, "If someone offers you that shit they ain't your friend, to be honest, they're your worst fuckin' enemy!"

I lit it up; it had a taste that I can't explain, except to say that it tastes like a coke cigarette only stronger, only better. It was called a "wula" and the high was euphoric. When we finished smoking the wula, the first thing I said was, "I want another one."

It's been said you don't necessarily have to get hooked from the first time you try crack. Well, I was on the other end of the spectrum. I was hooked from the very first time, like the vast majority of people who try it.

Finally, two or three days later when I made it out of Mount Vernon to see the rest of my family, my aunt and my cousins wanted to know why I hadn't kept in touch. It's hard to articulate, but I think that my dealing with Zenobia and Jake was changing me. I was becoming calloused and antisocial. I just didn't recognize the traits. In Millbrook projects crack was in full effect, everybody and yes, they mama, was smoking. At that time it was the hip thing to do. You would go to a house party in 1986 and people would be passing wula joints, and wula blunts all around the party, niggas and chicks, we were all getting high.

We didn't start to see the negative effects until you saw motherfuckers losing mad weight, and chicks that were bad as hell in high school, sucking dick for five or ten dollars. Worse than that, motherfuckers were in the news every day for doing crazy shit. Killing their grandmother for twenty dollars or selling their kids. I even heard some off the wall shit about my man Chase letting this gay cat named Bobby fuck him for a hit. On the other side of the coin were the niggas' who took advantage of the pandemic. The hungry motherfuckers who were already doing criminal shit like me when we were kids. The ones who didn't fuck with crack, even some of the nerdy kids got in on the act. They were all "Livin' La Vida Loca" with thick gold chains, expensive cars, and an air about them like they had a million dollars in their pockets.

For the next month, I went back to the finance office at Fort Hamilton numerous times requesting emergency funds or a cash advance. To top it all off, I was trying to get out of my last eleven months of service. I was a week AWOL when I got it together and decided to go to Fort Knox, KY. While I was in Kentucky finishing my tour of duty, all I could think about was all of that money dudes were making back home. When myself and the other soldiers would sit around and talk about what we were going to do when we finished our commitment to the military, I would say, "When I git' out I'm goin' home to sell crack." They were in the dark as I had been. They were all asking me what crack was. I described the way it looked and told them how you could get hooked from your first time trying it. Crack addicts have a saying and it goes like this, "The first hit is too many, and a thousand is not enough." Which is one hundred percent accurate.

Meanwhile, in Kentucky, I lost another rank which dropped my rank to E-2, private second class.That time I lost it because I hit a sergeant in the face with a glass in the club. The only thing that kept me out of jail is that I had no idea he was a sergeant. When I went in front of the Colonel to receive my second article 15, he looked over my record, demoted me and told me to keep my nose clean until I finished my tour. As I was leaving his office I grabbed my genitals as if to say "suck my dick," but a sergeant standing in the hall saw what I had done.

He snatched me up by my by the back of my shirt and took me back inside the colonel's office and said, "Sir as this soldier was leaving your office he grabbed his private parts in an obscene gesture."

My explanation to the colonel was comical yet simple, "Sir while I was standing in front of you; my balls were sweating. I had to scratch, Sir."

The colonel, whom I can only guess had seen and heard it all gave me an emphatic "Get the hell out of my office!"

The sergeant was furious, but with that, I was out the door.

The following day my company commander, Capt. Ray, called me down to his office and told me that he was going to put in the paperwork to start my dishonorable discharge papers. I pleaded with him to let me finish out my last four months, thankfully he agreed. Because of his act of benevolence, I am allowed to enjoy many military benefits, even now with my extensive criminal record, being a veteran carries a lot of clout.

The next four months went by very quickly. Before I knew it, my three years were up. Upon my exit from the military, I still had no GED, no driver's license, and I had only made it up the ladder one lousy rank. What I did have was a nickel-plated twenty-five automatic handgun that I purchased from a pawnshop in Louisville, KY. I had also picked up a work ethic that would elevate me above and beyond the average nigga on the street. Furthermore, I developed a certain charisma and ability to deal with, and interact with a variety of people on many different levels. Something that a lot of niggas weren't able to do. With that said, goodbye army life, and hello Crack City, NY. Here I come!

When I returned to Mount Vernon, Jake had custody of my youngest sister Charmane, and to my surprise, he welcomed me home. I immediately got a job working in a hospital as a cook in White Plains, New York. Nonetheless, it didn't last very long. I was getting high with my friends every night, and it was impossible for me to get my ass up for work the next day. Jake suggested that I get a job with the Department of Corrections. That was the third great piece of advice that he had given me in my life. First, was getting an education. Second, he let me know that if you hang with women rather than a bunch of hard legged niggas you would be less likely to get into trouble, and third, well you know, become a correction officer.

I don't know what I was thinking. Well, actually I wasn't thinking, I was focused on the streets and getting high. If I had gone the route of the corrections department, I would have finished my 20 years, three years military, seventeen years of civil service, and retired by the time I was thirty-seven. Not long after that, Jake moved his new girlfriend in and told me I would have to leave and go live with my mother. Jake had been the only father figure in my life for the last fourteen years since leaving Aunt Pat's house, but he still didn't see me as his son. If he had, he wouldn't have told me that I would have to leave so his girlfriend could move in. I humbly packed my things, thanked him for letting me stay there, and left.

When I knocked on Zenobia's door, this time, she said, "Hey, son. C'mon in." I mean it wasn't "Welcome home," but at least it wasn't "What are you doin' here?" She let me stay in the room that Vonnie used when she came home to visit from Albany, where she was now living with her father.

I would leave the house every day and go up to Mount Vernon to hustle and check on Charmane. Hustling came naturally to me, it was like I was a fish on land my entire life and when I started hustling I was swimming in open water. We had a term back in those days in Mount Vernon; the term was, "In power." If you were selling crack, crackheads would walk up to you and ask you if you were in power. I didn't realize what those words signified. I had control over someone's life. I was eating that shit up, but in reality I was in the same boat as them. I would work five hours a night, make up to two hundred dollars, and at the end of the night, I would smoke all of my profit up and end up hopping the train to get home the next day.

My first low point was when two beat cops came walking by me, and I swallowed the two caps I had in my mouth. That's what we called crack back then, caps, jumbs, jumbos, or plain ol' bottles. Later that night after I had smoked my P.C, I went into a parking lot, took a shit, and dug through my feces with my bare hands. Naturally, the bottles hadn't worked their way through my system yet, so I sifted through my own excrement for nothing. The only thing I had gotten was shit under my fingernails. I too was officially a crackhead!

The brother I was working for saw me slipping. He would ask me from time to time if I was ok to work. I would always tell him I was good. His name was Ra'Qan, and he had a younger brother named Unique. Along with crack, the Five Percent Nation had exploded on the scene. That's a religion where the followers declare themselves as Black men to be God which is a beautiful thing. It gave my generation a sense of pride in being Black, except for the fact that as "God Bodies" they were into the drug game and various other criminal activities.

While selling drugs in Mount Vernon, I would get arrested twice and sent to Valhalla, a county lockup in Westchester. There was a cop on the police force, Detective Evans, I swear this nigga was a crackhead. He had the look. Not the look of a cop pretending to be a crackhead, more like a crackhead pretending to be a cop. He was the one who arrested me for the first time as an adult. I had three hundred dollars and roughly fifteen bottles of crack stashed ten feet away under a car. He would have never caught me if this motherfucker didn't come out of the barbershop I was hustling in front of and volunteered to move his car. When I got to the precinct, there was only one hundred dollars and nine bottles in my arrest folder. Yeah, Evans was smoking!

So now at twenty-one, I had my first misdemeanor and now, subsequently, a burgeoning criminal record. Valhalla was like a boy's camp, so it was nothing to me. I thought that I had been to a real jail but I was in for a rude awakening when I started selling drugs in the Bronx and got a taste of Rikers Island. The last time I got a package from Ra'Qan I ran off with it. It was a five-hundred dollar package which wasn't much. Sadly, when I got my shit together and went back to Mount Vernon, I heard that both Ra'Qan and his younger brother Unique had been killed. Law enforcement agencies call their drug initiatives a "War on drugs," and that's exactly what it was, a war! A war in which young Black men were killing each other at astronomical rates, and the reality is, we still haven't gotten any closer to cultural, political, or financial independence.

I struggled to get my life back on track. When I tried to get off drugs, I had no support from Zenobia. She let me know in no uncertain terms that I was not welcomed in her house. She let me know plainly that I was a border, and I owed her rent. Whenever Vonnie would come from her father's house in Albany, she would walk into the living room and turn the television no matter what I was watching. Zenobia made it a point to let me know that it was Vonnie's home, and if I didn't like it, I could leave. Even with all of that, I still have to thank Zenobia, she made me determined to succeed at any cost. She used to do foul shit like taking food downstairs to her girlfriend's house so I had nothing to eat. There were times when I would take welfare flour, mix it with water, make flour balls and fry them for dinner.

It wouldn't be long before I felt strong enough to try hustling again. This time I hustled right down the block from Zenobia's building. This lame cat named Troy from the neighborhood introduced me to this young God body named Powerful. The name fit the youngster to a tee. Duke was only seventeen but he had our hood on smash. While I was in the military niggas were out in the world getting their weight up. Cats were copping guns by the boatload. Everywhere we went we had guns, to the store, to the barbershop, to school and especially the clubs. Powerful had gotten his rep by association from some of his family members busting their guns and holding it down, so authority just passed on to the young God. But make no mistakes, Powerful earned his name and his standing in our hood. He was wise beyond his years, and although I was five years older than him, I looked up to him. We all did!

When I met Powerful things changed once again. I was hustling hard from eight in the morning to two in the morning, seven days a week. Now you got some people who think that hustling is easy money, and to that I say, "No nigga." It can be fast money, but there's nothing easy about it. You got niggas catching cases, catching bodies and getting killed. Sometimes I would wear my underwear for two or three days. I would go upstairs and not even bathe and wake up the next morning and head out the door with the same clothes on. On top of that, that fast money will slow the fuck up.

When Troy and I started hustling for Powerful, we would sell maybe forty or fifty dollars' worth of product a day, so at the end of the week, we would get paid thirty-five dollars apiece. After a while, with me grinding hard, (this nigga' Troy would be in the house all day with his girl.) things started picking up. I told Powerful to hit me with my own package (since Troy wasn't doin' shit anyway why should he git' half the money).

While things had gotten better for me in some ways, I still wasn't making as much as I had in Mount Vernon. If we had one bad day, Powerful would come to the block with the fly ass leathers on and tell us what a bad week we had. Meanwhile, he would have a knot that could choke a fucking horse. We would all go up to Skate Key on Allerton Ave. and he would pull out a mint and pay for the whole crew from the block to go in. Now while I'm sure his intentions were good, to all the chicks on line watching this, we come off looking like his fucking sons, and he comes off like the man. From that moment on, I decided I wanted my own money, I would never depend on anyone for my survival or my lifestyle!

After the talk with Powerful, I had my own work. Troy and I also worked different shifts so we would be able to have some time off. It was cool with Powerful as long as the money was straight. Out of the blue one day, Troy, Darryl, and I were sitting in this private house that we were pumping out of, and Troy said "Let's roll a wula." I don't know what I was thinking, it had almost been a year since I had gotten high but the word that came out of my mouth was "Bet!"

Darryl rolled it up and passed it to me; I lit it up and passed it to Troy. Troy looked at me like I was stupid. Those two niggas' started laughing at me, telling me I was crazy for smoking that shit. They set me up, Troy out of jealousy, and Darryl because he was a follower. So naturally when Troy suggested that they play me, Darryl went along with it.

The next day Powerful told me that he heard that I was smoking, and he wanted to know if I was ok. I told him the same thing that I told Ra'Qan, which was "Yeah man I'm good," but I wasn't. I started dipping and dabbing, getting high off and on again.

Powerful took me at my word without a second thought because I was a "Git' money nigga." The thought of Powerful not firing me had Troy's ass tight. He wanted me out of the picture. I had seen him go to a pay phone and call police on niggas hustling down the block from us and say shit like, "My daughter was comin' home from school and these guys on such and such block tried to sell her drugs." Then, his bitch ass would stand off in the distance and watch the police pull up and harass them until they had to shut down. He found that funny, but there's nothing funny about niggas snitching.

I should have seen the writing on the wall. I was in the private house grinding like I did every day. Today, I had a young kid from my mother's building as my lookout. The young kid sends this Puerto Rican cat in. He was sweating up a storm, right away I knew he was a cop. He asked me could he get two nickels. The hairs on my neck stood on end. Not only did he look like a cop, his numbers were off. We were selling three dollar bottles. I told him I didn't have anything but out on the table in plain sight were fifty bottles of crack, a few hundred dollars, and a twenty-two revolver. When I said that I didn't have anything he reached for his gun and missed. He was nervous as hell, for a split second I thought it could have been a robbery. He reached for his gun again, pulled it from the holster and said, "Police, get on the floor."

Everyone that gets arrested for selling drugs knows it's the police when they get busted. There's no such thing as an undercover cop. We recognize the police as soon as we see them. They stand out like a bowling ball on a snow-covered football field. This would be my third arrest in less than a year. My lookout was a minor, so he was released into his parents' custody. As for me, I was taken to the Bronx central bookings and held for two days where I had my mug shots taken, asked my medical history, and assigned an 18b lawyer.

I stood in front of a judge who tells my legal aid that my bail is set at five thousand dollars, which to me at the time might as well have been five million. To be completely honest, most niggas standing on the corner don't have fees for a lawyer, forget about bail. So off to the Bronx House Correctional Facility I go. The Bronx House was a neighborhood picnic. It was all Bronx niggas so you were bound to bump into someone from your hood. I met this brother named Forever from 169th and Boston Road. He was housed in the dormitory next to mine. He would see me in the dayroom come over and shoot the shit with me. This particular day he approached me and asked me if he could hold my ring to go on his visit. It seemed innocent enough, but what I hadn't realized in the time that I had been gone from New York, was that along with the crack pandemic there also came a plethora of schemes and cons, and Forever was running a con on me. When it came time for me to get my ring back, he told me he let his man from his dorm hold it, and when he saw him later that night, he would get it from him. That night never came.

When I would run into Forever, which was few and far between, he would say that he hadn't seen his man yet. Needless to say, I never saw my ring again either. But you know the saying, what comes around goes around. Years later, Forever's girl said he put a .44 Magnum in his mouth and blew his brains out. The hood said she killed him. The griminess never ceases to amaze me, but, by no means am I suggesting that he deserved to die the way he did. I called Powerful from the Bronx House and told him to leave me in jail until my bail got reduced. I was chilling, eating good, playing cards, watching TV, and yucking it up.

Based on my experiences in Valhalla, and now the Bronx House, jail wasn't shit, or so I thought.

Watching TV sitting in the dayroom I hear the C.O yelling, "Atkins pack up."

I was confused, "Pack up for what?" I asked.

He was shuffling through his paperwork; to him, it was business as usual. "Rikers Island" was his reply.

Rikers Island! I couldn't go to the Island, fuck that! I ran to the phone and called who we all call when the shit hits the fan, mommy. I was begging her to call the lawyer, call Powerful, call anybody. There wasn't anything she could do; I was about to find out what jail was really like.

Chapter 5
Rikers Island

From the ride on the bus to Riker's Island I could tell things were different. It was no longer the happy go lucky atmosphere that it was in the Bronx House. Niggas whole attitudes were somber and more serious. I asked an old timer what his charges were and his reply was, "None of your fuckin' business." That set the tone of how shit was going to be. The reception areas in Valhalla, the Bronx House, and Rikers were basically the same. You were put into a cell with twenty or more inmates where you waited until your name was called. Once called, you would go into a room with tables and wait for correction officers. The C.O.'s instruct you to strip bare, lift up your feet, lift your balls, and spread your ass cheeks. It's invasive as well as demeaning, but it was 1988, and Rikers Island was a jungle. You had niggas who would conceal razors in their mouths, tapped to the bottom of their feet, or hidden in their anal cavities wrapped in toilet tissue. I even heard stories of uncircumcised inmates concealing razors in their foreskins.

Rikers Island is appropriately named. It's an Island in the middle of the east river with numerous inmate housing facilities. Some of the more notable buildings are the four building for the juvenile inmate population, the eight building, for inmates sentenced to a year or less, and the Women's House which is self-explanatory. I was sent to the now-shuttered infamous HDM, The House of Detention for Men, or as we inmates referred to it as, The House of Dangerous Murderers. The only building worse than HDM was the four building. The juveniles would assault and nearly kill each other over the simplest offenses such as cracking a joke about someone's mother, or more commonly, over a pair of sneakers. HDM was an assortment of robbers, murderers, rapist and drug dealers. At that time, (I don't know about now), the penal system didn't differentiate between non-violent and violent offenders. You might be facing a skid bid of six months, and be housed with a motherfucker facing twenty-five years to life, but you and he are housed in the same housing unit until you're sentenced. Meanwhile, you trying to do your bid and go home and this nigga don't have shit to lose if he sticks a shank through your neck for the phone.

I was housed in four block, side A. It had three floors of cells called tiers. The second and third tiers were closed because you had motherfuckers getting thrown over the railing. We had two small TVs out in front of our cells, and two thirty inch TVs in the dayroom where we would sit and play cards. Besides the guards, you had inmates who ran the house. Those inmates were called the house gang. If you wanted to get on the house gang, you had to bang a nigga out or blow a nigga up. Banging a cat is stabbing him with a shank, and blowing him up is cutting him with a razor. Shanks were called guns, and a razor was called an ox. If you blew a nigga up, his wound would be called a buck fifty. If you see someone on the streets of New York and they have a horrific scar across their face or neck, more than likely they've enjoyed the hospitality of Rikers Island.

The most appalling assault I've ever witnessed is when a new inmate came into our house and tried to lock shit down. The house gang consisted of this big brother named Magnetic, another nigga named Pete, and this one brother who took me under his wing named Sun-God. When the new inmate came in running off at the mouth all of the other inmates stood quiet and looked. The next morning after breakfast he went into the dayroom, got up on one of those long lunchroom tables and started doing pushups. Sun-God went into the dayroom behind him, closed the door, jumped on his back, spat a razor out of his mouth and began to cut a pattern on his back that looked like a jig-saw puzzle. In my mind, he had two options, one, try to turn over and fight and risk exposing his face, or two, lay there and let Sun-God turn his back into what looked like ground beef. He chose to lay there.

Some of the guards were as corrupt as the inmates. They could become a parental figure, ally, or enemy. They were the ones, allegedly, who supplied the Latin Kings with Gem razor blades. There was also an incident where a C.O. smuggled a handgun in to an inmate. Rikers took a toll on them as it did us. I remember laying in my bed with a sheet hanging up covering the front of my cell. I was lying there naked calling the female C.O. on duty. I pretended that I wanted to ask her a question, but what I really wanted to do was flash her. She cut that shit short before she even walked to my cell. She let me know that if I flashed her, "she would open up my cell, and let niggas come in and kill me." I told her never mind and to forget it. I knew she wasn't making idle threats. In any penitentiary, a C.O. can have an inmate beaten or killed. For example, whenever a rapist, child molester, or child abuser comes into a house, the correction officers let it be known to all the other inmates, and jailhouse justice is administered promptly.

My cell was all the way in the back of the cellblock so whenever there was any business to conduct it was conducted a few feet from my cell. One evening this big Puerto Rican and Black dude were talking. From what I overheard, the brother's wifey was supposed to smuggle in some heroin. Whatever the reason, she didn't come through with the drugs. The Puerto Rican cat let him know that if the drugs didn't make it through on the next visit, "He was gon' have a fuckin' problem." I had never seen a grown man shake before, but his fear was warranted. There were all kinds of weapons on our cellblock. Some a foot long and an inch thick. If I had to describe them, I would have to say they resembled homemade swords.

It's said, jail is a place for rehabilitation, and for some, it can be, but others go to places like Rikers Island and become better criminals, gladiators, and savages. The ludicrousness of it all is that even in an environment like Rikers Island, Blacks are still divided! Take the situation of the Puerto Rican nigga extorting the Black inmate. If it had been a Black inmate extorting a Puerto Rican inmate, the outcome would have been different. Hispanics and other races have a concept that we as Blacks haven't grasped yet. That concept is unity. If it had been a Black inmate extorting a Puerto Rican inmate, the other Puerto Rican inmates would have intervened. They wouldn't have to know him from a hole in the wall. That's the way it is.

For Black inmates, it's a different scenario. When a Black inmate walks into a house, the other Black inmates line up and decide who's going to take what, whether it's his sneakers, jewelry, or the clothes on his back. His physical stature is irrelevant. From the time he walks through the cellblock gates, if he has anything of value he's going to have to fight for it. On the other hand, when a Hispanic inmate walks through those doors; their people ask if they need soap, deodorant, or food. If they need to make a phone call, they get that also. After many years I've come to a conclusion that our lack of unity may be because we don't have a flag, language or country to unite us, and our history and color aren't enough.

I didn't have long in HDM. I was sitting in the dayroom watching TV, and this Jamaican nigga was a little funky.

So I said, "Damn, money stink!"

This brother named Islam, who happened to be the Jamaican cat's man overheard me and said, "Fuck you nigga, you be stinkin' too."

Haven't already made the mistake of running' my mouth, I escalated shit by saying' the worst thing you can say to a nigga, especially to a nigga in jail, "Suck my dick!"

Fuck it, I said it. I wasn't a punk. Yes, things had changed, but a fight is still a fight. I mean, I'm not Mike Tyson, but I can fight.

Islam got up and said, "What! Say it again."

So, I said it again.

"Suck my dick!"

I still hadn't learned my lesson about telling a man to suck my dick, but I was about to learn the hard way! When I said it again, he punched me in my face. We were going at it for a while. That's when I caught him in the mouth and knocked his tooth out. As the fight went on, I started to get winded from all of the cigarette smoking. In the middle of the brawl, I quit and ran out of the dayroom. I don't know why. Looking back, I guess I was out of my element. Truth be told, I wasn't aggressive enough.

I ran to my cell and laid down. Minutes later, Islam and this other nigga came to my cell and stood at the door. Islam had a shank in his hand. I jumped up out of bed and grabbed a sheet so I could wrap him up if he came in.

I looked at him and said, "If you want it, come in and git' it."

As he stepped in with the shank, I ran toward him. When I did, his hand moved fast. I felt the shank travel across the back of my head to the front of my face. Islam looked at me, turned around and left. When I looked in the mirror, I had a gash extending from behind my left ear to the front of my face just under my temple. The wound was so deep that you could stick your fingers inside and touch my skull. I picked up my tee shirt, put it to my head, and walked to the front of the cellblock.

As I walked to where the C.O. was sitting in the officer's bubble, an inmate looked at me and said, "Dammmn, yo' shit is leakin'!"

As I continued walking to the front, I saw Sun-God. I went over to him to give him a pound. He immediately backed away from me and told me he couldn't get any of my blood on him or he might be charged for cutting me. The medics hurried into our unit, placed me on a gurney and rushed me to the clinic.

With all of the numerous assaults occurring daily, Rikers Island was profoundly ill-equipped to deal with major trauma. As I lay on the gurney, I turned my face to look. There beside my head were enormous blood clots, some so huge, it looked as though someone had taken bloody globs of toilet tissue and flung them next to my face. I felt my stomach beginning to turn. I saw a light. Whether Heaven or Hell, I was on my way. I heard a medic say my skin and gums were turning pale. In my mind, at the age of twenty-two, I asked God to take me and end it all, but I cheat death once more.

Up to this point in my life, this had been my third encounter with death, and each time I've come away alive. The second was when Karen pointed the gun at me. The first was my being born prematurely. At birth, I weighed a little over four pounds. So again, I ask God why am I here? Unbelievably, as I recall, there was only one medic on staff who knew how to properly administer an IV. It was enough to keep me alive until I reached the hospital.

On the way to the hospital, the C.O. who was riding in the ambulance with me asked me what happened. I told him that I fell and hit my head on the edge of the sink in my cell. What else could I say? The criminal code of conduct is cut and dry; snitches get stitches!

He replied, "That must have been a pretty sharp sink."

I received four injections into the wound along with thirty-nine stitches, nineteen stitches on the inside of the wound and twenty stitches to the scalp. I stayed in the hospital handcuffed to the hospital bed for about a day and then it was back to the Island. I lay in the reception area holding pens for another day until I was well enough to transfer to my new facility, C-95, M-module, which was also known as, Murder-Mod. It would be another three weeks before I got the stitches removed and I was able to exercise. I gave the cigarettes up and started eating every morsel of food I could get my hands on. I ate up to twelve slices of bread a day, plus an extra meal whenever I could get one. I was getting ready for war. Islam had baptized me in blood.

The animal was awakening in me. I kept to myself and didn't socialize with anyone. There was no laughing or playing, and very little talking, just eating, silence, and exercise. I was getting huge doing a thousand push-ups a day. C-95 was run by the Latin Kings who were predominately Puerto Rican. The Crips and the Bloods hadn't reached New York, but they would eventually emerge as an answer to the Hispanic gangs dominating the Black population on Rikers. The only other influential gang on Rikers at that time were the Ñetas which were made up of both Black and Hispanic inmates. Murder-mod was a dormitory with beds lined up side by side, so if you had a beef with someone and you made the mistake of going to sleep that night, the next morning there was a strong possibility that they would find you in your bunk with a shank sticking out of your chest. So what the warriors and the wise did was sleep during the day, and walk the dormitory in the evening.

Since I kept to myself, the house gang would ask me if I had any input on matters in the dorm when they had meetings. I didn't give a fuck what went on as long as it didn't concern me. I only asked nasty motherfuckers to stop blowing boogers in the showers and leaving that disgusting shit on the walls. Otherwise, if I did say anything, it would be to the older inmates. What I did do was sit back and observe the daily movements of my dorm mates. I would see homo thug ass niggas bopping through the dorm all day, and later on that evening they would sneak into the shower with a fucking homo. (Not that there is anything wrong with that if that's your thing, I'm just saying.) Or, you had other niggas saying that a homo was their wife, and they would kill you if you said anything to them. All through the penal system, you had homos coming through with big titties and fat asses. (And yes, I can say that. I'm not gay, homophobic, or anti-gay, and again, I'm just sayin'.) What's ridiculous is the city and state will pay tens of thousands of dollars to give homosexual men hormone shots to make them look like women, who will then be housed in a men's facility. In that said facility, thousands of men are housed at the cost of up to fifty thousand a year per inmate. But that same city and state will cut music programs, art programs and other programs designed to give our children a head start.

In our dorm, there was this Puerto Rican nigga named Tattoo. He was what I would call a bona fide homo-maker. He would scare timid motherfuckers, or flat out rape them for that ass. One evening, this Hispanic inmate came into the dormitory wearing full motorcycle regalia. You know, the leather jacket, the boots, insignias emblazoned on the back of his jacket, and a full beard. I think he even had shades on. He was slim, but I'll admit he looked tough. I don't remember his motorcycle club, but he was an absolute disgrace to their colors. He made a critical mistake; he took the bed next to Tattoo. The next morning he got out of bed, shaved his beard off, combed his hair back and only got out of his bed to shit, shower and eat.

Eventually, Tattoo got his just desserts when this young Spanish kid named Freddie got housed in our dorm. As soon as he came in, Tattoo set his sights on making Freddie his bitch. He thought he was going to rape Freddie and turn him out, but little Freddie had a trick for that ass. When Tattoo approached Freddie and propositioned him, Freddie went into the bathroom and came out with an industrial mop ringer and split Tattoo's face wide open. That's what I'm talking about!

The only thing that comes to mind when trying to find a comparison to an inmate is a soldier in combat. By no means am I glorifying prison, but prison is where you separate the men from the boys, the strong from the weak, and the predator from the prey! You learn to make weapons from any and everything. Something as simple as taking water that comes out of a separate spout on the side of the water fountain at 180 degrees and throwing it in someone's face, to something as ingenious as melting the filter of a cigarette butt and sharpening an edge on it sharp enough to slice someone's face open.

The only deterrent to the wave of violence was an elite unit of correction officers. They have a comedic name for this unit, but there's nothing funny about these motherfuckers. They were called "The Ninja Turtles." They're called that because unlike the other correction officers; they wear green army fatigues. When they come into a house, you sit your ass down on your bunk and don't move until they tell you to. They are the biggest group of thugs on the Island, and they will *beat your ass like you stole something*! The guards for the most part just want to do their shift and make it home to their families unscathed, so in reality, the inmates ran the house on a day to day basis.

Things were usually quiet and monotonous, but a knucklehead is always in the wings waiting to break up the humdrum.

For example, a new inmate is barely in the dorm for thirty minutes when he steps into the dayroom, takes the mounted TV off of the wall, and smashes it on the floor. Now he was a big dude, so we all overlooked his transgressions, that is until the captain came into the dorm and informed us that we wouldn't be getting a new TV unless the situation got taken care of. As soon as the captain left, a Muslim brother named Karim picked the broken TV up off of the floor and smashed the TV over money's head. That's all it took for the whole house to start wailing on that ass. I've never seen a thug run so fast. An hour later we had a new TV in the dorm.

Time was quickly flying by. I had been on Rikers for three months now, and since I was quiet and kept to myself, I stayed out of trouble. In fact, the only time I got into an altercation was when I was with the house gang. We beat the shit out of this nigga, literally. It was like déjà vu all over again. Once again, a new jack comes into the house trying to run shit. Where do they find these motherfuckers? This time, we didn't wait for him to break the TV. The entire dorm is pounding on him with locks in socks, feet, and fist. I throw a right hook to his left side, and bloody feces comes out of his ass and splatters on the floor. I didn't realize it until he walked up to the C.O.'s bubble with a white towel wrapped around his waist and there were bloody red splotches in the area of his asshole. I was young, strong, and reckless. I would walk around the dorm in my boxers late at night trying to rap to the female guards on duty. When our dorm would have a shakedown, inspection for weapons, I would hop out of bed with an erection.

I never got the chance to fuck one of them; my game wasn't strong enough yet. I make that assumption because you had plenty of niggas fucking C.O.'s when they came home, and you even had a few who'd be fucking C.O.'s while they were locked up. Perhaps it is a testament to the fact that so many Black men are either locked up, dead, or strung out on drugs that a woman would risk her livelihood to have a man; or maybe lust is just a strong motherfucking emotion.

In between the daily routine, there would be court dates. The C.O.'s would get you up at four in the morning to go to court. You would be taken downstairs to the holding area until you ate breakfast, loaded up on the bus to go to the courthouse, and sit there for most of the day. You would finally see your lawyer for five minutes, the judge for three minutes, go back to the holding pens and then repeat the process in reverse. By the time you get back to your dorm, you've spent the entire day just to see the judge and your lawyer for a total of eight minutes.

In the holding pens, niggas would bump into cats they had a beef with, and somebody would end up stabbed or cut. If an inmate was known for cutting other inmates, he would be transported around the Island in specially made gloves so that he would have no use of his hands. Many institutions now have a chair that an inmate has to sit on to detect metal in a body cavity. I was coming from court one day, and it happened to be inmate family day. This one inmate was sitting at a table with his family, and everyone at his table had their back turned to him. Sitting there, was this pretty redbone chick sucking his dick right there in front of the other inmates, C.O.'s, other families, and everyone at his table. You could see her red lipstick on his dick. As I write this, I wonder what the ride back home in the car must have been like with her family. Shit, I felt embarrassed for her! Everyone in the holding cell sat there and watched until we eventually got called up to our respective units.

Before I knew it, I had been on Rikers Island for four months, until one day in September I went to court, and my bail was lowered from five thousand to fifteen hundred dollars. Two days later, Powerful had me bailed out, and I was on my way back to the streets with a refresher course in violence.

I.Y. WADE

Chapter 6
Back on the Block!

Powerful was happy as hell to see me. Niggas that I had never met knew who I was. You see, Powerful had been telling cats about me while I was locked up and my rep as a money maker was becoming established. The same day I got out of jail, I was back down the block chasing that paper. When I got down the street, there were some new niggas hustling. They were this family called the Jansens. There were five of them, three brothers and two cousins. Their mothers lived in the building we were hustling out of. I had no idea what made Powerful let them on the block. Before I got locked up, we would kill a nigga if they hustled on the block, it didn't matter if you lived there or not. I soon learned that they would die and kill for that paper just like us, so Powerful had no choice but to hammer out a truce and let them take a shift.

Our crew worked the twelve in the afternoon shift until twelve in the morning, and conversely, they worked the twelve in the morning shift until twelve in the afternoon. I learned a lesson from that experience which men have learned throughout history, and that is, truces are usually broken. The oldest brother was the head of their clique. Niggas called him Action, or Act for short. He was called that because he didn't give a fuck and he didn't do a whole lot of talking. From fist to guns he would git' in that ass, action first! The middle brother a few years younger than him was called Sleepy. He was a bully; you know the type, mean mugging niggas all the time, but if you stood up to him, or caught him by himself, he would back down. The youngest of the brothers was Marcus. I believe he was around ten years old, and he was already on the streets selling crack, and on top of that, he was a motherfucking troublemaker. It's because of Marcus that our crew and his family stayed in beef with each other.

Marcus would be out in front of the building hustling until it was me and my people's shift. We would obey the rules that were agreed upon, but Marcus's little ass would always want to sell a few more cracks.

I would tell him, "Nah shorty it's my shift." This little nigga would run upstairs screaming Sleepaay! Sleepy would come downstairs trying to intimidate me, ice grilling me and shit, but I didn't give a fuck. Wasn't anything, or anybody going to stop my flow. One day Sleepy gassed his man James up to test me. See, that's how you can tell how a cat is built, he wants to step to you, but he's leery, so he gets his man to fight you. James was stocky, but as I said, I was doing at the very least a thousand push-ups a day on the Island, and I was ready for the world. James was talking mad shit trying to beat me with his mouth, but I hit him with that old school gangster shit and said, "Whatever's clever nigga!" When I said that, he put his hands up and ran towards me. I snatched him up and slammed him. *Wham!* From that day on, Sleepy might talk shit from time to time, but he didn't want to fight me.

Then there were the two cousins, Malik, who was younger than Act, but older than Sleepy. He had a younger brother Ya-ya who was younger than Marcus. Malik had gone to prison and converted to Islam. When he came home, he started teaching Islam to Ya-ya. I converted to Islam long after I left Rikers. It had nothing to do with me finding religion while being incarcerated. In fact, when I was locked up on Rikers practicing Christianity, I would get upset if a Muslim brother tried to convert me to Islam. What I find amusing is that you'll have Muslims who will get on you about eating pork, you know the rhetoric, "I don't swine and dine." or, "No pork on my fork." but at the same time, they'll be quick to curse, sell drugs, use drugs, smoke cigarettes, have sex out of wedlock, and kill a nigga in a heartbeat. I include myself in that analysis. Now that's not to say

Christians are any holier, but at least they're not fucking with you about what you're eating.

Ya-ya was nine years old, and he was selling crack too. The whole family was off the fucking hook. They were 'bout that life before it was in fashion. These niggas would slap you five then walk up the block and rob your moms. Ms. Jane, who was Malik and Ya-ya's mother, was 'bout it too. She got into a fist fight with the super of the building and busted this niggas lip, and I'm talkin' both of them was in their fifties. You have to love it when a nigga's moms give a motherfucker a one on one.

The next day I did what I should have done as soon as I got home, got some pussy! There was an older woman who lived in the building named Corin. Corin was a beautiful tall thing. She had hairy sideburns, which I've always found attractive, light complexion and shoulder length jet black hair. I would put her in her late thirties maybe early forties. I was twenty-two and the thought of hitting that mature pussy after being locked up for four months had my dick rock hard. The only strike against Corin was she was a crackhead. No, not like someone who's dirty and sleeping on the streets but she was a head like me, a head on the low.

I paid her thirty dollars and gave Ms. Jane three jumbs to use her spare bedroom. When we went into the bedroom and Corin pulled off her panties, my eyes fell on those fat pussy lips. My mouth started to water. I told her I wanted to sixty-nine. The taste of her pussy was different from the young girls I had been fucking. I now know that as a woman matures the scent and taste of her vagina also changes. I laid her on her back, pushed her legs open and back and began to lick her from her clit to her asshole, only slowing down to tongue fuck her twat. After a while, I stood up over her, looked in her eyes, squatted down and slid my dick into her soaking wet pussy. She let out a small sigh. "Oooh." I was grinding in that pussy, slow, and deep. Making sure she could feel every inch. At twenty-two, I was learning how to master my stroke. As I got older, I learned that you don't always have to beat a pussy up to make it good. I also learned that size doesn't matter if you can't make a bitch cum. Her legs were shaking as she climaxed. When it was my turn to cum, she told me to lay on my back so she could ride me. She eased down onto the dick and started twirling in a circular motion. Mmmm, mmm, mmm! It was too much for me. I grabbed her waist and thrust my dick up in her. Slamming her pussy until I felt the nut overwhelming me. "Aaaarrgghhh!" Damn! I felt like a new man.

The next morning I got dressed and kissed her goodbye. When she saw me later that day, she acted as though she was my woman but, I mean, it wasn't like that for me. For me, it was just business and a motherfucking nut. Now I know plenty of readers out there are saying to themselves, "This nigga is nasty! Fuckin' a crackhead and eatin' her pussy and shit!" Truth be told they're right, but you had a whole lot of niggas fucking crackheads, especially the ones that looked good. The ones we wanted to fuck all of our lives, and now had the opportunity to do it. I'm just one of the few who's honest enough to let it be known. Besides, it's easy for us to look at a person who smokes crack as beneath us, but you'll have a cokehead who will spend more money sniffing coke and feel their high society, again, no pun intended, and think their shit don't stink. The flipside of the coin is, if a nigga spends five hundred a week smoking weed, he's a motherfucking baller, but a fiend spending two hundred a week on crack is a low-life crackhead. Go figure.

I would never fuck Corin again, and sadly, some many years later she would die from the second endemic that was wreaking havoc in our community; AIDS! I feel I would be remiss if I didn't mention the ruination that occurred simultaneously and almost left our people laid bare. Not long after I fucked Corin; I fucked her niece, Rachel. Rachel was slim, young, and pretty. She had hazel colored green eyes, eyes that sparkled with optimism. I hadn't seen that in quite some time in the ghetto. Yes, I know I'm descriptive when it comes to women, what can I say, women are the muse of life, art, and certainly men! As I reflect on this seventeen-year-old mother of two, I was awestruck that she still had hope, but with all that being said, Rachel was a hoe. My whole crew had run through her while I was locked up. Also, her oldest son looked like he could have been fathered by her youngest brother.

The first time I fucked Rachel was on Pebble Beach. She told me to talk dirty to her. This little thing was five years younger than me, but she was on some extra shit. I was happy to comply. "Take this dick you fuckin' bitch," I said, fucking her doggy style on the landing of the roof. "Throw that pussy back; you feel me splitting that pussy." As good as the first experience was, the second time, when I got her into the bedroom was a hundred times better. She rode the dick like a cowgirl, standing on her feet and riding side saddle. When it came time for the oral, man oh man, she was the first woman ever to suck my dick with devotion. She let it slide through her lips like a lollipop. I was hooked. Rachel would have the first of my eight abortions. No, she didn't have eight abortions stupid; I had eight abortions from five different women. I guess that makes me the one who's actually stupid!

When it was found out that Corin had died from AIDS some years later, Rachel and I had long broken up. She tried to play me by shouting out of her window that I had it too. I cut that shit short by letting it be known that if I had AIDS- she fucking had AIDS. In the building that we hustled out of there were eight cases of HIV, of those eight cases, six were in Rachel's family. Five of those cases resulted in AIDS and eventually death. In the hood, we call AIDS, The Monster! I'm touching on this subject because, in America,

Blacks make up 13% of the population, and we make up 50% of the new cases of HIV reported. A disproportionately higher rate than any other ethnic group. Therefore, I believe it affects the way we view ourselves, and also the way the world views us. Nine years after the death of Corin, I would finally get up enough courage to get tested. Thankfully the results were negative. Unfortunately, fear keeps a lot of people from being tested, and delay can be deadly.

Meanwhile, things were going alright for me. I was now making three hundred and fifty dollars a week, which at the age of twenty-two and the year 1988, was more money than I had made serving my country. Shit was good! I was making money, getting pussy, and had no problems on the block. Out of the blue, I started getting high again. This time, I was worse than before, and I had no one to blame but myself.

I would run off with Powerful's work only to come back and tell him I fucked his money up and he could do whatever he felt he had to do; even whip my ass if need be, but Powerful respected me for my willingness to take responsibility for my actions, so he never had anything done to me. Besides, I was still the top money earner in the organization. I hit rock bottom one weekend when I sat in a crack house with my foot up against a bathroom door and smoked up to thirty bottles of crack in one sitting.

I didn't eat for two days. The word on the streets was that Powerful and the rest of the crew were looking for me. The next morning I knocked on this old lady's door who lived on the first floor named Ms. Theodore. She was this nice old lady that would give us sandwiches and sodas while we hustled outside, but in my sickness, it didn't matter. It was about five in the morning, and I had on a pair of black gloves waiting for Ms. Theodore to open her door so I could strangle and rob her. Again, a force greater than myself kept Ms. Theodore from answering her door, thus saving both our lives, her from a brutal death, and me from a lifetime of incarceration and shame.

Later that day I went home to Zenobia's. I took off my shirt and looked at myself in the mirror. There was a skeleton looking back at me. If it hadn't been for this crackhead named Dina giving me a bowl of macaroni and cheese, I wouldn't have eaten a thing in two and a half days. This relapse would set me up for the next chapter in my life, sobriety. That night I asked Zenobia for a blanket and slept up on the roof of her building. In the middle of the night, it began to rain. The rain soon turned to hail. I lay up on the roof shivering and asking God for guidance. That guidance came to me in a clear and distinct voice, "Go to 42nd Street." In my mind going to the Deuce was incredulous. 42nd Street, pre-Mayor Giuliani was a haven for drug dealers, addicts, thieves, and prostitutes.

The next morning I woke up and went down to Harlem to see my grandfather. I hadn't seen him in years. Isaac took one look at me, and I suppose he could see I was strung out. He took his forefinger and pushed on the whiteheads that I had on my nose from not bathing in days. That gesture struck me as the most heartfelt and intimate moment my grandfather, and I had shared in my adult life. From the time we were evicted when I was thirteen, it had been nine years since I had seen my grandfather or any of my extended family besides my aunt and my cousins. My great-grandmother passed away while I was in Germany, and as of this day, I have not visited her or my grandmother's grave. My family tree is in utter disarray, much like this generation of children having children, and the crack babies who are now teenagers and young adults, full of resentment against their own parents and society as a whole.

I asked Isaac if I could stay with him and get myself together. He told me no, I would have to find someplace else to stay. With that said, he gave me fifty dollars to get something to eat and hold me down for a few days. That night I slept in the stairwell of his building. I remember sticking my ass out of the window and shitting on the roof. Funny the things we recollect. The next morning I got up and headed down to the Deuce.

That first night I slept in a bank vestibule. In those days, banks didn't require an ATM card to gain entry to banks in the evening. The outer doors would be open all night, so patrons had access to the ATM machines, and it was a regular occurrence to see homeless sleeping in banks. I slept on a cardboard box along with five or six other homeless men and women. That morning when the bank opened up, we all headed out the door and went to the nearest soup kitchen. While there, I saw a gentleman in a Salvation Army uniform. I told him that I needed someplace to stay. He directed me to the Salvation Army Adult Rehabilitation Center, also known as The Miracle on 48th street. I must testify, through all of my difficulties, God has always spoken to me. I only had to listen to hear him. Once I heard him, I had the choice to obey or not.

AIDS in Black America: A Public Health Crisis: NPR

www.npr.org/2012/07/.../**aids**-in-**black**-**america**-a-public-health-crisis...

Jul 5, 2012 - **AIDS** is the primary killer of African-**Americans** ages 19 to 44, and the mortality rate is 10 times higher for **black Americans** than for whites. ... A new Frontline documentary, Endgame: **AIDS** in **Black America**, explores why the HIV epidemic is so much more prevalent in the African...

I.Y. WADE

Chapter 7
Sobriety!

Going to the Salvation Army Adult Rehabilitation Center was the first time in my life that I made a conscious decision to become sober since I had smoked my first joint at the age of eight or nine. I was given a urine test to make sure I had no drugs in my system and by the grace of God I had managed to stay clean long enough to pass the drug test. I was then told the rules and regulations. In addition, I was told that there would be work assignments, and we would also be required to attend church twice a week. The Salvation Army was a real blessing. I learned about addictive personalities and some of the things that triggered my addiction. The main thing that set me off was boredom. I needed to stay involved in something positive. I needed to have goals. More importantly, I needed to put God first in my life. When I was getting high, I blamed God for my addiction, and in that reasoning, I turned away from God and truly hated him. Going to church exposed me to my higher power once again.

It was a co-ed rehab, and although the policies forbid it, you had plenty of fraternizing going on. It was forbidden as well for the Hispanic clients to speak Spanish. Some may disagree, but I feel that was just another form institutional racism.

The average person who gives money to the bell ringing Santa's and other personnel who stand on every corner in the shopping areas soliciting donations, dropping off clothing and furniture at a number of drop-off sites in the five boroughs, and around the world, probably has no idea how much money that organization generates. They take in money directly through donations. The clothing and furniture they receive, they sell, and the clients who are in the drug programs work in the stores and clothing warehouses. The pay rate at that time was approximately a dollar and thirty cents a day, but that's not to belittle the charity that the Salvation Army has done for countless victims of natural disasters, fires, and the drug addicted clients they have helped, and continue to support.

In the program there was an Irish drug counselor named Mark Dadey. Mark would shove the Narcotics Anonymous agenda down our throats, but when we would head to work in the morning and walk past his room, the scent of alcohol would be wafting in the hall. He would come to breakfast shit faced, cold in his eyes, his face would be red, and his head would be held low. He would be too humiliated to look anyone in the face. He was one of the counselors, as well as a client, in the program who had lived there for years. I was terrified that I would end up like that. Wanting sobriety so bad, that you would rather live your life in a drug program, too frightened to live life on life's terms.

While I had found sobriety and God, I couldn't escape lust. I fucked two crackheads from around the neighborhood, and I eventually hooked up with this Jewish girl named Martha from the program. Martha was short with long brown hair and pretty green eyes, but what was most striking to me about her was her fat ass. She had an ass like a Hispanic or a Black girl. The first time I fucked her was in a hotel on ST. Marks Place in the East Village. After that, we fucked in Central Park, under bushes, on benches and any secluded spot we could find.

Again, I was open. Pussy is a hell of a drug. Not long after that, I would leave the Salvation Army. I went back home to Zenobia's after an eight-month absence. My God, the last time I had spent the night at my mother's home I was smoking crack a hundred miles an hour and staying up all night puffing wula after wula under the covers in the bedroom. My lips and fingers would be brown from the weed and nicotine residue. I bought Martha to my neighborhood.

I didn't know what it was, but she acted differently when she saw how I lived. She was a young "Jewish American Princess" from Long Island. She fucked with niggas most of her life, in fact, she had two kids with some God body out on Long Island, but the South Bronx ain't Long Island. The Bronx is really hood, really poor. Not long after that, our relationship was over. That situation left me jaded. I was convinced that money made the world go round, from family to friends, to women.

For every dollar you have, that's how many motherfuckers you can count on. I was getting an education that niggas can't get in an Ivy League school and that education was self-preservation. Soon after, I left the program and began working at a TGI Friday's restaurant near Rockefeller Center in Manhattan. I had been a cook in the military for three years, but because I didn't have a work history for almost two years, the manager, a White guy named Mike, started me off as a dishwasher making four dollars an hour, the minimum wage in 88'. A week passed, and this young White kid started working alongside me as a dishwasher also. You'll see the relevance of race in a moment. Two weeks more passed, and he and I got chummy.

We're busy loading the dishes on the conveyor belt at work one-day talking shit, and I said to him, "I'll be glad when we get a raise."

He replied, "Me too, this five dollars an hour ain't makin' it."

"Five dollars an hour!" I said stunned.

"They started me off at four dollars an hour." There was an awkward silence.

Perhaps a week later a Reiss Corporation executive, which is who the Friday's, Taco Bell, and Pizza Hut franchises were owned by in those days, came to the back where we were working and said, verbatim, "Why do you have this blonde haired, blue eyed guy back here washing dishes when he should be upfront waiting tables." I couldn't believe my ears, but he said it in my presence without any hesitation, or consideration for how I might have felt, or about any legal ramifications for that matter.

Once upon a time, I had been naïve enough to debate with my mother and tell her that racism didn't exist in New York. That belief changed one day when I went into a deli on Grammatan Ave. in Mount Vernon to buy a pack of cigarettes. A young Italian kid behind the counter told me the cigarettes were five dollars a pack.

"Five dollars!" I said a bit flabbergasted. At the time cigarettes were roughly two dollars and fifty cents.

His reply, "I forgot that's a lot of money to you people."

While that comment had flown over my head, on a subconscious level, it also slapped me in the face. A decade later I would run into another type of institutional, and economic racism when I applied for DeVry Technical Institute. I met with an admissions counselor at DeVry and expressed my interest in becoming a computer programmer. He stated, without giving me any type of aptitude test, that I would be better suited for the computer technician course. I again, let that offense pass. These situations happen to so many Blacks on a daily basis, and many of us let them slip by without acting upon them. Occurrences like security guards following us in department stores while we shop, driving while Black, or walking into expensive stores, or auto dealerships, and being overlooked by staff. Other times the incidents cannot be overlooked, and we as a people will file lawsuits, press for criminal and civil charges to be filed, and in the extreme, riot! On the flip side, so many of us are indoctrinated into a position of fear and subjugation. Our employers speak condescendingly to us, the police harass and kill our Black men, and the school system continues to under-educate our children. Teaching them that the vast majority of our people have contributed little to civilization.

It wouldn't be long before my White co-worker was promoted to bartender where the average weekend tips were triple what we were making as dishwashers. A month down the line I would be promoted to a cook, making six dollars an hour. In total, I worked roughly six months for the Reiss Corporation before I asked for a raise. When I was denied, I quit and went back to the streets where I could control my own destiny. In retrospect, the money wasn't a deal breaker, but along with the racist comments and atmosphere of inequality, I had enough!

I hooked back up with Powerful and started hustling again. There was a whole slew of new niggas who were following the young God. One was an older brother named Excellence, his younger brother Grill, this young brother named Pap and Powerful's sixteen-year-old cousin, a pretty boy named Sha'born. It was the summer of 89'. The money was plentiful, the guns were bountiful, and the streets were lawless. I came back focused. Although Powerful had leadership skills, he didn't have the business acumen to ensure money was made and everyone ate, so I was the one who showed the organization how to keep books. Up until then, Powerful would buy an ounce of crack and estimate how much profit should be made. I approached it from a numbers perspective which made it more precise. I would have the figures exact, give or take a few dollars. If we spent seven hundred dollars on an ounce, I would tell the niggas bottling up that we should make back twelve hundred. If the bottlers only made eleven hundred, then the bottles should be fatter. That way I could monitor if a nigga was stealing. It wasn't rocket science, just common sense, or business sense if you will. With that business sense, I soon became the go-to nigga on most business decisions.

Though I had never gotten involved in the Five Percent Nation, I learned their number code which is called Mathematics, and their alphabet, which is called the Supreme Alphabet. It's that code that I used when bookkeeping, so if and when the police raided our drug houses, they would have no idea of what they were looking at.

I was now getting paid approximately five hundred dollars a week whenever Powerful decided to pay us. That was still my biggest problem with him; he didn't like to pay a nigga. Anyway, one day a few of us were sitting on the block, me, Sha'born, this cat named Gee and that bitch ass nigga Troy. Troy had left Powerful's organization some time ago. When I came back from rehab, he had left the block to go Upstate New York to a town called Poughkeepsie. Troy was making money out of town selling heroin. He just came through to hang out with niggas. These two Puerto Rican homies' named Miguel and Alex came walking down the block and gave us all pounds. When they left Troy told us, "Yo', my moms said Alex and Miguel robbed her last night." None of us said anything since we were cool with them niggas, and Troy was a pussy anyway. When Alex and Miguel came back up the block, Troy approached them.

"Can I holla' at y'all for a second?" Troy asked.

Miguel said, "Yeah go ahead, what up?"

Troy told him what he told us.

"My mother said y'all stuck her up last night."

Before he could say another word, Alex got hype. He got in Troy's face.

"You gon' give me a pound thinkin' I robbed your moms, what kinda' shit is that?"

When he said that he smacked the Gucci bag that Troy had been swinging back and forth, and knocked it out of his hand. They were tussling for the bag on the ground when Miguel pulled out a machete and told Troy to back the fuck up. Alex picked the bag up, reached in it, and pulled out a chrome nine- millimeter.

He pointed the gun at Troy and told him, "If you want it, come and git' it nigga you can have it!"

Alex and Miguel walked towards the projects, and Troy walked down the stairs to Third Ave.

Sha'born told me and Gee he was going up the block to see this bitch then head to his crib and chill. Since he was Powerful's cousin, he didn't have to stay on the block with us anyway. Besides, his young sixteen-year-old ass was smoking crack so Powerful didn't want him handling the drugs or the money.

Not even an hour later, Sha'born comes back down the block and tells Gee and me that this cat named Clay came to his house and told him that Troy came to his house and pulled out a gun while he was sitting there with his mother. I don't care where you're from or what race you are, there are certain things you don't do, and disrespecting somebody's mother is one of those things! We were all going to sit back and watch Troy and Clay shoot a one on one. I had no idea how Clay got involved in the shit anyway but fuck it, who doesn't want to watch a fight? What we didn't know was that Troy went and got this O.G. nigga named Cherokee. Cherokee was an old timer from my mother's generation, and Zenobia had already schooled me that Cherokee was a killer.

When Troy came downstairs with Cherokee, Cherokee had on a sweat hood with a bulletproof vest on under it. He didn't say much of anything. Nothing except, "It's gon' be a fair fight, and nobody's jumpin' in." That wasn't my intentions anyway, so I didn't give a fuck, but regrettably, Sha'born being young, had to open his mouth. He said the two words that would be his last. "Fuck that." When he said that, Cherokee didn't even reply. He lifted up his sweat hood, pulled out a .38 and fired one shot. *Pow!* He hit Sha'born in the stomach. When he fired, we all started running. Cherokee looked around to see if anyone else wanted some, me included. It didn't matter that he and my mother had grown up together. If I wanted it, I could get it, without hesitation.

Cherokee hollered up to his kids looking out of the window and said, "Throw me my car keys." He got into his car and casually drove off as if he was going to the supermarket. This brought the war home for our organization. One of our own had been gunned down. That was the first time in my life that I realized that anyone was vulnerable. Sha'born lay there on the ground gasping for air, eyes glazed over, pitch black and soulless. I could see his life leaving him, breath by breath; it abandoned his young body. We watched as the EMS put him into the ambulance and rushed him to Lincoln Hospital.

When our crew met up at the hospital later that night, Powerful wanted to know what happened to his younger cousin. All of the yes men around him let him blame Clay and Troy for Sha'born's death but the truth was if Sha'born had kept his mouth shut he would still be alive, and I told him so. We attended Sha'born's funeral dressed in all black. Outside of the funeral home, Powerful told the crew that the police would be watching us for a while so we couldn't retaliate right away. In my opinion, and I could be wrong, Powerful didn't want any part of Cherokee, so we let the situation play out which culminated with Troy heading back to Poughkeepsie, never to step foot in our neighborhood again. Clay went down south only coming back to New York for days at a time, and Cherokee turned himself in after his youngest son died in a fire. The neighbors in my mother's building said he believed that God had punished him for killing Sha'born.

In the mid to late eighties, throughout New York and America, drug crews were gaining notoriety, and rightfully so, Fat Cat

Nichols and the Supreme Team were in Queens, Alpo, AZ, Rich Porter and the notorious Murder Inc. crew were out of Harlem. In the Bronx, we had the Wild Cowboys, Cypress Russians, Boy George, and the infamous Larry Davis. Brooklyn had the Decepticons, Lo-Lifes, Fifty cents, and a wide variety of criminals. I planned to make my mark as quietly as possible. Though I was becoming as volatile as any nigga in the hood, I preferred diplomacy, and besides, when I went to rehab, I jumped bail for that drug case, so I wanted to keep as low a profile as possible. In the meantime I met this young girl named Linda who would become the mother of my son, although I didn't plan it that way, as usual, I was just trying to get some pussy.

Linda was a shy fifteen-year-old beauty from 168th street, and I was twenty-three. At the time, I didn't have a grasp on the concept of age. When I got with Linda, I was renting a room in Mott Haven projects on 141st Willis Ave. On our first date, I took her shopping. She was so nervous she just picked out anything. I don't think one piece of her clothing was coordinated, but she was happy. Linda's mother didn't buy her or her two younger sisters much when they were growing up. In fact, she was hardly ever home. She was usually at one of her two jobs working, and when their mother did come home, she drank, slept, and kept a filthy house. I would tell Linda that I wouldn't spend the night if she didn't have her room cleaned when I came over.

My sweet little baby would do everything she could to please me, and somehow I still found fault in so many of the things that she did. I often criticized her for things that she had no control of, like the way she dressed, or the way she acted. What I failed to realize was that she was still a child and in the end, I made her miserable. The first time I hit that young pussy, I had her sliding all over the living room floor of her mother's house, but the truth is, she loved it rough and hard. The harder I fucked her, the harder she wanted it. I would suck on her chocolate pussy forever making her cum in my mouth until her body would quiver. Then I would turn her over doggy style and pound her pussy from the back until juice would literally run out from between her legs like someone had turned a faucet on. I have no idea if it was the sex, money, or the wining and dining that she was being exposed to for the first time, but Linda was falling in love but I still felt that she was too young for a relationship, and every time I tried to tell her that, she would break down and cry. Her tears were enough for me to stay.

Meanwhile, the young homie Pap started coming to Franklin Ave. on a regular. He lived in Powerful's building, and he was trying to get a spot on the block. Pap was seventeen and off the fucking chain. He was already on probation for a gun charge, and his attitude was arrogant as hell. He idolized Excellence and Grill, and the three of them were all over six feet tall with violent personalities to match. The thing is, Pap had no reason to hustle. His mother and father provided him with everything, but the lure of the streets was too much to resist. Like many hustlers who are spellbound by the status of ghetto celebrity, we become addicted just like the fiends we served, infatuated with the money, power, and notoriety that comes along with it. Pap got some diesel (heroin) from Grill, who got it from his man Alejandro and put it out on Franklin. Pap heard about these Spanish cats down on Third Ave. who were also selling dope. When Pap went and confronted one of the dudes, the guy said what anyone would have said. "I ain't nowhere near your block partner." Pap didn't say anything, he just grabbed the nigga up by his collar and pounded him out. He finished him off by putting his head through a sheetrock wall. That shit was like a Hollywood movie.

The kid's man was acting like he wanted to jump in, but I told him "It's a one on one nigga'." Although Pap was wrong; I still had to have his back. Two days later, homie came around with a Mac-11 and said, "When you see your man let him know it's on." I didn't say shit. I mean, I didn't want no beef, I'm a vegetarian. When I told Pap what happened, he was like, whatever. If he was scared, he didn't show it. For the next week or so Pap came to the block with a Glock nine and a bulletproof vest on. In the hood, we have more guns than jobs, more niggas with guns than high school diplomas, and we can get guns before we could get credit.

I can recognize the caliber of most weapons by the sound it makes when it's fired, but ask me the capital of Mississippi, and I'll be like, "Huh?" The drama with Pap and the Spanish dude eventually died down, he accepted the loss and kept it moving. With that situation being resolved, we finally had a period of quiet, but you know the cliché, there's always the calm before the storm. That storm was a Dominican nigga named Disco. He had already killed a few other dealers in our neighborhood to take over their operations, and he now had his sight set on us. Our foothold was Franklin and 166th street. That's where the building that we hustled out of was located, and it's also where we had one of our stash houses, but we controlled an area going north from 166th and Franklin to 168th and Franklin. South to 165th and Franklin. The direction going east to 166th and Boston Rd., and west to 166th street and Park Ave. for a total of eight blocks. Boston Road was the main avenue in our neighborhood, and it was considered neutral.

Anyone could set up and sell drugs as long as they respected the code of the streets. Disco decided to make a power move. He opened up shop on 167th and Franklin and began selling pink tops. Powerful was furious! He went up to 167th by himself with a .44 Magnum and put the gun in one of Disco's lieutenant's face and told him, and the nigga with him, to get the fuck off the block! Our click gave Powerful props for going up the block without asking for backup, but we were also upset because he should have given us a heads-up that he was about to go up the block and start a drug war!

Chapter 8
Drug War

The next day, Tone Black, Gee, Pap, and I were in the stash house (headquarters) having a meeting in the kitchen when there was a knock at the door. Tone Black tip-toed up to the door and looked out of the peephole. Thank God! Rule number 496, when you are involved in any illegal activities, always look out your motherfucking peephole before you answer the door. The people whose apartment we were in were named Juanita and Al. I met Juanita two years prior when I first began hustling on Franklin. I was selling tres', three dollar bottles of crack, and she handed me three bloody dollars. I asked her why her money was bloody. She told me that she was drinking and she fell down and cut herself. When she left, the people's whose home we were selling drugs out of told me that her husband Al would get drunk and beat the shit out of her. I was fuming. I wanted to go knock on their door and beat this nigga senseless, but everyone told me to stay out of it. I did for awhile, that is until Al took a pot of boiling hot water and scalded Juanita's breast. I didn't pound on him then, I should have, but I did let him know that if he put his hands on Juanita again, I would kill him, and I meant it.

Juanita and Al were like most crackheads who would do almost anything for a hit. We kept our drugs in their apartment for little more than twenty-five dollars a week. As time went on, and I took over the operation, I would ensure that people got paid substantially more for putting their lives on the line. When Tone looked out of the peephole, he saw four niggas standing in the hall with handkerchiefs over their faces. He came back and whispered to Gee. Gee crept quietly up to the door and looked out of the peephole. He walked back into the kitchen with his finger to his lips and said, "Shhh." He was whispering, telling us Disco and his people were at the door with masks on. We were all scared. Not so much because we were scared of them, but because we didn't have any guns in the stash house.

Powerful made it a point of telling us not to have weapons in the stash house with drugs in case we were raided. In those days, if drugs and guns were found together the case would be turned over to the FBI or the Boogeymen, as they're known. We sat in the kitchen as quiet as a house mouse until we were sure we could leave. The next morning we met up at Powerful's house early in the morning and had a meeting about the shit that happened the night before, it was Tone, me, and this fat Puerto- Rican kid named Gordo. Gee didn't show up to the meeting; maybe he was scared. I don't know, he had stabbed Linda's uncle in the stomach the previous summer, but Disco wasn't just some drunk crackhead. I don't remember the details of the conversation, just what I said, and that was, "When I see anyone of those motherfuckas' I'ma' let them have it. Disco, his lieutenants, or that crackhead bitch Pam that brought them on the block and let them hustle outta' her apartment." Usually, Pam would have been an innocent bystander, but she was the one who put the idea into Disco's head about moving on our block. The very next morning as I'm walking down the block, voila, I see Pam standing on the stoop of her building talking to her neighbors. I had personally advised her against getting involved with Disco weeks before we had an altercation with them, and still, she decided to let them hustle out of her apartment, because of that, she was accountable too.

I approached her and asked her rhetorically, "Didn't I tell you not to bring those niggas' on the block?" She looked at me wide-eyed as I pulled out the nine- millimeter. I squeezed the trigger. *Blam!* The first shot hit her in the stomach. She turned to run into her building. *Blam!* I shot her in the back. She spun around and faced me. *Blam!* I shot her in the stomach once more. She fell off of her stoop and onto the ground in front of her building. I stood over her and put the next round into her face. I looked at her body for a second. The adrenaline rush was incredible; it was incomparable. I had become the savage that I needed to become to ascend or descend to something greater than myself.

I took off running down the block back to the building we hustled out of. I ran upstairs to Powerful's girlfriend Sophia's house and banged on the door.

She asked, "Who is it?"

I yelled, "Open up it's me Llord."

She let me in. I told her that I just shot some bitch and I needed to get off the block. Sophia and I had been alright, not close, but cordial. She called a cab while I paced anxiously, looking out the window from time to time. When the cab pulled up, Sophia walked downstairs and held the back door open for me. I dove in head first as if I was Superman. Sophia rode with me as I lay on the floor of the cab. I could see the police activity from the reflection of the lights in the cab's partition. The cab made a right onto 166th and headed up towards Boston Rd. As we headed south on Boston Rd. I could see a police car pulling up behind us. I told Sophia if the police pulled us over, to step out of the car; I was going to shoot it out with them. I had five bullets left, and I wasn't going back to jail without a fight.

The cabby listened, not saying anything. All Sophia could say was, "Alright boo." I sensed she felt saddened for me. It had barely been a year since Sha'born had gotten killed, and here I was a killer ready to shoot it out with police and be killed at the age of twenty-three. I don't know if it was God or Satan's scheme, the police cruiser rolled by us, and again my life was spared. Sophia dropped me off in Millbrook projects, gave me a hug and said be safe. When I knocked on the door, my cousin Karen opened the door, and she greeted me with a smile. My cousins were always happy to see me. My Aunt Pat wasn't there, thank God, at least I wouldn't have to explain what I was doing at her house so early in the day out of the clear blue sky. I told Karen and Asia what I had done. They listened quietly without saying much. Asia asked me what I was going to do. I had no idea. I ate lunch and walked home to my room on Willis Ave. That evening, Powerful sent Gee to see me and hit me with some money. He also wanted to pick up the gun so he could get rid of it. Gee told me Powerful said to stay out of sight until he figured something out.

A couple of days later Powerful met up with me and told me as far as he knew, no one was talking, but I should go out of town until shit blew over. I told him it was cool with me. Somehow Darryl had hooked up with Troy in Poughkeepsie and had put Powerful on to the earning potential. I had time on my hands, and I was still the top money earner, so I was sent out of town to oversee this new business. This would be my first trip out of town to sell drugs. Shit was great. The profit was double what we would make in the city, but like a bad soap opera script, this time, Darryl started getting high again. I can't say it enough, what comes around goes around.

I used to send Darryl out on the street to hustle while I would stay in the house and bottle up. The stash house was the apartment of this chick that Darryl had hooked up with out of town named Theresa, who I later found out was also getting high. Darryl would be out all day and come back to the house with a sob story about how he lost this, or that got stolen, and I'm in the house trying to get his girl to fuck me for a hit. I have to say she must have loved Darryl because although she did pull her pants down and let me see her ass, she never let me fuck her. As fine as Theresa was, I stopped hitting on her once Darryl and I got close. I finally got fed up waiting for Darryl, so I went out on the strip myself. When I did, the income tripled. In those days when a nigga from New York would go out of town, shit was a wide open market. The police were slow, the town folk were slow, and neither of them could handle the influx of the drugs or the thugs coming from New York, but there were problems. One of the main problems, jealousy.

The town natives, the criminals anyway, had a problem with us coming to their town, cutting into their profits, and fucking their bitches, and I have to admit, it's our fault. New York niggas always go out of town and act like fucking gangsters, but they wouldn't step to us face to face. Instead, they would set you up to get busted. At least in those days, now these cats out of town will lay your ass out. They ain't slow anymore. So whenever I went out of town, I kept to myself and didn't fuck with anyone. Niggas out of town could never get close enough to me to figure me out. Although Zenobia has done some trifling shit to me, she has also taught me some valuable lessons on life. Never let your right hand know what your left hand is doing, and never kill anyone over money. Now while I have done some very violent things, in my mind, it has always been over principle, never over money.

I was standing on Main and White, an avenue in the heart of town when these hustlers from the area got together and started jumping niggas from New York. I had a small team consisting of myself, Darryl, and Linda's cousin Corey. Corey was a big nigga, six foot five, about two hundred and thirty-five pounds. Though I had been careful not to bring anyone where we rested our heads and kept the drugs, the cats from the town had grown up with Theresa, so they knew where to find us.

When they started whipping New York niggas out, Darryl and I slid off, but they came straight to Theresa's house and began banging on the front door. Darryl was a skinny cat, but when shit hit the fan, he had your back in any situation. He opened up the door and asked the mob outside, "Whassup?"

Some short and stocky, dark-skinned kid said, "Come outside."

That's when I stepped up and asked, "For what nigga?"

He didn't respond. He pulled out a .38' and started talking shit. When they began beating on the door, I went to the kitchen and grabbed a butcher's knife and stuck it in my coat pocket, just in case. It was roughly ten of them, but Darryl and I were going to get it in. Thankfully it never came to that. Corey ran out of the back door and left us. When the niggas outside saw him running, they forgot all about me and Darryl and shouted "There one of them niggas go! Les' get him!" Darryl slammed the door, and the two of us started cracking up. It was fucking hysterical. Corey was big for nothing.

When I got back to the city and told the crew what happened, Corey's name was mud. He was finished as muscle for the organization. When I told Linda what happened, she was upset. She said she wasn't fucking with her cousin anymore. A few days later I went back up to Poughkeepsie with two more cats from our crew. A brother named Banner and his man named Juju from Webster projects. Banner had a Mac-10 and Juju had a 9mm. As soon as we stepped on Main and White, this townie was staring me down.

I approached him and asked, "What up? You know me homie?" When I asked him that, he lifted up the 40 ounce he was drinking and motioned liked he was going to smash me in the face. Before he could hit me, Banner pulled the Mac-10 out. The dude and the niggas he was with froze in their tracks and took off running down the avenue. Banner said, "Yeah, it's about to be on." Those faggots stopped at the first cop cruiser they saw and told them that we had guns. Within seconds, the block was flooded with cop cars. They approached me with guns drawn. My fourth arrest.

When I got to the precinct to be booked, I gave them an alias and being that these were the days before computer fingerprinting, my warrant for my old case for bail jumping in the Bronx didn't pop up, and I was released the next morning with a summons. Juju never got arrested. When he saw the police coming, he ran into someone's yard and tossed the gun. For Banner, it didn't go as well. When the officers caught him, he had the Uzi in his hand. He did eight months for the gun charge. That experience left me with a bad taste in my mouth. I was from the school of thought that if you were involved in streets, then you handle shit in the streets. I'm not referring to the stop snitching campaign, which is absolutely insane. If you're an average working class citizen or anyone who's not involved in criminal activities, I'm going on the record and saying, if you see something, say something. You're not snitching. That's the problem today; everyone wants to be something they're not. It would be eleven years before I would consider going out of town again.

When I went back home, it was business as usual. I had no stop button, only go, and go at 100 miles per hour. I was back on Franklin two months after murdering Pam. My reputation was growing. The people in the neighborhood now had respect for me, as well as a healthy fear of me, but Jay-Z said it best in one of his songs, "You can't ever let your guns grow cold," which to put it in layman's terms, no rest for the weary. This nigga Pap tries to put pressure on me for twenty dollars because I had two bags of his dope in my pocket when I shot that bitch Pam and he felt that I should pay for them. Forget the fact that I was doing him a favor selling his dope for him while he was home bullshitting. Not to mention we were in the same crew.

Pap saw me on Franklin, walked up to me and asked, "Where my money at?"

I honestly didn't know what the fuck he was talking about, so I asked him, "What money nigga?"

He got a little closer up on me and said, "The money you owe me for my two bags of dope nigga."

Did I tell you that Pap was nicknamed after Fat Cat Nichol's man who was crazy as hell, Pappy Mason! Motherfuckers are comical. I've killed someone, left for two months, and when I return, the first thing he wants to do is question me about twenty dollars.

"Look Pa, I ain't got your twenty dollars," I told him.

Now I could have paid him the twenty dollars, but this wasn't about the money, it was about respect.

Pap hit me with that elementary school shit, "When you git' off at 3:30 you better have my money."

I kept it short, "Aight' we'll see."

This time, when 3:30 came around, I was ready. I went downstairs and waited for Pap to hit the block. When he saw my face, he knew I wasn't having it.

He extended his hand for me to slap him five, and said, "Don't worry about that twenty spot homie."

I hesitated, gave him a pound and said, "Aight' Pap."

Shit, I was glad. I didn't want to fight his big ass anyway.

From that day on Pap and I were joined at the hip. If I walked across the street, he would be there to hold me back to make sure no cars were coming. He was a big dude, so he took on the role of being my bodyguard, although I've never needed, or wanted one. I've always handled problems on my own. Pap soon quit the heroin game and started working for Powerful. He became my right hand. I was the brains, he was the enforcer, and Powerful was the figurehead. My loyalty to Powerful was fierce, but Pap forced me to come to a realization, that while Powerful was the leader of our organization, his true allegiance was to himself and the almighty dollar. I didn't come around until I caught Pap stealing. I let him know that if I caught him stealing again, I would tell Powerful. Like that was going to stop him. When I caught him stealing again, he showed me how much money he was making on the side. I was like, fuck loyalty. Pap and I were rakin' in the dough, boy, but my conscience was fucking with me so Pap suggested that we pay Powerful three thousand a week if he let us run the day to day on Franklin and he would never have to step foot on the block again. Powerful was glad to accept the proposition. He didn't do much anyway, but now he was guaranteed a paycheck without the aggravation.

I was now making more money than my parents had made working their entire lives combined. Pap and I had come up with the idea to sell two dollar bottles of crack, or as they were known on the streets "Deuces". We tried to bring the notion to Powerful, but his response was, "We ain't no two dollar niggas." He couldn't see the forest for the trees. Despite the fact that we would sell our product cheaper than anyone else in the hood, our rationale was that a crackhead could get three dollars quicker than five, and following that line of reasoning, two dollars quicker than three. On that note, we decided to go ahead and sell deuces anyway, and when we did, shit got crazy! The cheese lines were bananas.

I moved out of my room on Willis Ave. and into a studio in the Castle Hill section of the Bronx paying five hundred a month for rent, which was an exorbitant sum of money in 1990. Shortly after that, I asked Linda's mother if Linda could move in with me. She said yes of course. She knew I would take care of her daughter.

We were making twelve to thirteen thousand a week in profit. We were the main niggas in the hood. We didn't have to worry about the police because the narcotic squads, or TNT as they were referred to as were a joke. They would conduct bust twice a week, on Tuesdays and Thursdays, if they came by at all. Those two days the hustlers in the neighborhood would be on high alert. The NYPD were the equivalent of the Mayberry police force. However, we did have one thorn in our side, this nosey bitch named Ms. Jessie. She would be in her apartment in the building across the street from our spot taking pictures of our crew out of her second-floor window and giving them to the police without our knowledge. We would be out front chilling in front of our building, and a flash would be seen coming from her window. I don't know why we didn't kill her old ass, but we should have, but that's what Pap and I were doing, standing in front of the spot, lounging.

Two blasts from the past walked upon us, my niggas Sleepy and Action. We squashed the beef with their family a while back and came to an agreement that if they ever wanted the night shift, it was theirs, and they told us if we ever needed extra firepower they were there for us. Sleepy asked if we wanted to make some money. Now we knew the only things these two niggas were good at were robbery and fighting. They weren't any prizefighters and their hustling days were behind them, so it had to be a stick-up, and although Pap had robbed niggas in the past, that wasn't my thing. Besides, we were getting money, and we definitely didn't need to rob anyone.

We went along for the ride anyway. Me, because I liked to keep that edge, Pap, because he went where I went. We stopped in front of this after-hours gambling spot on 137th and 8th Ave. in Harlem. Sleepy pulled out the sawed-off shotgun and passed me an empty bag to put the swag in. He gave Pap a .45, and Action had a .22 automatic rifle with an extended arm. What it didn't occur to me was that I was the only one without a fucking weapon. Sleepy knocked on the door while we stood off to the side. When the bouncer looked through the peephole and saw him standing there by himself, he opened up the door to reveal a mini Atlantic City in that motherfucker. Niggas were shooting dice, playing cards, slot machines, and playing pool. Action pushed pass Sleepy and hit the bouncer in the head.

He yelled, "Everybody git' down on the fuckin' floor!"

He began waving the rifle around. Sleepy was moving through the spot making sure no one made a move.

"Throw your wallets, purses, jewelry, and any money you got in your motherfuckin' pockets in the bag my man is holdin'. If we find anybody stashin' on us, you gon' haf' to suck my man's dick." Action said pointing in my direction.

I pulled out my dick for emphasis. This freak in the back said, "Ummm."

Any nigga that had money hidden started coming out of their socks with it. It was hilarious. I was glad that we didn't have to shoot anyone. I'ma a hustler not a stick-up kid. In the streets, you're going to be one or the other, or you'll spend the rest of your life looking over your shoulder for some nigga you've robbed.

When we got back to the Bronx, I told Sleepy and Action they could keep my share. They ain't give a fuck. I know it's crazy, but I Just wanted to know what it felt like to rob a motherfucker. Pap ain't hesitate to take his cut though. He and I got out of the cab in front of his building, while Sleepy and Action continued on towards Franklin.

Pap looked at me and asked, "Yo, what you woulda' did if a nigga had to suck your dick?"

We both laughed, gave each other pounds and went our separate ways.

Time had flown by so fast. Linda and I had been living in the studio for over a year living the good life. We were going to restaurants and the movies every weekend. We wore all the latest fashions, plus, we were fucking like rabbits. I was the first one to introduce her to oral sex. Now you can't get her to keep a dick out of her mouth. Smile, just playing Lin. One evening while we were laying in bed, she told me she was pregnant. I was thrilled. At the time I felt as if I was getting old, although I was only twenty-five, most of my homies had kids by the time they were seventeen or eighteen. Now, let a bitch tell a nigga that she's pregnant. That shit is like a jail sentence. A nigga will be sad as a motherfucker. The only disappointment I had was that we weren't married. Linda was becoming a fine young woman, and I didn't want her being another, baby's mama, we have enough of those.

As soon as she told me, I started looking for a bigger place. I found it on Quimby Ave. A beautiful two bedroom with a huge living room and kitchen for nine hundred a month. Before we moved in, I had wall to wall carpet installed and I furnished it with all new furniture. Linda was happy, and so was I, but with the sun must come rain.

Pap used to let some of his buddies from Morris High School hang out in our stash house, and I take full responsibility for not being sterner with him about our place of business not being a hangout. He and these young cats would be up in the stash house smoking weed all day long, blunt after blunt. He, them, and two of our lieutenants, L.A., and Pap's right-hand man, Money Mark, were in the stash house bottling and getting blunted with Pap's two young homies Wes, and Jay. The both of them were sixteen, but they were already getting paper on their block and busting their guns.

I left the five of them in the house and jumped in a cab to go to 149th and Park Ave. to the smoke shop to cop some more bottles. When I was returning, I noticed two detectives who rode around in a Christian Brothers cab doing a stop and search on a vehicle, a big white cop, who I was on a first name basis with, named Dave, I can't recall his last name, and his partner Ramirez. When I pulled up to the building Rachel's youngest brother Taylor was outside of the building crying uncontrollably. I exited the cab and asked what happened?

"They killed him; they killed him." Taylor uttered in between sobs.

I thought Disco and his boys had come and done a hit on us, but no, Pap was playing with a gun, and he accidentally killed Mark. When I opened the door to the apartment, I saw Mark sitting in the living room with his left eye hanging out of his head like a fucking slinky. His eye was hanging on by nerves and tendons. He had an exit wound that had blown a piece of the left side of his head off, and there was brain matter on the couch and wall. The sight of him sitting there turned my stomach; I had to get out of there.

Juanita was screaming, "I kept tellin' him to stop playin' with those damn guns."

She was right; we had all told Pap to stop playing with those damn guns, but I didn't have time to sit there and discuss it with her, I had to get out of there. I ran downstairs.

When I got to the first floor, Dave and Ramirez were coming in with their guns drawn yelling, "Don't move, put your hands up!"

I ask as if I didn't know, "What's going on? I'm just coming from my girlfriend's house." but they're not buying that.

They escorted me back upstairs and pushed open Juanita's door.

When they see Mark on the couch with his brains blown out, and his eye hanging on his cheek, Ramirez said, "Holy shit!"

They pulled Juanita aside and ask her what happened. She said she didn't know; she was only renting out the room to a border. Juanita was true to the streets, and rule number 103 in the streets is, never volunteer any information to the police. In other words, lie your ass off. I was lucky that Pap and L.A. had the frame of mind to take the majority of the drugs up to Sophia's house, but they left about ninety bottles of crack with purple colored tops on the table combined with the thirty packs of empty bottles that I had just bought, and two plus two equaled, I was fucked!

The cops had me in the hall out in front of Juanita and Al's door for about an hour when Ya-ya and Malik's mother came downstairs, looked me in the face and asked, "I guess it ain't gon' be no more purple huh Llord?"

Shit! I couldn't believe it. After all the shorts I had given her. People will fuck you over for no reason at all. When she said that, the detectives and the officers standing there turned and looked at me as she sashayed down the stairs, sure she would never see me again. Ten minutes later they asked me if I would come down to the station and answer some questions. Sure, like I really had a choice. Well actually I did have a choice, but I didn't know my rights at that time. I wasn't aware that I had the right to have my lawyer present if I had one, which I didn't, and in the real world the police don't inform us of our rights like they do on the TV show, "Cops."

That afternoon I learned quite a bit about what the police thought they knew, and what they really knew. First of all, I gave them an alias, something simple and easy to remember, Lamar Anderson, but I didn't think that one through. It was the same name I had given the Police in Poughkeepsie, and since I never went back for my disorderly conduct summons, there was a possibility, if NYPD did a warrant search on that name a warrant could pop up. That would give them cause to fingerprint me. Which again, would result in my warrant for bail jumping on my drug case in the Bronx to come up also, but they didn't, and even if they had, it would have taken days or weeks for a warrant to come back.

Dave had me sit in a corner facing a wall while he checked his files for a criminal record on a Lamar Anderson. I would look up and see him visibly frustrated. Six hours later they took me into an interviewing room and brought in this Black detective who told me he was Mark's stepfather. He said that he was aware that Pap and his stepson were friends, but he was more concerned about the drugs in the apartment. While I found that statement strange, I told him I knew his son and Pap were like brothers, but I didn't know his son that well. I explained that if Pap was involved in his son's death, it had to be an accident and as far as the drugs in the apartment, I told him I didn't know anything about them. I was visiting my girlfriend who lived in the building. I told him no more than that.

Without anything to hold me on, they eventually released me. It was around 1 p.m. when they took me into the precinct and close to 9 that night when I walked out. Almost eight hours being questioned and sitting in a corner facing a wall like I was in kindergarten. I headed back to Franklin to confront Ms. Jane. I asked her why she would say something like that in front of the police. She retorted that she was commenting on a purple leather jacket I owned. She looked me in my face and lied without missing a beat. It didn't matter what she said, from that moment on I knew she couldn't be trusted. I went back to the comforts of my home and Linda, who was now six months pregnant. I had no idea that incident would change Franklin Ave., and my life forever.

Chapter 9
On the Map

The next day when I spoke to Powerful on the phone, I told him I couldn't imagine what might have happened. I explained to him that I wasn't in the apartment when shit went down, I was at the smoke shop buying bottles. Powerful was upset; Money Mark was his first cousin.

He was screaming, "I told y'all niggas' don't have no guns in the fuckin' stash house. Now my cousin is dead, and the fuckin' block is gon' be hot. Pap fucked shit up!"

What could I say? He was right. Powerful told me to go to Sophia's house and see what happened to the drugs. When I got to Franklin Ave. the police had torn Juanita and Al's place apart, and they were still being held. I went upstairs and knocked on Sophia's door.

Sophia's question was one that we all had which was "What happened?"

I could only tell her what I knew, that Pap was playing with a gun, and he accidentally shot Mark in the face and killed him. I asked her what happened to the drugs? She told me she flushed them down the toilet. She was scared; the police were all through the building knocking on people's doors. I told her I would let Powerful know, not to worry about it.

"Shit ma', I woulda' have done the same thing," I told her.

Days later Pap called me and told me that he was sorry that I had been taken to the precinct for questioning. If the police would have kept me, he would have turned himself in. I told him it was nothin' and that it came with the game. I asked if he was alright.

He answered in a pained voice, "Nah man I'm not."

This was the first time that I had ever heard anything in Pap's voice besides arrogance or obstinacy. I asked him the million dollar question.

"What happened man?"

Pap took a deep breath and began to tell me what happened.

"We was gittin' blunted while L.A. and Mark was bottlin'."

I interrupted him, "That's what y'all were doin' when I left, so what went wrong?"

Pap went on, "I was playin' wit' the tec-9 pointin' it at niggas bullshittin' when Mark told me to stop playin' wit the fuckin' Uzi cuz if I shot him he was gon' press charges on me and go to court everyday til' I got sent up North."

He was babbling now, "I had the safety on, but when I pulled the trigger, the bullet just exploded. Mark never had a chance to scream, and Jay and Wes didn't say a word when the gun went off. They picked up their book bags and was out the door without lookin' to see if Mark was dead or alive."

I thought about what he said before I spoke.

"It's partly my fault homie. I shoulda' let it be known if a nigga ain't gittin' money wit' you, he ain't got no business in the stash house, hangin' on the block wit' you while you hustlin', or goin' wit' you when you re-up. Truth be told, when shit hit the fan, niggas ain't gon' do the time wit' you, and I don't need no fuckin' co-defendant.

Although Pap was listening quietly, now wasn't the time for me to lecture him, he was going through enough. We talked a bit longer. Pap said he was going to turn himself in, but first, he wanted to speak to Mark's mother and get a lawyer. I told him I had his back and to let me know what he needed. A week later, Pap walked into the 42nd precinct with his parents and a lawyer. His decision to man up took the heat off the block so I could open up shop.

When I contacted Powerful, I told him I was ready to open back up. He said I should lay low for a while, but I couldn't; I had bills to pay, and I had a baby on the way. I let him know flat out.

"I can't walk away. I'ma haf' to slap an H on my chest and handle it pa."

He said he wasn't fuckin' with Franklin anymore, and if the Feds came he was out of it.

"But listen to what I'm sayin' Llord, I don't want that nigga Pap on the block, ever!"

That was it. I didn't put up much of an argument. Although Pap was my man and I didn't want to see him locked up, I was glad I wouldn't have to split the profit with him. I was now the HNIC of Franklin Ave. no boss, no partner. Greed had me anticipating getting all that cake for myself. I couldn't wait, but as usual, it didn't go as planned.

Franklin Ave. was on fire! The police were coming through the block five to seven cars at a time, up to four times a day. Money was slow, and the crew was scared. Was I afraid, sure, but hunger, or my aforementioned greed as it were, kept me fighting the tide of the police onslaught. Dave and Ramirez would drive through the block, get on the squad car P.A. system and yell, "Llord enjoy your freedom while you got it." I was terrified, but every day I would go out and face the insanity of crack addicts, gun violence, the threat of going to jail or even death. I wasn't' your average drug dealer, at least in my mind. I would go over and over problems in my head until I reached a solution. Then I would go to the experts for advice, my customers. I would ask questions like "How did this dealer git' arrested? Or how did so and so git' bagged?" I would listen like a student studying for an upcoming exam, which I was, but if I failed this exam, there would be no re-testing.

I went to RadioShack and purchased Walkie Talkies which were common with the Dominican dealers in Washington Heights, but Black and Puerto Rican dealers still had lookouts on the corner yelling "Teddy or five-o." What separated me from the niggas on the corner and the Dominicans, is that when I purchased the Walkie Talkies, I also purchased a police scanner and a manual which contained codes for each of the precincts throughout the five boroughs. These were also sold at Radio Shack. The only drawback was that the narcotic units had codes which weren't listed. A small hindrance at best.

I had twenty people working for me. The person who did hand to hand in most crews were called a Pitcher, but in my crew, I instructed my lieutenants, or "Captains" as they were referred to as, that the "Pitchers" were to be called the "President", whom we had to protect with our lives. The "Lookouts" were called "Scouts", and the "Couriers", or "Mules", were to be called "Runners." This gave everyone on the team a sense of importance, responsibility, and dedication. I understood the importance of programming as a tool of leadership and control. I ran my operation like an elite military unit, which we were. We called the marked blue and white police cars, The Yankees, and the unmarked vehicles the Mets. Franklin Ave. was home plate, Third Ave. was first base, Boston Rd. was second, and the various other blocks were third base, infield, etc. That way, we could openly communicate over the Walkie Talkies and discuss where the police were setting up.

I would take Pap's mother money for lawyer fees when I could, but things were rough. I had done the best I could to stay off the radar, but with Mark's death, I felt like I was public enemy number one. During the Dinkins administration, Mayor Dinkins reinstated the Beat Cop, which helped to slow the flow of drugs in the community as well as the Wild West mentality that we had in the streets as far as the brazen shootings anytime, anywhere. However, when the officers left their post, we would open back up undeterred. On the horizon, two new adversaries were in my future. A rookie cop named Officer Manning. He was young and just as determined as we were. By himself, he made close to thirty arrests in our neighborhood and would earn the name "Robocop." In the end, time and promotions would make him less of a threat. The other would be a new mayor named Rudolph Giuliani; he would prove to be both a motivating factor and an impediment to criminals and poor minorities alike.

Linda was now almost nine months pregnant, and her due date was sometime in mid-December. On the night of December 10th, 1992, Linda called me, "Llord come home quick; my stomach is killin' me. I think I'm having contractions."

I told her, "I don't think you gon' have the baby. Call your mother."

It wasn't that I thought she wasn't in labor, I believed her, but at that moment I was at a motel on 14th street with a stripper named Precious. I had met her at a strip club a few days earlier, and she was laying on the bed playing with her pussy, but Linda wasn't that docile little girl anymore. I couldn't feed her any line of nonsense over the phone.

"I'm not callin' my mother for shit. You need to git' your ass home and take me to the hospital motherfucka'!" she yelled at the top of her lungs.

I knew she was right, but I wanted to fuck Precious, especially since I had already paid sixty dollars for a short stay at the motel. While I was on the phone arguing with Linda, Precious was getting dressed. I told Linda I would meet her at the hospital and to call her mother to drive her there.

"Hurry up I'm gittin' dressed." She said hanging up the phone.

With Linda out of the way, I turned my attention back to Precious.

"Why you put your clothes on?" I asked.

Precious put her hand on my cheek and said, "I'm a woman first. You need to be at the hospital with your girl."

She turned and walked out the door. I called a cab and headed uptown to Metropolitan Hospital on 99th street and 1st Ave. When I got there, Linda was sitting in the emergency room with her mother, sisters, and her cousin Yolanda. I played the role of the doting father to be.

"Lin' how you feelin' boo?" I asked, without betraying the fact that I had just left a seedy motel some thirty minutes earlier.

"I'm fine. As if you care!" she said rolling her eyes.

"Come on don't be like that. I'm here right." I said giving her a kiss and rubbing her swollen belly.

That night Linda was admitted and given an epidural to ease the pain. I slept alone in the waiting area until five in the morning. I sat there fidgeting trying to get comfortable on a chair when a doctor came around to speak to me.

"Mr. Atkins, my name is Dr. Heinrich. I'd like to let you know we're looking at perhaps another five to six hours before your wife will be ready for delivery; why don't you go home and get some rest."

I sat up in the chair.

"Are you sure doc?" I asked.

He replied. "Yes, sir, but be sure to be back between 10 and 11 a.m. tomorrow morning. She'll be fine."

With that said, I made the worst mistake of my life, at least as far as Linda was concerned, I left and went home.

I was home for less than an hour when the phone rang.

"Mr. Atkins this is nurse Getel. Your girlfriend is here alone sir. She needs someone her to comfort her."

She sounded cross. I explained to her what the doctor had said to me.

"Excuse me, nurse, a Dr. Heinrich told me I could come home and get some rest, and besides, I just climbed into bed. I'll be back early in the morning."

Again, she responded with an annoyed tone in her voice. "Well get back here as soon as possible. She needs someone here by her side," she said hanging the phone up in my ear.

I woke up four hours later, jumped in the shower, got dressed, and was back out the door. When I reached the hospital, I went to the cafeteria grabbed some breakfast and headed upstairs to the Obstetrics ward. As soon as I entered Linda's room, the nurses were instructing me to hurry up. I put the hospital scrubs on over my clothing and went into the delivery room. Linda was already on the birthing table pushing, grunting, and deep breathing. Dr. Heinrich was calmly coaching Linda. "Push mommy; you're starting to crown, I can see the head." Linda clenched her teeth and pushed. Screaming loud and long. Ten minutes later there he was, my first, and only child. "Messiah Ilyas Atkins."

There are events in a person's life that are life-altering, and the birth of my son would be one of those events. While violence had become a part of my daily life, and I was capable of switching from charming to a miscreant in the blink of an eye, I now felt wholly responsible for someone other than myself. Someone whom I would be connected to for the rest of my life. That was something that Jake and Zenobia had robbed me of, that feeling of unconditional love and family. The next afternoon Linda's family was gathered around the hospital bed admiring our beautiful baby boy, when a nurse of Indian descent entered the room.

"Hello, mommy how are you doing today?"

Linda smiled and answered, "I'm fine thank you."

The nurse continued, "We have to run some test on baby Atkins. It appears he may have Syphilis."

When she said, that the room fell silent. Before anyone could say anything, I flew into a rage.

"You fuckin' bitch! What the fuck you talkin' about? You outta' your mind comin' in here announcing somethin' like that?" I shouted with spit flying out of my mouth. "You're supposed to pull us aside bitch. Git' outta' here and go git' a fuckin' doctor."

I walked behind her and slammed the door. Linda's family hadn't seen my temper before, although her cousin Yolanda knew me from the streets because she was dating Grill and she heard about my temper. She, as well as Linda's family hadn't witnessed it firsthand. Moments later a doctor came in to speak with me.

"Mr. Atkins my name is Dr. Canton, nurse Tetrad said there was a problem,"

I replied using both a lexis and demeanor that made me approachable. "The only problem is your nurse ignored professional protocol, such as doctor-patient confidentiality, and the common decency of pulling me and my child's mother aside before announcing something as personal as our child having syphilis. I should have my lawyer give the hospital's ethics committee a call."

I was bluffing, I didn't have a lawyer, but I wanted to shake the staff up. I believed that immigrants come from other countries, don't face the same racial barriers that Black Americans face, surpass us, look down on us, and have no visceral empathy for us.

"Mr. Atkins that won't be necessary. I'll personally run the testing myself and see to it that nurse Tetrad is reprimanded."

I thanked him and told him that I and my wife would appreciate that. A day later the test came back negative, and Linda and Messiah came home. I stayed home for the next week giving Linda a chance to get some rest while I got to know my son.

Though Linda's family had been to the hospital every day, my family hadn't called yet. The last time I spoke to Jake was over four years prior when he asked me to leave his home. It had been a year since I had any dealings with Zenobia and Vonnie, who screwed me out of twenty thousand dollars in a business deal. As for my Aunt Pat and my cousins, I had no idea why they hadn't come to see my son yet.

To be honest, I share some of the blame. I began to distance myself from them as the years went by. As my finances grew, it became a regularity for Karen and Asia to ask me for money. One occasion Asia asked me for three hundred dollars to pay her bills so she could hang out with her money. Wanting to please what little family I maintained ties to, I would give it to her, but an eye-opening moment for me came when my Aunt Pat asked me for the combination to a safe that I kept in her house. When I said she didn't need the combination, she broke down crying.

"You don't trust me; I don't believe you boy. I would never steal from you." she said in between tears.

I tried to explain to her, "It's not that I don't trust you, auntie, it's just that God forbid anything happened you wouldn't be responsible."

She continued crying.

I asked her. "How can I make it up to you auntie?"

That's when she said something that would change the dynamics of our relationship, even if only a little.

"You can buy me a coat."

When she said it, it stung me; I couldn't tell her no. I would never tell her no, not for anything, but I was hurt. It seemed like she was playing on my loyalty and my love for her.

With Karen, it was also money and something like an episode out of the "Twilight Zone." When I was on Rikers Island, I dreamt that Karen had a child on a hot summer day, but her baby was born in a freezer. When I woke up, I called Karen, told her about my dream, and asked was she pregnant. She laughed and replied, "No crazy, I'm not pregnant." A year and a half later, Karen's man got killed. He was a heavy player in the drug game. He lavished Karen with expensive jewelry, furs and plenty of money. He called Karen one Thursday evening and told her he was going to meet up with one of his friends that kept calling him. When he went uptown to meet his friend, it was a setup; they robbed him and shot him twice in the face. Not long after that, Karen found out that she was pregnant. Eight months later in the month of May, she began having labor pains, and her water broke. My aunt rushed her to the hospital where her baby, a baby boy, was delivered stillborn. Worse than that, she was told that she would never be able to have children again because of an ectopic pregnancy. Thus the baby born in the summer, but born in a freezer.

Soon after that, she began to lean on me more and more for finances and for years I would help her, partially because of love and partly because of pity. When my son was born, and she hadn't called me, I drew the line, and she too distanced herself from me. Zenobia and my sister Vonnie were a different scenario. As I stated before, they fucked me over in a business deal. I put up twenty thousand dollars to open up a restaurant. I put all of the licenses in Zenobia's name and had her sign all of the legal documents. All she and Vonnie had to do was open up, keep it stocked, and pay the rent which was a measly seven hundred dollars a month. The location was prime, right next to Morris High School. Business was booming. We had fried shrimp, burgers, hot dogs, fish sandwiches, and fries. It should have been our first step towards establishing a legal business and giving us a leg up. Yeah, right!

Rule number 234, never fuck with friends or family when it comes to business. I began to notice that they were opening up later and later. On top of that, they would do nigga shit like not keeping the restaurant re-stocked. People don't realize that having a successful drug business is like running any other company. If you sell out of the product, you have to re-stock, or as we say on the streets, re-up before, emphasis on before, you run out of an item. When I spoke to Zenobia about it, things got ugly.

"Ma, I don't understand why you and Vonnie are running out of food. If we're sellin' food, there should be money to replenish what was sold and why ain't you opening up until 12 O'clock? If we gon' be successful, we have to open up a lot earlier."

It was a principle that I was adamant about. If one of my crew members came to the block late, I would dock their pay twenty-five dollars for every half an hour they were late.

She gave me an excuse that keeps average people average or worse than that, poor people poor.

"Listen Llord; I can't do everything by myself. If the suppliers don't deliver on time, then there's nothin' I can do."

I had taken a second before I answered her.

"Ma, it's simple. If the suppliers don't deliver on time, then you jump in a cab, and you go to them."

After a while of going back and forth, I had heard enough.

"I'll tell you what ma, you put my name on the paperwork and I'll give you and Vonnie 40% of the profit. I'll take over runnin' the restaurant; you and Vonnie won't have to do anything at all."

She wouldn't even consider it.

Vonnie snatched the phone from our mother and said, "You can git' your name on the papers when you pay us the money you owe us for workin' in the restaurant."

What? How could she be so fucking ungrateful? She had been working in restaurants like Fridays, and Uno's for minimum wage most of her adult life. Here I was giving her an opportunity to run her own business, and she was talking to me about money I never saw. I never took a dollar from the business. Meanwhile, she and Zenobia were walking through the neighborhood with new clothes on every time I saw them. I was done.

"Put mommy back on the phone," I said.

When my mother took the phone, I told her, "you know what ma', before you and I become enemies, you keep the restaurant."

A few months later the restaurant was closed. With that said, I wouldn't speak to them until the birth of my son.

Pap was locked up. He copped out to a three to six. The guilt of killing Mark was too much for him to go through sitting through a trial. Besides, he couldn't face Mark's family. I had so much drama going on I could barely think straight. The birth of Messiah. The block was on fire. The beef with Disco had never been resolved and I was out of twenty thousand dollars. So, I did what I did best, I hustled. I would leave Linda and the baby at home from 7:30 in the morning and return 10:30 in the evening. My poor young wifey. At the time I didn't think about what she was going through dealing with a newborn by herself. She was suffering from postpartum depression alone while I was out running the streets. I didn't know it at the time. Not until I found a suicide note that she had written to Messiah.

Eventually, the police pressure eased up on Franklin Ave. They had no choice. I knew that. I constantly read the newspaper looking for information on a new drug offensive and how much money they had in their budget. If the police union wanted a raise, I knew that it would affect financing for their other projects. If the jails got overcrowded, it meant they would have to slow down their arrest. I surveilled them as well as they surveilled us.

To me, at least, the police are conspicuous, never undercover. Their unmarked cars are obvious; the undercover officers stick out like sore thumbs. Coming into our neighborhoods wearing green, yellow, red, and orange wristbands to identify each other. They had to, well the Black cops had to. In years past there was an incident where a Black officer was on a buy and bust operation, and the White police officers who he had been riding around with all day entered a building where a buy and bust operation was in progress, saw the Black officer with his gun drawn, and shot him. Hahaha, God bless America. I love it! The police weren't a threat to me; I was more concerned with the FEDS, so I did my best to stay off the grid; If you can call waging a drug war with Disco and his crew off the grid.

Although he never retaliated against us for Pam's murder, he never shut his operation down, and that shit irritated me to no end. I couldn't let him continue if I wanted to maintain respect on the streets. When the incident with Pap happened, L.A. stopped coming around. He was a funny style nigga, so it didn't matter. He was the type of cat who would be in his house smoking weed, you go by to holler at him, and he would have his wife lie and say he wasn't home. Also, he was a part of Pap's inner circle anyway, so he wasn't a loss to me.

I put together a new crew, my crew. A crew of young guns. When Pap got sentenced, most of the guys he brought with him after we took control of the block left quietly without saying anything to me. They just stopped showing up to work. The new crew consisted of Ya-ya and Marcus Jansen, now in their early teens, another young cat from Washington Ave. named Roc, Ya-ya's man, Trouble, and one of my homies from Millbrook projects named Stan. We were busting our guns on a fucking regular. The crew followed my example. It's like it says in the Bible; if you keep the company of violent men, you yourself become violent. Our block was put on the 42cnd precinct's list of high priorities, but that didn't stop us. I paid Rachel's uncle Jimmy, a crackhead, to cut the power to the street lights on Franklin Ave. from 165th-166 St. so the entire strip would be pitch black. Jimmy was once an electrician for the city before he got strung out on drugs. I would pay him to open up the face plates on the street lights and cut the live wires. It was fucking outrageous. The beat cops would walk through our block petrified with their hands on their guns.

On top of that, I had another crackhead tint the windows in the hallways of our building. The pitcher could see out, but the police couldn't see in. I was getting my crew prepared for war. A war with Disco, the police, and any other organization that wanted what we had, and I aimed to be victorious, which meant staying alive, staying free, and being profitable.

Chapter 10
The Chickens Come Home

I was home with Linda one Sunday evening when the phone rang.

"Hello, who's this?" I asked.

It was Ya-ya.

"Yo' Llord this nigga Elroy and his crew robbed me for my moped," he said frenzied over the phone.

"How the fuck did that happen?" I asked him.

"I was ridin' my moped on 169th when this nigga Elroy ran up on me wit' the u-wop (Uzi) and stuck me the fuck up."

Ya-ya was one of those hardheaded niggas who didn't' believe shit stunk. I told him before about riding that fucking moped all hours of the night, but no, he had to be the man. Now, 11:30 at night he's calling me to come and help him. Although I was lying in bed, I had to go meet him. What was absurd was that this nigga Elroy had his left leg blown off at the knee while attempting to rob someone in the past, and here he was still out robbing niggas, crutches and all.

"Lin', I have to run out and take care of somethin'," I said as I was getting out of bed to get dressed. "

Where you goin'?" She asked.

"I got some man business to handle," I answered.

That's what I always said to her when I was doing something that might get me jailed or killed, and I didn't want her to worry. I grabbed the two tec-9s out of the closet and called a cab. I had the cab drop me off halfway up the block on Franklin between 166th and 167th Street. As I got nearer to the steps on 166th and Franklin, I saw Ya-ya, Stan, Roc, and Trouble standing there waiting for me.

"What's good?" I asked.

Ya-ya started running off at the mouth.

"This nigga Elroy gon' run up on me as I'm comin' out of the bodega on 169th put a gun in my face, and robbed me for my fuckin' moped," he said pacing back and forth.

I thought to myself, "How many times I told this nigga not to be out ridin' that fuckin' moped all times of the night, up and down the hood."

The truth is, half of the motherfuckers don't, or won't listen, and the other half don't give a fuck. It was a waste of time. I just asked where Elroy was.

"He's down the steps at the Cannonball Club," he said pointing.

I told him to go inside the club and get Elroy to come outside. Ya-ya went down the stairs and started banging on the club door. It was a hole in the wall coke spot and gambling spot where the local hood rats and scrub nigga's hung out.

"Yo' Elroy! Yo' Elroy, come outside motherfucka'," he yelled while pounding on the door.

I stood there running my mouth with Stan and the rest of the crew.

I had the Tecs stashed in a garbage can across the street when Ya-ya yelled up to me, "Git' ready he's comin' out."

This is how things generally went. Nigga's waited for me to initiate the violence. When the door opened, I ran across the street to grab the guns. I ran down the stairs like I was the fucking terminator. A Tec in each hand. I got about forty feet away when this bitch named Gloria from my mother's building reached out of the doorway, grabbed Elroy's jacket, pulled him back in the club, and slammed the door behind them. Now most people would agree since I pulled a weapon on Elroy I would have to kill him, but I never gave shit like that a second thought. Why? Simple. Most of the time if I did something to a motherfucker they had it coming, and niggas accepted it. If they didn't like it, then I was prepared to go all out. Even if it meant killing a nigga or dying in the process.

Life on the streets always ran in cycles for me. I would have the bountiful cycles when the money would come so fast it was like it was falling out of the sky. Then there would be cycles when it was a fucking drought, and I would be starving, usually in the winter time. The times I dreaded the most were the violent cycles. Not only was this the beginning of a violent cycle, but it was also the winter.

Later that week out of the clear blue sky, Disco's henchmen came up the stairs leading from Third Ave. to Franklin and shot the men's shelter up; wounding an innocent homeless man in the process. That act officially ended the unspoken truce that allowed both crews to make money. I didn't understand why these dickheads couldn't leave well enough alone. Later that night my crew and I met up at our headquarters; which was still Juanita and Al's place. While we no longer kept drugs there, it was still the place where we held our meetings, did payroll, and yes, kept guns.

"What the fuck them niggas start wildin' for?" I asked although I knew the answer.

The same as it always, jealousy and greed. My man Trouble was hype.

"Fuck why," he said, "Them niggas' been up the block gittin' money next to us long enough. We don't allow nobody to eat next to us. They been gittin' fat and dissin' us for a long time, it's time to go to war!"

He was right something had to be done.

"Gimme' the burner," I said to Stan.

It was around 8 o'clock in the evening. I took the gun, stuck it in my pocket, and walked up the block to 167th and Franklin by myself, to the building where Disco's cousin Chuchie ran red top's other spot, pink top. Their headquarters was on the first floor of the building in this little Puerto Rican cat named Frankie's house. It was the same building that crackhead Pam had lived in. Frankie lived there with his grandfather, but I didn't give a damn. If he opened up that door, I was going to shoot whoever was in the apartment. If I couldn't get inside the apartment, I was going to shoot through the door.

As I stood on the stoop waiting for someone to come out of the building, a police car slowly rolled by. I stood there looking up at a window like I was waiting for someone to come down and let me in. The cruiser headed down Franklin towards 165th street. When they merged onto Third Ave. heading towards the precinct, I couldn't wait any longer. I let off four shots through Frankie's first-floor window. I ran back in the direction of 166th street to Zenobia's building. Ya-ya was there waiting in the courtyard. I passed him the gun and said, "I'm out."

He put the gun in a backpack and said, "Git the fuck outta' here. Everybody is gon' be on point for tomorrow, stay low til' we hit you."

The call never came, so I went to the block the following morning to see what was up. When I got there, shit was already jumping. Ya-ya and Roc caught Chuchie trying to sneak out of the building around 10:30 that morning, and that was all she wrote. Trouble and Ya-ya were arguing with Roc saying he almost shot one of them by accident. Trouble filled me in.

"Me, Roc, and Ya-ya saw this nigga Chuchie comin' out of pink tops buildin' and jump in his girl's car. His ass was sittin' there like shit was sweet. We ain't say a word, we ran upstairs and got the toast. Roc had the .38, I had the .9milli, and Ya-ya had the tec.9," Roc cut in.

"Chuchie must have seen us comin' in the rearview mirror and told his girl to pull off, but it was too motherfuckin' late. I was on one side of the street, and Ya-ya and Trouble was on the other side. We started blazin' at her ride. That bitch did a motherfuckin' burnout," he said, still a bit on edge.

"That's how you almost shot us, nigga! We on one side of the street and you on the other side shootin' in our direction." Ya-ya said trying not to laugh.

"So what happened nigga?" I asked him.

"Bullets was hittin' that bitch's car like crazy," he said making a *ting-ta-ting-ting* sound.

We all started laughing when he made the sound effects.

"Y'all niggas is stupid," I said still laughing.

The truth is, I was happy they were coming into their own. The next day when we opened up shop, the whole crew was on the block. Everyone was prepared, ready for red top to retaliate. That's when Chuchie approached us with his hands up asking if he could talk to us. He had a proposal, an alliance between Pink Top and Purple Top.

"I can't front, I'm tired of this beef between me and your peoples. I'm always lookin' over my shoulder, and my fuckin' cousin be sittin' in his house givin' orders like he some kinda' kingpin or somethin'. Besides that, y'all niggas' git' it in," he said finally lowering his hands.

He seemed sincere, but I didn't trust him as far as I could see him.

"How do I know you ain't tryin' to set me and my peoples up?" I asked him.

"I'll prove it to you Llord. I'ma go wit' you and your peeps down to Washington Ave. and set it on one of Red Top's lieutenants. I'll do whatever. I on't give a fuck," he said.

"Aight' homie, it sounds good, but if you tryin' to set me and my people up, we gon' be strapped and we gon' all out," I said to him humbly, but sternly, looking him in the eyes so that he understood I meant every word I said.

Later that night we met up with him on 166th and Washington Ave.

"You ready pa'?" I asked him.

I have no idea why, but when it's time to get down to business I'm so hype, I can barely speak. Me, Roc, Trouble, Ya-ya, and Stan were all dressed in black. The only time most cats dress in all black, again, is for funerals, or war. Tonight was going to be a combination of both. We saw a young Puerto Rican kid standing on the block counting money. He couldn't have been any older than sixteen, but his age wasn't of any consequence to me. He was one of Disco's workers, therefore he was a soldier and an enemy combatant. Stan had a husky voice to go with his husky frame. He wanted to get out of there, so he was the first to speak up.

"What you gon' do homie?" He asked keeping it short and to the point.

Chuchie didn't reply. He pulled out a .45, cocked the hammer back and let off a round. It sounded like a cannon. *Booom!* The shot echoed breaking the night's quiet. The young kid had his back turned to us. He never saw what hit him. It struck him in the back of the goose down jacket he was wearing. The shot blew him ten feet away. Feathers were everywhere. He lay there on the ground moaning like the baby he was. Then came the blood. That fucking blood was flowing out of his mouth. That fucking blood that's followed by death. We stood there for a few seconds watching the kid as he lay there dying. Then it was time to move.

"Les' go homies, we out," I said.

I had to get my crew out of there. I didn't give a damn about Chuchie. What he didn't know was that if he didn't step up and shoot one of his cousin's people, we were going to kill him. No question about it. Someone was going to die that evening. That night finally brought the cycle of violence to an end. For the time being anyway. Chuchie ran in one direction, and we ran back towards Franklin Ave. to put our guns up.

"Damn Chuchie lit shorty the fuck up," Roc said handing his gun to Ya-ya to put in the safe.

"Yeah, he lifted little man off his feet wit' the fifth," I said empathetically.

Since the birth of Messiah, I couldn't shake the thought of, "that could be my son."

"I'll see y'all niggas tomorrow, same bat time, same bat channel," I said slapping niggas five as I left out.

From that time on, no one would come up against us, and the violence, as far as the drug wars, subsided. We began getting the lion's share of the drug business in our neighborhood. We still had the occasional problem of a worker running off with a package, or the pitcher coming up short, which I overlooked for the most part as long as they didn't make it a habit. If they did, they would get their ass whipped like a foster child. The streets were talking. We were the hood superstars. We were making money hand over foot, and with that came women. I was fucking all type of women, Black, Puerto Rican, Jamaican, and Dominican. I was fucking chicks just to say I fucked them. Some of them, I can't even recall their names, others I'll never forget.

Noreen was one of the unforgettable ones. She was about five feet tall, fat ass, sexy legs, shaved pussy; pretty brown nipples, and a beautiful complexion that favored liquid gold, which complimented her long black her. She was a friend of my cousin Karen whom I had known since I was a teenager. Whenever she would come over to my aunt's house, and I was there, I behaved like an anxious little boy watching her every move. Yes, I had a childhood crush on her, but now I was a twenty-seven-year-old man with a baby, and although she was thirty with a child of her own, I was ready for her now. Our first date was typical, dinner, roses and drinks. Dinner conversation wasn't spectacular either, but desert was delicious. I booked a Presidential suite at the Marriot hotel in New Jersey. It was a hundred and ninety dollars for an overnight stay on a Saturday, and while neither of us could stay the entire night, she was worth every penny.

The room was magnificent. It had two bathrooms, a kitchen, large living room, and a dining room area. She led me into the bedroom and turned on the radio. She put on "The Quiet Storm." I watched her as she got undressed. A lump rose up in my throat. It was the anticipation of years of lust and a hunger for her joined into one carnal urge. I went down between her legs and started sucking her pussy. She let out soft and sweet moans as I opened up the lips of her vagina and tongued her clitoris. Sucking on it while sticking my tongue in and out of her pussy letting her pre-cum run down my chin. I wrapped my arms around her legs and pulled her further into my mouth, licking, sucking and spitting on her clit. She turned over doggy style and told me to ease my dick in nice and slow. She was in full control, and I loved it. I stuck the entire length in her slowly, deep to my balls, and pulled it back out just as slowly so I could suck on her pussy. It was a technique that I called, the fuck and suck. We fucked like that for hours, sweating, intertwined until her pussy was swollen and my dick was numb, but she wasn't finished with me. She had a treat for me that I hadn't yet experienced, anal sex.

I still hadn't cum, and my dick was throbbing painfully. She reached into her purse and took out a small tube of lubrication. She squeezed a little on the tip of my penis and slid her hand up and down the shaft until it was glistening. Then she put a little on her finger and began to finger her ass as I watched stroking my dick until she was ready.

"Come here, Lloyd." She beckoned me.

I laughed. I found it funny to hear her call me by my given name.

"Take your time baby, my ass is tight, be easy," she whispered.

We laid on our sides, her leg over mine as I moved slowly. I felt her ass tightening on my dick as she started cumming anally.

"Fuck me harder daddy, "she said.

As delicately as she wanted me to fuck her in her pussy, she now wanted me to fuck her in her ass twice as hard. I was slamming my dick as hard as I could. She was screaming,

"Yeah, yeah, that's it. That shit feels so fucking good. Fuck that tight ass daddy."

Juice was running out of her ass as she came. I fucked her harder. With each stroke, I could feel the nut rising up from my toes.

"I'm cumming baby!" I yelled, my legs shaking as I came.

I would get together with Noreen a few more times after that, but nothing would measure up to our first encounter. All these many years later, while I still fiend for her, she acts as though I no longer exist. She would call me from time to time, fuck me, then ask me to leave. The way a man does with a woman after he's done using her. A real-life "Boomerang." Yeah, it hurt my ego, but I was making money, and I had no shortage of women. Unfortunately, I still equated my self-worth with, sex, money, and violence. It would take me years before I realized that with all of the women I slept with, I still needed fifty cents to buy a newspaper.

As the years flew by, me and Linda's relationship became strained. While we had plenty of good times, things at home were hectic. Linda was lazy, and maybe I bear some of the responsibility, giving her two hundred dollars a week allowance and not pushing her to finish school. She would sleep all day, ten to twelve hours a day. Messiah was three years old now, but at three, he was old enough to feel something was missing. When I came home in the evening, he would have ten pictures drawn. Out of those, nine would be for me and only one for his mother. I asked my baby why he would draw so many pictures for daddy and only one for his mommy.

His answer at three years old was, "Mommy treats me, different daddy."

He broke my heart, at three that was his way of verbalizing that his mother wasn't attentive enough.

When he was a newborn, Linda and I would take turns feeding and changing him at night. When it was my turn, I would feed him and change his diaper, and that would be that. On Linda's nights, Messiah would be up crying through the night. For the most part, he was a great baby. That is until he started teething. He would cry endlessly through the evening. It drove me insane. I would put ice on his tiny feet to keep him awake during the day; I had so little patience. When he was two, I would force him to sleep in his room by himself, unaware that many babies are scared to sleep alone. I beat him every time he came out of his room. It didn't dawn on me to stop until I heard a noise coming from his room around 11 p.m. When I got up to go check it out, I saw something that cut me to the very core of my being. He was in the dark playing in his toy box. He would rather play in the dark by himself, then face another beating.

I was now doing to Messiah what Jake had done to me. As much as I loved my son, I too was walking a fine line between discipline and abuse. That's the story of my life, hot and cold, good and evil. Seeking to be pious, and ease my guilt, I would buy a kid from the neighborhood whose parents were getting high a winter coat. I wouldn't sell drugs to anyone too sick, too old, too young, or pregnant, but the worldly side of me would fall victim to temptation. I was fucking bitches by the boatload, and still, I would watch pornos and beat my dick so much, that I would have to break the DVD and throw them away because I had no self-control. I view things like that as both weak and sick.

I've since come to understand that I am a product of my environment, as we all are. When N.W.A., Ice Cube, Snoop Dogg, and Tupac hit, the east coast niggas in New York started gang banging again. With music videos and west coast rap, came the Bloods and Crips. Before that, it was the bang-bang shoot em' up westerns, followed by the gangster cinemas, Bonnie and Clyde, John Dillinger, and Baby Face Nelson to name a few. Art began to imitate life with fictitious characters like Michael Corleone from Mario Puzo, and Francis Ford Coppola's the "Godfather" trilogies as well as "Tony Montana" from Brian De Palma and Oliver Stone's "Scarface." Those movies would influence a generation of criminals, rap artist, urban, and suburban youth alike. Everyone wanted to be a gangster. It would come full circle with movies like "Juice", "Boyz N The Hood", "The King of New York", and "New Jack City". Hollywood would become a springboard for spreading the gang culture, violence, and drug trade across America. So yes, we're all products of our environment. Whether you were molested by your babysitter, or you were exposed to music, movies, or videos with graphic content; nudity, sex, and violence are ubiquitous. We've invited debauchery and depravity into our homes, but I don't blame everything on circumstances, or happenstance.

I believe God puts things in our paths and gives us choices. It's like he's playing chess with our lives. On the one hand, he'll throw crack, AIDs, and gang banging in the mix, and on the other hand the re-emergence of the Nation of Islam. In the midst of all of the booty shaking and rapping about drug selling and gun busting, a segment of Black America was searching for a solution. I believed we had found it in a leader named "The Honorable Minister Louis Farrakhan." Here was a man who preached Black unity and pride. I along with hundreds of thousands, if not millions, were captivated by his persona and charisma. I purchased tickets to hear him speak at the Jacob Javits Center in Manhattan New York. He spoke about being accountable to our children as well as our communities. He told us that we were not animals or menaces to society, as the media would have us believe. He said that we were kings and soldiers as well businessmen who could control our own destinies and become self-sufficient entrepreneurs.

He spoke to the heart of what many Black men and I were feeling and still feel. That sentiment is that the American plutocracy doesn't care for the wellbeing of a large demographic of Black Americans, economic or otherwise. My friends and I had been watching videotapes of Minister Farrakhan speaking in forums across America, and we were taken in by his message of Black empowerment. The year was 1995, and the minister said that the time to act was long overdue. He and the Nation of Islam were organizing a march on Washington D.C., a "Million Man March."

I told Linda that I would have liked to take Messiah, but I thought that we might have to fight to get into Washington D.C., or maybe Minister Farrakhan would get a million or more of us gathered together and tell us to burn D.C. to the ground. In either case, I was ready. But on the contrary, the Washington police departments were courteous and very helpful.

Excellence, Powerful, Grill and this other brother named Absolute rode in one car, me and Ya-ya rode with another homie named Spencer. Although I had known Spencer for years because he was a driver for members of both of our crews, as well as my personal driver, I had never been to his home, or he to mine. The reason for that was rule number 331. Niggas don't need to know where you rest your fucking head. Since I had never been to his crib, the thought that he might have been an informant was at the forefront of my mind. Down the line, our crew both immediate and extended came to believe that Absolute, whom Powerful held in close confidence, was the alleged federal informant.

The evening was historic. Speakers such as Jessie Jackson, Al Sharpton, Maya Angelou, and the grandchildren of Thelonious Monk were all in attendance. Another speaker was a young sister who spoke to us and said our daughters were not our girlfriends to be molested and abused. But the standout speaker of the night was this young brother who asked us to go out and fight battles for Black America, come home and tell our sons of the wars that we've fought and of the victories we've won. The atmosphere was one of unity. All around me, there were Black men saying, "Excuse me brother, can I get by?" or, "Do you need a hand Black man?"

There was a brother trying to climb a tree and beneath him were outstretched hands giving him a lift to see the stage. The Million Man March destroyed the crabs in a bucket myth. To my amazement, Black men were unified like days of old. I hadn't seen it first hand in my lifetime. I had only read about it in history books or seen old news footage of the civil rights movement. It was as if our culture began with slavery and ended when Martin Luther King and Malcolm X were assassinated.

The march wasn't a Muslim march; it was a march of all denominations, all-inclusive. The Reverend Jessie Jackson spoke about the lack of home ownership due to the scarcity of homeowner loans being given to our community. At the time, he said less than three percent went to Black applicants, which combined with the practice of the economic double standards towards the Black community, was no surprise to me. For example, if I walked into a car dealership and wanted to buy a car with less than perfect credit and twenty- five hundred dollars down, nine out of ten times, that dealership would let me finance that vehicle for five hundred dollars a month, no problem. Now take that same scenario, but now I'm trying to lease that same vehicle for three hundred dollars a month, usually, that salesman will come back with a credit readout multiple pages long and just as many reasons as to why I'm not eligible to lease that vehicle. The question that I ask you and the rest of America is why is my credit good enough to assume a debt of five hundred monthly and not three hundred?

The march culminated after many speakers, musicians, poets, and a speech by Minister Farrakhan, the new voice of Black America. I remember the secret service standing on the White House steps watching one of the biggest events in recent history. As Minister Farrakhan took the stage, the sea of approximately a million men grew quiet. Honestly, I don't recall much of what was said. But, in my opinion, it was irrelevant to much of what was happening in the streets of America. It was nothing more than rehashed rhetoric and conspiracy theories. Before it was over, we were asked to make donations. There were large hefty sized garbage bags full of money, being passed up to the podium, and now almost two decades later, Black America is not much better off than we were before.

I became disillusioned with the minister a few years later when I saw him doing an interview with a major network news channel sitting at home in an opulent mansion, that was lavishly decorated. While I'll be the first to say that I don't have a problem with our leaders or anyone for that matter enjoying the fruits of their labor, to me, it seemed that he had gone the route of so many of our activist. Once their belly was full, he had forgotten about the cause. To be fair, I've heard that he has done tremendous things in Chicago, and for the Nation of Islam nationally, but there were men from all across the country in Washington that day, and again, men from all denominations. That being said, I've seen little change in the inner cities and poor neighborhoods in this country. Do I have reservations to write these things? Yes!   Am I scared that there may be repercussions from the Nation of Islam? Yes, but the questions must be asked, what happened to all that money, and what the fuck happened to the movement?

I have spoken to numerous people on the subject, and they all say the same damn thing, "Maybe Farrakhan made moves on the low because he was scared of retaliation from the government." To that, I reply, bullshit! In our neighborhoods, we see ads for clothing, liquor, cigarettes, and a whole lot of other nonsense. Why not advertisements for homeowner loans, business loans, free government grants, and other opportunities? Everyone always responds by saying one or two things, "You have to do shit like that under the table." Or, "If they find out, the "they" being the government, they gon' sabotage you." Niggas are so scared of White authority it's laughable. Always worried about what the White man is going to do. The Nation of Islam has tried to duplicate the magnitude of that march, but with little success. For what it's worth, Minister Farrakhan made us stand up, look at ourselves, and our communities. He gave us the desire to want to become more than pimps, gangsters, and hustlers. He gave us the aspiration to become men again. He gave us back our dignity.

Chapter 11
The Winds of Change

It was 1996, Pap had done four years of his three to six-year prison term before being released on parole. While he was locked up, I continued to give his mother money for his commissary and pay for his daughter's school tuition. Being that I held my man down, as soon as he got out, it was back to business as usual. Powerful had left the streets long ago to pursue a career in music, so he had no say on Franklin, but he objected to Pap coming back to make money on the block. I told him Pap was my man, I had to let him eat, besides Pap was different now. Prison had changed him. When speaking to him, I remember commenting on how much he had matured.

"Pap welcome home partner! How you?" I asked giving him a hug.

"I'm good bro,' I'm just contemplating my next move homie," he said.

"I see that. You on some real laid back shit huh pa'?"

Pap looked at me for a few seconds.

"Yeah, Llord, I had four years to think about a lot of shit, about the mistakes I've made, Mark, my daughter. She was five when I left; now she's goin' on ten years old. I missed a lot of her young life because of somethin' I coulda' avoided. While I was in prison, I found Allah. I got deep into Islam and myself. I got my focus back nigga. I'm ready to git' this paper and make moves. Power moves."

I heard the candor in his voice and more than that I could see the genuineness in his eyes.

"Aight' pa'," I said. "You know you my ace boon coon. If I'm gittin' money, you gittin' money. Ain't shit changed, but les' enjoy ourselves tonight. Have a few drinks, and we'll talk business tomorrow. Now c'mon and check out my new ride nigga," I said jingling my car keys.

We headed to our man I-born's strip club on 166th and Third Ave.

Pap was sitting at the bar having drinks while I was in the back of the strip club in the VIP room getting my fuck on. I-born had made it a point of telling me that every bitch I see in the club that I wanted to fuck, make sure I fucked her so she could never walk by me on the street and act saditty. I had this light skin chick twisted the fuck up putting serious dick in her. She called her girlfriend, who's over on the opposite side of the room giving a nigga head to come over to take a look at my dick, but her girlfriend tells her she has her own business to tend to. Long story short, honey can't take the dick, so she don't want to let me get my nut off, and she don't want to give me none of my money back. It was only fifty dollars, but me, being petty and drunk, told this sister selling herself dirt cheap that I want twenty–five dollars back. Naturally, she said she shouldn't have to give me back a motherfucking dime, and she was right. So we walk up to the front of the club and tell I-born the situation. He listened and said what any real nigga would have said, "C'mon Llord, forgit' about that short paper." But now I'm beyond reason, more accurately, I'm being a fucking shithead going back and forth with the sister for twenty-five dollars.

Pap saw me and shorty arguing, and comes over to see what's up. He stands there not saying anything. This beautiful, black, chocolate sister walks up to me and says something. I couldn't hear her, but Pap told her to mind her fucking business. When he said that, she grabbed a champagne bottle and struck him in the chest with it. Fuck. I realize she was trying to have her homegirl's back, but Pap had put on at least fifty pounds, and he weighed 270 if he weighed an ounce. When the bottle hit Pap, I reacted first. I hit her with a straight left jab hard enough to break her jaw.

Pap snatched her up by the flimsy blouse she had on, and we beat her mercilessly. Stomping her like she was a man. We left her bloodied on the sidewalk and walked to my car. As I was getting in, I saw this older brother from the neighborhood named Ed standing there; he had seen the whole incident. At that moment I felt ashamed of what we had done. I can try to blame it on the alcohol, but I have no idea why Pap and I beat the sister the way we did. Maybe it's the same reason why she felt the need to swing first. We live with so much self-loathing and anger and the only way we think to resolve our differences is with violence, or maybe like I've stated before, it's just human nature. I called Pap the next morning to tell him that I was feeling guilty.

"Damn nigga'. We wilded the fuck out last night. We should'na pounded honey out like that," I said while looking in the medicine cabinet for an Alka-Seltzer, but he didn't give a fuck.

Yes, it was four years later, and he had matured as far as getting money and other things, but he was still the same nigga when it came to pounding a motherfucker out, man or woman.

"That bitch had it comin'. If she woulda' minded her fuckin' business, she wouldn'a got that ass beat," he said in a matter of fact voice.

You see Pap's reasoning process is why I love, and simultaneously dislike niggas like him. Shit is too elementary to them. Someone violates, they get that ass beat. No gray area, no in between. As for me, I wanted to remain inconspicuous, at least until things quieted down. Not that I feared any retribution, I was just mortified. It was Sunday, and the block had to be opened up the first thing Monday morning.

"Pap do me a favor dogs. Go to the hood tomorrow and make sure these cats open up on time?" I asked reluctantly not wanting to put him back in the mix so soon after his homecoming, but his answer was what I expected.

"No problem homie, I got it."

Shit was like he never left. The "Dream Team" was back together.

While some of the headaches of the block were taken off of my shoulders with Pap being back, things with Linda had continued to get worse. I tried to run my home like I ran my operation, but I didn't do it purposely. I was young, getting money and I felt that my way was the only way. I admit, that it was pretty arrogant of me. Linda was growing up and growing tired of my shit, but it wasn't all my fault. She was still sleeping all fucking day, twelve to fourteen hours a day. In a nutshell, she was lazy, and I was getting tired of her being tired all of the fucking time. What I didn't realize that while she was maturing, she was eight years younger than me, and she had a lot on her plate dealing with motherhood and depression. We would have drag out, smack down fights. One of the worst was her going into the closet and grabbing my Tec-9. That crazy bitch was going to shoot me! Messiah was in the next room sleeping.

It was after 10 pm and freezing outside. I recall all of those details, but the one detail I don't remember is why the fight started in the first place. I think I initiated the physical violence by jumping off of the bed, choking her, and smacking her in the face. She ran to the closet grabbed the gun, and tried to load the clip into it. I tussled with her trying to wrestle the magazine from her grip. When she let it go, I cracked her in the motherfucking head with it. A stream of blood spurted from a gash on her head like a fountain.

She fell to the ground yelling bloody murder.

"Motherfucka', you goin' to jail," she was screaming at the top of her lungs. Mind you; we lived in a private house with the landlord and his family living directly above us. Messiah came out of his room rubbing his little eyes asking, "Daddy what's wrong with mommy?" I yelled at him and told him to go back to bed. I threw on a pair of fatigue army pants, no underwear, my green pilot bomber jacket, no shirt, and a pair of Timberlands with no socks. I grabbed the other gun out of the closet, threw them both in a garbage bag along with my small security box containing six thousand dollars. I ripped the house phone out of the wall and ran out of the house before she could call the cops. It was preposterous how I always took whatever money I had in the house with me whenever Linda and I got into fights. That was that street shit in me. I didn't trust anyone. Not even the mother of my child after being together for seven years.

We eventually made up, but not long after that, we went our separate ways for good. It happened on Messiah's first day of school. I had started to dabble in the music industry, and Linda was going to enroll in college. The day started out beautifully. Linda and I got up early that morning to take our baby to school.

"Llord after we drop Messiah off, I want you to take me to Monroe College on Fordham Road so I can register for fall classes," she said.

"No problem baby. I just have to go to a meeting with some record executives downtown around 2 o'clock. If you ain't back, I'll check the answering machine to see if you need me to pick Messiah up." He had to be picked up no later than 4:15. "If you ain't leave a message, I'ma hit the streets and be back around four."

As I'm writing this, the thing that comes to mind is how most niggas plans for making it out of the ghetto was one of two things, music or sports, and oh yeah, the fucking lottery. With that said we headed out the door. Linda had mixed emotions since it was our baby's first day of school. I, on the other hand, was smiling ear to ear since it was a step in regaining some of my freedom. That afternoon around 2:30, I came home, checked the answering machine and found no message. I went back to the block to make sure things were in order and returned home around 4:45 that evening.

I check the answering machine again, and this time I hear multiple messages.

"Hello, this message is for Messiah's parents. It's now 4:37, and no one has come to pick Messiah up. It's his first day of school: this is not a good sign."

When I heard that message, I ran outside and jumped in my car. I was doing at least sixty miles per hour and running red lights driving to his school which was eight blocks away. When I entered his classroom, the teacher informed me that Linda has just come and taken him home. I coolly tell her "thank you," but on the inside, I'm fucking fuming. I drove to her mother's building where I run into her and her sister Lillian. Without thinking, I reached out and grabbed her by the throat. I was trying to choke the life out of that bitch. Meanwhile, Lillian is trying her best to keep us apart and calm me down.

"Llord what's wrong with you? Let her go!" she said getting in between the two of us.

The people coming in the lobby of the building were acting as though they weren't paying attention to us, but I was yelling at the top of my lungs.

"This bitch gon' have my son watin' for almost a fuckin' hour. I'ma kill her ass!"

Linda's ready to fight now that she has gotten her bearings, but Lillian is holding her back.

"Just go Llord," she said while holding onto Linda.

Linda said something that would be indicative of what things would be like dealing with her as my baby's momma.

"Take your son with you motherfucka'."

The slight implication didn't occur to me which was; she wasn't ready to be a full- time mother. In hindsight, I think she had Messiah for me, and she wanted her life back. When she said that, I snatched my son from her arms and left without saying a word.

My world was becoming topsy-turvy. The streets were beginning to change. In hip-hop, rap music had transitioned from, party songs, to conscious rap, to rap about drug dealing and balling, to becoming infused with lyrics about gang banging. The streets followed the trend blindly. In New York and all across America gangs infested the neighborhoods like roaches. The Bloods and Crips had come to New York wreaking havoc. At the same time, an intimidating character by the name of Suge Knight, a co-founder of "Death Row" records started a beef with Puff Daddy the CEO of "Bad Boy" records which escalated into a beef between the East and West coast. It led to rap fans choosing sides between the two coasts from all over the nation. It ended with the death of Tupac Shakur on September 13th, 1996. His death would lead to more acts of violence. It was alleged that Suge Knight and his henchmen forced one of Puff Daddy's associates to drink a champagne glass full of piss. It was also rumored that a New Jersey rap artist from the group the "Outlawz," who were signed to "Death Row" records, was gunned down as a result of this rap beef.

Six months after the murder of Tupac Shakur, "Bad Boy's" preeminent artist, and friend of Sean "Puffy" Combs, Biggie Smalls, was killed in Los Angeles, California on March 9th, 1997. It took the mothers of these slain artist to hold a joint news conference to ask for a halt to the senseless violence, but it was too late. The seeds had been planted. The West Coast had made its presence felt, and gang-banging was here to stay.

The Patriarch or father figure of our organization, Excellence would learn this the hard way. He made the mistake of starting a war with another powerful organization. Let me back up and restate the facts. I wasn't there when shit went down, so this is a second-hand account or hearsay. A heroin dealer named Cubano was making millions on the streets, and it was rumored that he was in business with a gentleman who was politically connected. Cubano himself was an ex-corrections officer whom purportedly started making so much money selling heroin that he quit the corrections department. He and his partner opened a restaurant/nightclub in the Fordham section of the Bronx called the "Speak Easy Café."

It was the place to be seen at the time. Excellence had the mindset a lot of thugs have. If you weren't known for being violent, then you had no right to make money on the streets. As the story goes, Excellence approached Cubano and tried to extort him. He told Cubano if he wanted to stay in business, he would have to pay a thousand dollars a week. Realistically, a thousand dollars weekly was chump change to Cubano, but it wasn't about the money. It was about principle. If Cubano wanted to stay in business, he would have to hold his ground, and holding his ground wasn't even an issue. Cubano's right-hand man was a ruthless killer named Paulie. Word on the streets was that Paulie had six bodies under his belt by himself, not to mention the hits he had ordered. Of their organization, Cubano was the businessman, and Paulie was the enforcer. He was also the head of a notorious sect of the Bloods gang called, More Money, More Murder.

These niggas were organized from selling drugs, to prostitution, and yes, murder. When Excellence propositioned Cubano, Paulie stepped up.

"You tryin' to extort us, nigga'? I'll kill you where you stand."

Before Excellence could respond, Cubano put his hand on Paulie's chest and told him, "Let's go, this nigga ain't on our level."

Which was true. Excellence made the same blunder most niggas make, which is spending every dollar on clothes, cars, jewelry, and pussy. He didn't have any money put up for lawyers or war, but it was too late, the ball had been thrown into play, and Paulie wasn't going to let it rest. Over the next few months, a hit was placed on Excellence's head. The bounty? Whoever killed Excellence could have whatever price they asked for. Two attempts were made on his life in Harlem. One, while he was in a restaurant, and the other while he was riding home in a yellow cab. Neither attempt was successful. Excellence escaped physically unscathed, but mentally he was scarred beyond repair.

After those two incidents, I did something that I never did. I invited Pap, Grill, Powerful, and Excellence to my home for a sit-down. We ate dinner which I cooked myself, spoke about the situation that was facing Excellence and our organization. I laid my cards on the table. They had the option of listening to me, or not. You see, I was still only mid-level in our organization, and I was connected through Powerful and Pap more so than to Grill and Excellence. While Pap and I had our own crew, our crew was young, and we were the main muscle. Powerful, Grill, and Excellence each had their own crews, and each one of their crews was strong in their own right. I stated my case.

"Fellas', we need to go over to Bronx River and spray everything wearin' red. That's the only way we gon' come out on top of this shit. From the youngest to the oldest, if a nigga' old enough to flag, then they old enough to die."

They listened to me without saying much, but ultimately the call was up to Excellence to make. He hesitated for a moment before speaking.

"I wanna' git' this shit squashed. I'm always lookin' over my shoulder. Everywhere I go, I have to walk wit' security and a gun. This shit got a nigga' stressed. I wanna' let this shit die down before I make a move."

In saying that, our meeting was over. As for myself, I grew to understand the fact that for every killer there was another killer waiting in the wings to test him. The only thing a nigga can do to impress me or make me fear him is to show some me bulletproof skin.

Some months later Excellence was dead. He was killed coming out of this club called "The Dungeon" on 138th street and the Grand Concourse. The details surrounding his death were cloudy. From what I heard, once again hearsay, Powerful had called Excellence and told him he was going out to the club, but he thought Excellence should stay home.

Now don't get it twisted Excellence had said to all of us that he wasn't going to hide from anyone, no matter how many times we said he should stay off the scene. He would always tell us that he wasn't pussy! This particular day he wanted to come out and get some air. When he arrived at the club shit was jumping as usual. He was glad to be out amongst the family, but less than an hour later he was dead. Shot multiple times and Powerful was charged with his murder.

Pap called me as soon as he got the call. It was a little after 11 p.m. His voice was stoic, it betrayed the gravity of the situation.

"Llord, Excellence got returned."

It took a minute for his statement to register in my mind.

"What?" I asked making sure I heard him correctly.

"Excellence is dead," Pap repeated.

"What happened?" I asked, half in a state of shock, half in disbelief.

Pap told me he wasn't going to speak about it over the phone, but he would meet me at Lincoln Hospital. I made a call and told Linda what happened. I asked would she mind coming over to spend the night while I go meet up with Pap. I arrived at the hospital around 12:30.

Pap was there with Grill, Grill's mother, and some of Grill's and Excellence's crew. Pap pulled me to the side and gave me the rundown.

"I on't know what happened. Shit is up in the air right now, but Powerful is locked up, and niggas' is sayin' he killed Excellence."

This shit was unbelievable. We were all family, but like all families, niggas sometimes squabble amongst each other. Powerful and Excellence's beef was over an issue that many of us had with Powerful, money! Powerful still hated to pay a nigga. Excellence was providing security for Powerful and Powerful owed him money. My first thought was perhaps Excellence tried to press Powerful about the paper that he had coming, or, maybe Excellence threatened him. Powerful being a man, might have lost his temper and shot him, but I kept those thoughts to myself.

"Where's his body?" I asked Pap.

"It's in the morgue downstairs in the basement. C'mon I'll take you downstairs," he said pressing for the elevator.

It was three floors to the basement. During the ride, that took less than a minute; my mind went over the different scenarios of what could've happened. Before I could come to a conclusion that made sense the elevator doors opened.

"The morgue is down the hall, c'mon," Pap said putting his arm over my shoulder.

The morgue doors were locked, but I could see the bodies lying on the metal gurneys covered in sheets. I smelled the scent of death seeping from under the doors. I don't know if it was the cold temperature or the eerie atmosphere, but the hairs on the back of my neck stood on end.

"Damn Pap, which one is Excellence?" I asked in a whisper as though I might wake the dead.

"He's the one on the left," Pap pointed, his voice slightly cracking.

As I stared at the lifeless body of the man that I had tried to emulate lying there on a table, I felt a void inside. Sure I felt remorse. Even outrage, but the feeling of loss far outweighed any other emotion that I had. As for retaliation, Grill would have to make the first move, but before anything could be done, we had to get the facts straight. When Pap and I went back upstairs, I walked over to Grill and his mother. I hugged Grill and gave his mother a kiss on the cheek. I told Grill I would holler at him in a day or two. I had no idea what to say to him or his mother.

Grill was his mother's last son or her last son alive and free. His older brother Jaron went to prison when he was sixteen. He had been imprisoned since before Grill was born, which was over twenty years ago, and he would probably be an old man before he saw the light of day. He was sentenced to life in prison with the possibility of parole after forty years for a murder that happened during the commission of a robbery. What can you say to someone who has lost a child or a sibling? I walked over to where Pap was sitting in the lobby and placed my hand on his back.

"I'ma call you first thing in the mornin' homie," he didn't reply.

He gave me a pound and nodded his acknowledgment. On the drive home, I had time to reflect, but I was wasting my time. The only ones who knew what really happened were Powerful and Excellence. When I got home, Linda was in my bed sleeping.

"Lin' wake up."

It was 2 a.m., but I would have to put her in a cab if she wanted to head back to her mother's house before Messiah woke up. She turned over wiping the sleep from her eyes and asked, what happened at the hospital? I told her that Excellence's body was in the morgue, and Powerful was in jail charged with his murder.

Without blinking, she blurted out, "See! I told you I never liked that motherfucka'!"

Her dislike was, again Powerful's, me first attitude. I didn't say much. I didn't want to judge my brother without knowing all of the facts, so every once and awhile I would shake my head in agreement, or say "Uh-huh." We talked for most of the night. Our conversation soon turned sexual and talk soon turned physical. It's so funny how you'll dislike certain things about someone, whether it be their personality or some annoying habit, but if the sexual chemistry is there, you'll overlook all of that shit. Linda and I didn't have good sexual chemistry; we had great sexual chemistry. I couldn't wait, I missed the taste of her. We spent the rest of the night sucking and fucking. I banged her pussy until it was dripping.

"I'ma about to cum Lin'," I said as I pulled my dick out of her pussy to let it drip on her stomach. "Damn I miss this pussy."

Linda did what she always did. She got out of bed, went to the bathroom to clean herself up. When she was done, she returned with a hot washcloth to wipe me down. I looked at her the way I sometimes did. Appreciating the little things, and still, in the back of my mind wanting, no more like longing for her, Messiah, and I to be a family once more.

That night we fell asleep in each other's arms. No sooner than I closed my eyes, the phone rang.

"Mornin." I managed to mumble.

"Llord git' up man."

It was Pap on the other end.

"Nigga, what time is it?" I asked looking out the window at the sun shining in through the blinds.

"It's 7 a.m. homie. Time to rise and grind nigga. I'ma meet you on the block so we can talk. Besides, we still gotta' git' this money," he said.

I rolled over and looked at Linda. She was in a deep sleep.

"Lin', Lin', wake up mama."

I was shaking her gently; she could be a bitch in the morning if I started her day off on the wrong foot.

"What now boy?" she asked a little irritated.

I understood, both she and I were exhausted.

"Would you mind spending the day with Messiah? I have to meet up with Pap again."

She shook her head yes, and dozed back off. I was relieved. It was Saturday, and it would give her and Messiah some much needed alone time together.

I reached Franklin Ave. in less than an hour. Pap was already there with the pitchers and lieutenants setting up shop. Excellence was a mentor to Pap. He had taught him much of what he knew about the streets, but here he was, business as usual. I admired Pap's quiet strength. He spoke his mind no matter what. He didn't give a fuck who liked it. Some of the time he was tactless. Other times he was wrong, but he was always straight to the point.

"How you bro?" I asked although I knew the answer.

"As good as I can be given the situation," he said pausing for a second before he filled me in.

"From what Grill told me last night at the hospital, Powerful and Excellence was outside the club talkin'. Motherfuckas' heard gunshots and ran in the direction where the shots came from. When the crowd got there, people said Excellence was lying on the ground dead, and Powerful was runnin' up the block wit' the toast in his hand. He ain't git far before the hot boys jumped out on him."

I interrupted him. "Wasn't nobody from our squad there wit' them?"

"Nah," Pap said. "Jus' some of Powerful's people, and they ain't talkin' yet," Pap continued. "But from what I understand, niggas' is screamin' for blood. They wanna' lay Powerful out."

This shit was crazy! Like an episode of a fucking soap opera.

"What Grill have to say about all of this?" I asked.

"It ain't Grill, it's the guns that's loyal to Excellence that's ready to react," Pap said. "They even talkin' bout' killin' his brother Joel."

I had heard enough. Joel was a good nigga. While he would go clubbing and hang out with niggas from the hood, he was square. A cat who worked a nine to five, although, on occasion or two, he would take the reins and run the block when Powerful had other shit going on. I had never known him to be a troublemaker, and he definitely wasn't a shooter.

"Joel, I on't think Joel had anything to do wit' this. I ain't never seen the nigga' have a fight. I'ma go build wit' Grill and try and straighten shit out." I said walking towards my car.

 "What you need to do is mind your fuckin' business!" he yelled out behind me.

Maybe he was right. Maybe I should have just let things work themselves out. After all, I didn't have anything to do with it. It's just that I fancied myself a peacemaker of sorts, but you know the saying, no good deed goes unpunished.

While I was cool with Grill and his crew, those niggas were true thugs with no off button. That wasn't my scene. I did the best I could to stay out of shit, and those niggas loved the drama and the limelight. I pulled up in front of Grill's building, went upstairs, and knocked on the door.

"Who is it?" A deep voice asked from the other side of the door.

"It's Llord," I answered.

When the door opened, Grill's man Snake was standing there with the chrome plated .50 Cal. Desert Eagle at his side.

"Excuse my left," he said giving me a pound with his left hand.

"It's nothin' homie. Where's Grill?" I asked.

He pointed to a room down the hall. Grill's crib was the neighborhood house party, strip club, and flophouse for the niggas in his crew. The place where you might find your daughter, sister, or in some cases your girl. The bitches loved this nigga. That's why we started callin' him, Grill. It was short for, Gorilla Pimp. The bedroom door opened up, and Grill came bopping up the hall. I gave my nigga a hug.

"Grill, what's good daddy?" I asked walking past a half-naked hood rat sleeping on the couch in the living room.

"Ain't shit," Grill said embracing me back.

In all the years that I had known Grill we had been cool, and as the years passed, we had gotten closer, but in all of that time, this was the first time that he and I had a one on one conversation.

"Yo' I'm sorry I didn't hang around las' night. I didn't know what to say to you and your mother homie."

"That's nothin' my dude. I understand. Sit down homie."

I picked up the dirty clothes off of a beat up recliner in a corner.

"What you want me to do with these?" I asked him holding up clothes and a bunch of socks that smelled like they could stand by themselves.

"Throw that shit on the floor nigga."

The next words that came out of his mouth were, "What you think about the shit that's goin' on?"

I thought back. I heard Powerful say once before that if Excellence wanted it, he could git' it, but every nigga' talk shit when they're mad, so I kept that thought to myself and said,

"I on't know pa', shit don't add up. The only ones who know what happened is Powerful and the cats that was wit' him when the shit went down."

Grill had tears running down his face now. You see every killer, gangster or thug is someone's son, brother, husband, or father. Grill, like most niggas in the hood, was bout' it–bout' it, but here he was crying like a baby. It was too much for me.

"Yo' pa' I'ma' call you later," I said as I walked back down the hall toward the door.

"Aight' Llord, if you hear anything holla' at me."

That was it! I was out the door, but for some reason, maybe it was Grill's tears, or maybe it was because I felt I had to be that nigga who had to put his two cents in everything, whatever the reason, I stopped when I could have walked out.

"Grill, I'ma, keep it funky wit' you. I heard Powerful say that if shit ever got hectic between him and Excellence, he would wild out if he had to. I don't know if he was talkin' shit outta' anger or what, but I heard him say it more than once."

While Grill didn't react to what I said, as soon as the words left my lips I felt as though a dark cloud descended over me. Grill listened without saying a word. He gave me a pound and told me he would get up with me later.

When I told Pap what I said to Grill, he lost it.

"You said what nigga? Yeah, you bumped your fuckin' head! I told you to mind your fuckin' business!"

Pap was going on and on with the "I told you so shit," but, he was right. I fucked up. I should have stayed out of it.

"Listen, man," Pap said, speaking with more composure, "What you gon' do is wait for Powerful to come home. If and when he comes home, you gon' tell him what you told Grill. So from the jump, either Powerful gon' hate you and stop fuckin' wit you, or he gon' git you smoked for runnin' your mouth," he paused. "Or, the last possible scenario, he gon' respect you for comin' to him as a man and let shit ride, but I highly doubt that shit nigga."

"You know what Pap, fuck you, nigga'," I said sticking my middle finger up. "I'ma tell him and let the chips fall where they may."

Powerful was locked up for two weeks. When he came home, he laid low. When I finally met up with him, I told him about the conversation that Grill and I had. He didn't flip out, but he let his feelings be known.

"You know that you coulda' go me killed right?" he asked looking at me with an expression of both disappointment and distaste.

I could only say, "You're one hundred percent right, but trust me when I tell you, I wasn't trying to stir up no beef between you and Grill. I was jus' tellin' him that I didn't think you set Excellence up. You know, maybe shit got outta' hand, you felt disrespected, and you had to wild out."

I tried to explain the rationale behind my actions, but the damage was done. Powerful was angry but more than that he was hurt.

"You know Llord, were supposed to be brothers. We don't lay hands on one another, and we definitely don't go to the guns against each other and for your information brotha, the gun I got caught wit' was Excellence's hammer. He dropped it when he got hit, and I picked it up to chase the niggas that shot him. On that note, I'ma holla' at you later."

He left without giving me a pound. I can't say that I blamed him. There are rules on the streets that must be obeyed to the letter if you are going to survive. Many of these rules apply to life as well. Rule number 37, mind your fucking business and keep your mouth shut whenever possible. I had violated that rule, and I was lucky to be alive.

Nothing was ever mentioned again to me by Powerful or Grill, but one of Powerful's associates said something a little sketchy to me once, but it's not worth mentioning, it was such a minuscule offense.

Excellence's funeral was attended by hundreds, if not thousands of mourners. While the FEDs also attended the funeral taking pictures of the attendees, Excellence's murder was never solved, but the streets said Paulie had him killed. Consequently, our family was torn apart by the death of Excellence, Powerful's implication in his murder, and me running my fucking mouth!

Chapter 12
The Return of Disco

Mayor Giuliani was a motherfucker. I had been hustling for the last eight years, and I was used to the frenetic routine of going head to head with the NYPD, but Giuliani had beefed up the police force to unprecedented numbers and had given them free reign to bring drugs and crime to a standstill. While it didn't exactly stop niggas from selling drugs, it did change the way we sold drugs. Pap and I stopped selling deuces and went back to selling nickels to slow the stream of traffic, but that didn't put a dent in our flow. We still averaged six thousand dollars a day, and eighty-five hundred on the 1st, 3rd, and 15th of the month, but the most noticeable change was the way the NYPD policed the community.

They conducted stop and frisk all day, every day. They would stop ten individuals and say they were looking for a robbery suspect. I'll give New York's finest the benefit of the doubt, but I have to ask what did the suspect look like? Out of the ten people, they would stop, most would have different physical traits. I'm short, Pap was over six feet tall, and some niggas would be light skinned, others would have a dark complexion, and many would have different builds. So, who was this ambiguous suspect? Was he a fucking Chameleon? I'll admit, to the Mayor's credit, crime plummeted, but at what cost? With drug sweeps escalating from twice a week to seven days a week, the courts were pushed to full capacity. Arrestees sat in precincts or holding pens for days at a time without seeing a judge and lastly, but certainly not least, the police rode around like they were untouchable! Giuliani gave them unrestrained authority. The end results were the deaths of Anthony Baez, Amadou Diallo, and the sodomizing of Abner Louima. These were just a few of the high-profile incidents of police brutality run amok.

Not long after, we began to feel the noose getting tighter, but as usual, Pap and I brainstormed until we came up with a solution.

"Aight' Pap. We know the main problem is the police ridin' around every day, but we also know Franklin Ave. ain't their main focus. It can't be. They have up to thirty other crack spots in our hood alone, and their patrol area is from as far south as 161st and Third Ave. to as far north as 174th and Boston Rd. Also, as far east as Bronx River Ave., to as far west as Clay Ave. There's no way in hell they're gon' be able to sit on us all day. It jus' ain't feasible."

"Yeah, Llord we know that, but we also know niggas is still gittin' hit, and the team is scared to death nigga," Pap said frustrated.

The wheels in my head were turning at full speed. I was thinking and rethinking every angle. I had it.

"Remember how I told you how I would follow Robocop wherever he went when he was a beat cop?"

"Okay, so what?" he asked sarcastically.

"Okay, so what?" I asked him back facetiously. "Nigga, all we have to do is expand that concept. Git' our lookouts bikes and have them ride around a four-block perimeter every thirty for forty-five minutes. If they spot the hot boys, they hit us on the Walkie-talkies, and we shut down for an hour. Like I said, they can't sit on us all fuckin' day!"

I saw that flicker in Pap's eyes. That look he got when he knew I fixed the problem. Pap used to tell me he didn't need to know the numbers. All he needed was to see me smile and that was enough for him.

People underestimate the mind of a hustler. A hustler is an entrepreneur in their most rudimentary form. A hustler is intelligent and determined. A hustler doesn't just sell drugs; a hustler can sell Bibles to the devil and a new religion to God. The drug dealer has tunnel vision, and thus, he is destined to spend his days in and out of jail and in the end, spend his last days with nothing but memories.

What I hadn't thought through was the, Buy and Bust. Granted it had been a tactic that the police employed frequently, but Mayor Giuliani and his militia took to using addicts and informants to apprehend dealers as well. His proverbial, "better mousetrap," was a thorn in my side.

That morning in May of 98', our pitcher was late, and me being the general that I fancied myself to be, took the package and began to pitch. Pap volunteered to pitch, but I said what I always said, "I needed to stay sharp," and besides, it would be good to let the crew see me in the trenches when shit had to be done. Our spot that day was in some bushes in front of a private house on the block. It was 1 p.m., and I was on my sixth pack when a crackhead came up and informed us that he saw the narcotics unit driving through the hood five cars deep. The thing was, he had a skinny Puerto Rican with him that no one recognized. I asked did he know the dude he brought with him.

"C'mon Llord, would I bring somebody wit' me I ain't know?" he asked. But he set me up, not only was he working with the police, but the cat that he brought with him was an undercover cop.

"Pap do me a favor. Jump on the bike and do a perimeter check homie. I'ma shut down til' you git' back." I said as I handed the head two nickels.

I waited until he and the Puerto Rican cat with him turned the corner and headed up the block before I put the stash away. As I walk out of the bushes, a police van pulled up. The doors opened, and the narcotic officers' jumped out, guns were drawn, "Put your hands on your head."

I did what most niggas do; I acted as though I didn't know what I was being arrested for.

"What's goin' on officers? What ya'll jumpin' out on me for?" I ask trying to sound as sincere as I could.

"Shut the fuck up and put your hands behind your back," was the officer's reply.

That's when I went into my routine which was to call the officer by name so I could establish a rapport with him or her. It's a propaganda tool to make the arresting officer feel at ease with you. See a stupid motherfucker will tell you, "Fuck the police. I ain't got shit to say to them." Some will curse, or go to the extent of fighting with the police, but I figured once I was in handcuffs, I might as well get what I could out of the situation.

"Excuse me Officer Sharpe; you don't have to curse sir. I was just asking what I'm being arrested for."

Instantly, the officer's demeanor changed. First, I called him Officer, second, I called him by his name, and third, I called him sir!

He was at ease now. That's when I asked him to loosen my cuffs, which he did. When the transport van pulled up, the van doors slid open, and there staring at me with a look that said, "We fucked up," was Pap already on the chain gang. Once we got to the precinct, Pap and I started talking about what went wrong.

"When I see that crackhead, I'ma fuck him up," Pap said pacing back and forth in the holding cell. I was worried. I had to get in touch with Linda so she could pick Messiah up from school.

"Pap, I know you tight man, but I gotta' call Linda. She gotta' go git' my little man."

I was becoming concerned. Not that I wasn't upset at myself for getting arrested, but I understood that was a consequence of doing business.

"Excuse me, officer, I need to call my son's mother and ask her to pick my son up from school."

The officer hardly looked up from his desk as he was doing the paperwork to process Pap and me.

"Just give me a minute," he said returning to his paperwork.

The door swung open to the entrance of the room leading to the holding pens and standing there with a grin on his face was my old nemesis and friend, Officer Manning, A.K.A., Robocop!

"Well, well, well. If it ain't the almighty Llord and his trusty sidekick Pap," he said cynically.

"What they in for? As if I don't know," he asked the officer that was finishing up our paperwork.

"We have the big guy for steering, and his partner got a direct sell," the officer replied still typing.

Robocop asked him to open up the cell so he could take Pap into the interrogation room. The officer finally finished typing up the arrest report and was ready to fingerprint me, but before he did, he let me make my phone call.

I spoke to Linda, told her I was locked up and asked her to pick Messiah up from school. She said, of course, she would pick him up and take care of him until I got released. On my way back to the holding cell I saw a few officers with tee-shirts on that read, Warriors of the Wasteland. I surmised they were all from the same unit.

I stopped a burly cop with one of the tees on and asked, "Pardon me officer, but where's the wasteland?"

His answer was concise, "This, this is the wasteland."

With that, he trotted up the stairs. His statement summed up how a vast majority of the New York police department views the communities they are sworn to protect and serve. After a few days of bullpen therapy, I was interviewed by a legal aid before seeing a judge. This process which by law states that you must be seen by a lawyer and a judge within the first twenty-four hours of your arrest generally takes seventy-two hours. I eventually ended up getting off with five years' probation, but it wasn't for the current case. Those charges were dropped due to a lack of evidence. When I exited the bushes, I was clean. I had no drugs or money on me. I had thoroughly stashed them. Remember Rule number one, stay clean! The probation was for the case that I jumped bail on almost a decade earlier. I plead guilty to a felony. What an idiot. I should have fought the case. After all, ten years later, who knew if that cop was still on the force?

Pap's case was dismissed. As for me, I was ordered to report to the department of probation upon my release. After reporting to my probation officer, I formed a new game plan. First, I was going to take a step back and let Pap handle the day to day operations while I played the system. I signed up for a GED program and a class to get my real estate license, which I acquired within months of each other. I had my P.O. eating out of the palm of my hand, but that was part of my superficial charm. I only show most people the fluffy shit on the surface. I'll know someone for years and not even know their fucking name, and yet when they see me, it's as though they've bumped into a long lost relative. In the meantime, I asked Pap to give me a thousand a week to help me stay afloat until I got a foothold in the real estate game. I also had a little cushion. A twelve thousand dollar cushion put up for a rainy day.

While I was able to organize my life as far as goals and money, my personal life was in disarray. I was sleeping with Linda and any other woman I could bed, but I still had no one special in my life. That is until I met Joharra. I was out shopping one day when I saw her. I was hypnotized. She was absolutely gorgeous. Skin so yellow it was as if she was a daughter of the sun. Her hair was a reddish-blonde tone, and her hazel eyes accentuated it all. The avenue was full of shoppers that summer day, but it was like she stood alone, illuminated like an angel. I parked my car as soon as I saw her. When

I walked up the block towards where she was standing, I got a better look at her. Oh my God! She was the most beautiful woman I had ever laid eyes on.

"Excuse me, but I don't usually approach women on the street like this (a lie), but you look absolutely gorgeous. Please, tell me your name."

At first, she looked taken aback. Perhaps nervous, but then she looked into my eyes, and I guess she saw something she liked, something that put her at ease.

"My name is Joharra. What's your name?" she asked with a thick Spanish accent.

"My name is Llord," I said trying to sound smooth.

That's when she hit me with that real hood' shit.

"Your mother ain't name you no Llord."

I had to laugh.

"My name is Lloyd, you happy now?"

She smiled at me and said, "I like that. Lloyd, it sounds smart."

I looked at her and said, "Wow your game is tight. You pimpin' me huh? Can I git' your number?"

She told me that she didn't like to give her number out to guys on the street, but I seemed nice.

The rest of that day I couldn't stop thinking about her, but I didn't want to seem thirsty, so I waited until the next day to call her. We spoke on the phone for hours getting to know each other. I asked if we could go out on a date. She said she would love to as long as she could bring her cousin along. The following Saturday I picked her and her younger cousin up on University Ave. We went to 125th St. to this Spanish restaurant on Broadway. Her cousin Elisa was eighteen, and she was impressed with my manners and my money. I knew the way to most female's hearts is to get in good with the family, friends, and kids. That night we laughed and got further acquainted. When we pulled up to her building, Elisa got out and said, "Thanks for dinner. I had a really nice time."

I told her, "No problem, we'll do it again sometime."

Elisa went inside while Joharra and I talked for a bit longer. Before I pulled off, I asked for a kiss. She gave me her cheek. I couldn't believe it. Most women were usually overwhelmed with my aggressiveness, but she held her ground. She was indeed a young lady. I have to say; I was pleasantly surprised with her strength and innocence.

Our next date was dinner and a movie. We kissed through half of the movie and talked through the other half. She told me that she had a two-year-old daughter named Jamila. I told her that I was also a single parent raising a six-year-old son named Messiah. She smiled and asked me where his mother was. I told her that she had given me custody some years ago.

"Wow," she said. "I could never give up custody of my daughter,"

I said that my son's mother wasn't ready for a child, but she helped out when I needed her.

"Yeah, Jamila's father is a deadbeat dad too," she said disappointingly. "He didn't want me to have Jamila, so he became abusive when I told him I was pregnant. He used to beat me and tell me he wanted me to lose my daughter. I hate his ass."

Her pretty face had a look on it that I hadn't seen before.

"Look ma', I ain't no killa,' but if duke ever put his hands on you again, let me know, and I'll take care of it," I said looking into her eyes to reassure her that I meant business.

"Lloyd I don't want you gittin' into any trouble. You just met me, and you have a son."

I placed my finger on her lips. "Shhh baby, it ain't no trouble at all. I'm not gon' allow no man to put his hands on any woman I'm wit.' Promise me you'll tell me if he bothers you again."

She made me a promise and then she said something that I hadn't expected. "I'm really into you. Please don't hurt me."

My goodness, standing in front of me was a young woman so beautiful and so fragile. For the first time since Linda, I was falling in love.

"I'm feelin' you too baby. I give you my word I'll never hurt you."

Without missing a beat, she said, "If you do, I'ma' cut you, boy."

In that instant, I fell in love with her. She had an air about her so street, you would think she was born in Harlem instead of the Dominican Republic.

We changed the subject and began talking about our kids again.

"So you got some type of God complex namin' your son Messiah and callin' yourself Llord?" she asked wringing her neck back and forth.

"First of all, I didn't give myself the name Llord. My sister Vonnie gave me that name. Second, I named my son Messiah because it was a word play on my name." I said wringing my neck back at her. We both laughed.

"Come on, it's gititn' late. Let me take you home mama." I said turning on the car.

On the way to her house, I asked if she and Jamila would like to come with me and Messiah to Florida for vacation.

"Are you kiddin' me? You better not be playin' wit' me boy," she said with her skin turning flush with excitement.

"I told you, baby, I got you," I said smiling.

We were riding on cloud nine. I could see her, our kids, and myself as one big happy family, but one evening as I was dropping Joharra off, standing in front of the building next to hers, was Disco. She opened up the door and gave me a kiss. As she got out of the car, he made it a point to let me know that he had seen her and me together.

"What's up Joharra?" Disco asked, smirking while looking at me from the corner of his eye.

"Hi, Lozario," she said calling him by his real name.

A name that I hadn't known in all of those months of warring with him and his crew. I hadn't seen this motherfucker in years. I thought he was dead or in jail, but here he was on my baby's block no more than thirty minutes away from where he had killed countless motherfuckers. It's ironic how such a big world is really so small.

"Joharra, go in the house baby. I'll call you when I git' home."

As I slowly drove off, I called Pap. I felt as though I had seen a ghost. I was on pins and needles. Not for myself, more so for Joharra and her family. I knew what Disco was capable of doing.

"Pap you ain't gon' believe who I jus' saw!" I said talking fast.

"Who?" Pap asked calmly.

"That nigga' Disco," I yelled into the phone.

"Disco, I ain't heard that name in years, so?" Pap asked like he had no idea what I was talking about.

"What you mean so?"

I had forgotten that Pap was locked up during the whole drug war episode with those Red and Pink top niggas.

"Oh shit, my bad homie. I forgot you weren't here when we were goin' at it wit' this cat, Disco. Him and his people's was bustin' they guns hard body homie." I said anxiously.

Still hoping that my voice didn't betray my fear.

"So you sayin' you think this nigga' gon' be a problem?" Pap asked.

"I don't know, but when I saw him on Joharra's block, he gave me a funny look. I jus' ain't tryin' to sleep on him. For real, that nigga' is dangerous."

Pap did what he could to reassure me that if things got bad, we would handle it like we always did, "An eye for an eye."

While it eased my mind a bit, I still felt worried for Joharra.

"Besides, if you scared, git' a dog nigga." Pap said continuing to try and lighten the mood.

"Nah I ain't scared, jus' cautious," I said. "I don't want to have to kill this motherfucka', but you already know it is what it is. Ain't nothin' changed."

With that said, Pap and I hung up the phone, but in the pit of my stomach, I had an uneasy feeling.

Chapter 13
And the Music Stopped

It was quiet for the next month or so. Joharra and I were enjoying getting to know each other. We spent a lot of time together shopping and preparing for the trip to Florida, buying swimsuits and flip-flops for her and Jamila and anything else they might have needed. We headed to Florida that last week of August. When we touched down at Daytona Beach, the weather was beautiful! The sky was clear, and the sun shone brightly on the setting. We arrived at our hotel, the Holiday Inn. It was literally right on the beach. I had been hustling for the last eleven years, but this was the first vacation I had taken since my last leave from Fort Knox, Kentucky in 1986.

Everything was perfect as we stepped out of the hotel onto the beach. It was surreal, from riding ATVs up and down the coastline, walking on the soft pink sand, enjoying water so blue that it looked like a scene out of "Miami Vice." Our trip lasted a week. A week of relaxing, eating at top-notch restaurants and taking the kids to Disney World and other theme parks in the surrounding area. The only problem we had was me. I got upset with Joharra because I felt she didn't get into the water as much as I thought she should have. I was such a controlling asshole.

"Joharra I can't believe you came all the way to Florida just to sit on the fuckin' beach," I said with disgust in my voice.

"Lloyd, I just want to sit and get some sun baby. Maybe I'll get in the water with you and the kids later."

While what she said was perfectly reasonable, my stubbornness compounded by ignorance made me feel as though I was always right. No compromising. I woke up later that night to find her staring at me.

"What the fuck you lookin' at?" I asked raising my head up off of the pillow.

"Nothing. I was just watching you while you slept." she said wiping tears from her cheeks. "Lloyd, why are you so cold? Everything is so fuckin' 'whatever' with you. It's like you're incapable of emotions."

I answered as candidly as I could.

"Look, I've seen, and been exposed to so much crap in my life. What can I say, I think this world is a fucked up place. People you trust will stab you in the back, and even your loved ones will fuck you over for money and in a lot of cases, when that's gone, so are they. I don't know what else to tell you."

The next day I told her I needed a break when we got back to New York. She cried and told me that she loved me, but at that point, I didn't give a fuck. When we returned home, I avoided her calls. Weeks had passed before we spoke again. That is until her birthday when she called me.

"Today is my birthday, and you wasn't going to call me nigga?" she asked angrily.

I was glad she called. She was more of a woman than I deserved. I was falling over myself apologizing.

"Baby, I'm so sorry. I'll make it up to you I promise."

We talked a bit longer. Mostly about Jamila, Messiah, the trip to Florida and how we were going to make love when I got my hands on her. I also told her she didn't have to worry about me acting up anymore.

"I'ma treat you like a queen mi corazòn, mi vida. I'll call you later so we can meet up."

I gave her a big wet kiss over the phone before hanging up.

"You better boy. I told you I'd cut you," Joharra said jokingly.

Later that day I went to a jewelry store and purchased a beautiful 18 karat gold and diamond necklace as a birthday and makeup gift. When 9 p.m. came and went, and I still hadn't heard from her, my stinkin' thinkin' took hold.

"This bitch is probably out wit' the next nigga." I thought to myself as I turned on the TV and channel surfed.

I came across a news story that reported that the body of a young woman had been found emolliated on the roof of a building in Spanish Harlem. News like that was typical in the 90's in New York and America as a whole, so I thought nothing of it, besides, I wanted to get bed early. I had to pick Messiah up from Linda's house to take him school shopping the next morning.

I was awakened at 6:00 that morning to the sound of a ringing phone. My first thought was that it was Joharra calling to say she was sorry for standing me up the night before.

"Hello, Lloyd?"

The voice on the other end of the line asked crying. A voice, that wasn't Joharra's.

"Who is this?" I asked.

"It's me, Elisa," the voice on the other end said.

"Elisa, what's wrong? Why you cryin' boo?" I asked her, rising out of bed.

"Lloyd its Joharra, she's dead."

Her words went through me and ripped the soul from my chest. I dropped the phone and fell on my knees crying.

"No! No! No!" I picked up the phone. "Elisa, what happened?" I asked barely able to speak.

"I'm not sure. All we know is that the police found her on a rooftop on 105th street last night. Someone set her on fire."

I couldn't believe my ears. It's inconceivable how life is often stranger than fiction. Who would have thought that the story I was watching on the news the night before was about my beautiful baby?

"Elisa, can I call you back please?" I asked choking back tears.

"Yes, Lloyd." I could hear the empathy in her voice. "Call me later," she said hanging up the phone.
The first person I called, as usual, was Linda.

"Lin, can you come over to my house?"

Linda wasn't an early riser, so the first thing out of her mouth was, "Llord why the hell you callin' me this fuckin' early?"

I started crying.

"Lin, the police found Joharra dead last night. Whoever killed her set her body on fire. Please come over; I need you, I can't be alone."

Without a second thought, she said, "Llord let me wake Lillian up and tell her I need her to watch Messiah, and I'll be right over."

Within the hour she was at my house taking care of me. Trying her best to get me to eat something, but I couldn't. She stayed with me throughout the day while I made the calls to tell Pap and my people about Joharra's murder. Pap being my consummate protector was ready to act. I told him I would come to the hood the next day.

Soon after Linda left that night, I got a call from Elisa.

"Llord how you feeling Papi?" she asked.

"I'm fucked up ma'. I can't believe my baby is gone. If I find out who did this, their ass is meatloaf!" I said yelling into the phone.

"That's why I'm calling you. I heard a rumor in my neighborhood that I need to put you up on."

I could hear the angst in her voice.

"Aight' ma, I'll be there around 9 o'clock tomorrow night. I need to go to my hood and tie up some loose ends. Then I'ma come through and holla' at you."

I was about to hang up when she cut me off.

"Wait I almost forgot to tell you, Joharra's mother and stepfather want to talk to you."

I didn't feel ready to talk to her parents, but I understood their need to speak to me.

"Do you know what they wanna' talk to me about?" I asked.

"They want to know if you knew why she was going to Manhattan. Just come over and talk to them. Then you and me are gon' take a walk, and I'll tell you what I heard." she said.

"Talk about what?" I asked now a little frustrated.

"Llord I don't want to talk about it over the phone." Once she said that, there was nothing more I could say.

Rule number 482, never say anything over the phone that you don't want to come back and bite you in the ass.

"Ok. We'll talk tomorrow night," I said and hung up the phone.

That evening was one of the longest nights of my life. Joharra's beautiful face haunted my sleep. When I awoke, I hoped that it was all a horrible nightmare, but it was all too real. The next morning came fast. I got dressed without eating breakfast. I don't think I could keep anything down if I did try to eat. In fact, I could barely walk. I called my man Spencer and asked him to pick me up. I filled him in and told him I wasn't up to driving myself around. When I got to Franklin Ave., the crew was there. Everyone gave me their condolences and let me know they had my back. I told Pap how scared Joharra was of her daughter's father, so his first assumption was that he had something to do with her death.

"Llord if her daughter's father did this sick shit what you wanna' do to the nigga?" he asked.

"I'ma kill him," I said in a monotone voice.

I was numb from crying, as well as weak from not eating.

"I'm gon' blow his brains out," I continued. "Then I'm gon' pull my dick out and piss on his face," Pap just listened.

"Whatever you do, or, we do," he corrected himself, "We gon' do it smart. Now go home and git' some rest partner, you look like shit," he said giving me a pound.

"Aight' homie, I'll git' back to you later."

I told the rest of the crew good looking out for their well wishes, but I let them know I would be back to work the next day. Pap had definitely grown up since the incident with Mark. I had the business mind, but I also had a temper and a I don't give a fuck attitude. Plus, I was quick with a gun. Pap, on the other hand, was the type who would pound a nigga out on impact if he felt he had it coming, but he wasn't hot-headed like me. He also wasn't a natural born hustler like me, so together we were like salt and pepper. We brought out the best in each other in everything we did.

As I climbed into Spencer's car, I asked him to take me to the liquor store and then over to my Aunt Pat's house. I bought a bottle of Alizè Red and started swigging it down like water. By the time I arrived at my aunt's house, I was drunk and reeking of liquor. When I knocked on the door, my aunt could see something was wrong.

"What's the matter with you boy?" she asked sternly in that no-nonsense voice that she would often speak in when things were serious.

"Auntie they killed my girl," I said moaning.

That's when Karen came out of her and Asia's room.

"What? What happened?" she asked empathetically.

She had endured the same pain that I was going through. Well, actually, while my situation was similar to hers, in reality, her pain was much more tragic than mine. She had been in a relationship with her man for eight years when he was killed. I had known Joharra for less than a year, but the agony I felt was no less diminished.

"I on't know, Karen. They found her dead in Spanish Harlem," I answered taking another drink.

"Who killed her?" My aunt asked.

"I don't know auntie," I repeated. "I think it was her daughter's father. If I find out that it was that nigga, I'ma fuckin' kill em'!" I said slurring my words.

Karen knew I was angry since I rarely cursed in front of my aunt.

My aunt interjected. "Boy, what you talkin' about? You talkin' crazy. You have a son you have to take care of. That's who you need to be worried about," she said pointing her finger at me.

"Auntie, I on't care. If I find out he killed my baby, he's dead."

What my aunt said made sense. I was talking crazy, but I didn't care. I was out of my mind with agony.

"Auntie I gotta' go take care of some business, but I hear what you sayin'. I love you."

I put on my jacket, kissed her on the cheek, and was out the door. When I got downstairs, Spencer was sitting in the car waiting.

"Where you at?" he asked.

Spencer was a funny type of cat. He mostly kept to himself, but every once and a while he would give me his opinion. Now wasn't one of those times.

"Take me to 198th and University," I said. "I'm goin' over to Joharra's mother's house."

When we pulled up, I told Spencer to keep the car running. I didn't want to be there too long.

I stepped out of the car and got myself together before I knocked on the door.

"Quièn es?" A male's voice asked from the other side of the door.

"Soy yo, Llord," I replied back in Spanish.

When the door opened, standing there was Joharra's mother, stepfather, Elisa, and a slew of Dominican dudes.

"Hola Señora," I said as I reached out and embraced Joharra's mother.

"Còmo estàs Señor?" I asked while I shook her stepfather's hand.

The other niggas had a look of all business on their faces, and although I understood why, I still felt the need to keep my guard up. One of them said something to Elisa in Spanish, and while he spoke too fast for me to catch what he was saying, I could pick up on the aggression in his tone.

"Llord this is my cousin Henry," Elisa said pointing to the oldest looking male. "He wants to know when was the last time you spoke to Joharra."

Her translation wasn't as demonstrative as his, but I felt the tension just the same. I explained to her that the last conversation Joharra and I had was on her birthday. She said she was going shopping with one of her girlfriends. She didn't tell me with who, but we were supposed to meet up later that night.

"That was the last time I spoke to her," I said, my voice trailing off.

It was at that moment her cousin's demeanor began to soften. They saw the sadness in my eyes, on my face, and they heard it in my voice. Two of the other cousins walked over to me and placed their hands on my shoulder.

"Cuìdate," one of them said.

"Gracias, y tù tambièn," I replied.

I again embraced Mrs. Castillo and looked into her eyes. There was nothing I could say to her except goodbye. Elisa told her relatives she would be right back. Once outside she told me what she had heard.

"Llord I heard that Lozario had something to do with Joharra's death," she said speaking quickly, as if she didn't, she wouldn't be able to get it out.

"What? Where you hear that shit at?" I asked furiously.

"This girl who's a friend of mine, Joharra, and Lozario's girl told me," she said.

"Ok, where did this friend of yours get her information?" I asked.

"She got it straight from Lozario's girl," she said a little agitated. "Why you actin' like you don't believe me?" she asked with a frown on her face.

"Ok, well what's Disco's girl's name?" I asked still not sure what to think about what she was telling me.

"Niña, her name is Niña," she huffed.

My mini-Inquisition was annoying her. I had to be 100% sure. I couldn't jump to any conclusions. That was a lesson that I had learned the hard way. The way I learned most things. There was an incident when I was doing the books and Ya-ya and Stan were on the block collecting money from this female pitcher named Renita. Those two fuckin' knuckleheads called me and told me that she had come up short on a pack. Normally, if a pitcher comes up short, it's no big deal. We usually deduct the money from their pay at the end of the week, but Renita had been coming up short frequently, so subsequently, I told niggas if she came up short again, to beat her ass. After going over the books myself, and counting the money that was brought to me, I realize these geniuses made a mistake. Renita wasn't short at all. Before I could get in touch with anyone, they'd broken both of her arms. Regrettably, all I could do was apologize. Luckily she didn't lose her life. From that mistake I learned, don't jump to any conclusions, don't assume, and check shit out for yourself.

"Alright mama, if you're positive, I'ma go handle it, but I gotta' question tho," Why didn't you tell your family or the police what you just told me?" I asked not fully convinced.

When she answered me, it was with a brashness that caught me off guard.

"For one, my cousins are actin' like they niggas from the streets, but they fresh off the boat from D.R., Second, my family has been through enough without involving them in any more drama. As for the police, I want that motherfucka' to die for what he did to my cousin. Jail is too easy for him. Joharra didn't deserve to die the way she did. No one does." she began crying uncontrollably.

I put my arms around her.

"Shhh, don't cry nena. It's gon' be alright. I'ma take care of everything. Just make sure you don't tell nobody what you told me, understand? If Disco finds out that there's a rumor goin' around that he had something to do wit' Joharra's death, you, his girl, and your fuckin' girlfriend gon' end up on a milk carton."

Elisa shook her head in acknowledgment wiping tears from her face. Before I left, I gave her the necklace I bought for Joharra.

"I want you to have this mama. I don't want it. It's jus' gon' remind me of her," I said handing the necklace to her.

"Before you go nena, how can I find Disco's girl?" I asked.

"She lives three blocks from away from here," Elisa said, "and she goes to Monroe College on Fordham Road, right off of

Jerome Ave. If you meet up with me on Monday, I'll point her out to you."

Rule number 56, be careful who you double-cross, you never know when or where you'll bump into them. It turns out, Disco's girl went to the same college that Joharra attended, and Linda never finished.

"Aight' ma' that sounds like a plan. What time do you want me to meet you on Monday?" I asked, again getting that funny feeling in the pit of my stomach.

"I think she gets out of class around 9:00, meet me at 8:00," she said turning to go back into the house.

"No problem mamita, but if you ain't able to git' up wit' me for some reason give me a call don't have me waitin'," I said getting into Spencer's car.

I immediately called Pap and told him I would get up with him the following day and let him know how the meeting with Joharra's family went. Spencer drove me home without saying a word. On the radio, Brian McKnight's song "Anytime" was playing. It was like the shit was scripted. The song brought back thoughts of Joharra. I took another swallow of Alizè to help me forget. When Spencer dropped me off, I found myself alone. Sleep came hard that night. I tossed and turned, reliving the last few days. As I slept, I dreamt, and in my dreams, I could see Joharra begging for her life. I wanted to make sure Disco suffered.

When I met up with everyone the next day, the mood was quiet and somber. No one knew what to say to me. I was the first to break the silence.

"What up fellas?" I asked slapping everyone five.

Pap asked me what happened the night before.

"You ain't gon' believe this shit nigga," I said. "Remember when I told you I had a bad feelin' when I saw that nigga' Disco?

Well, I was right. Joharra's cousin told me Disco's girl been goin' around runnin' her fuckin' mouth sayin' Disco killed my baby."

I barely got the words out of my mouth.

"That motherfucka' is crazy," Ya-ya said. "Why would that nigga' kill your girl?" he asked.

"He don't need a reason," Trouble said. "That nigga' is off the fuckin' hook. How many people he killed around the hood?"

He was right, Disco turned out to be a sociopath, but I was fine with that.

I talked to the crew and explained my plan for Disco.

"This is what it is. I'm gon' meet up with Joharra's cousin Monday night. She's gon' point out Disco's girl. I wanna' snatch her up and hold her dumb ass until I can git' Disco to meet me somewhere," before I could finish, Roc cut me off.

"What's this I and me shit nigga?" he asked. "We a team, you ain't doin' shit by yourself."

I had mixed feelings. On the one hand, I was glad to have their support. On the other hand, I didn't want to jeopardize anyone's life because of my personal shit.

"Aight then if y'all wit' it, then this is what it is. Like I was sayin' we gon' snatch her ass up and send word to Disco that we got his bitch. If he love her, he gon' git' back to us. If he don't, then it don't matter, this bitch is collateral damage. Either way, it's a win-win situation."

Even as the words rolled off of my tongue, I knew there weren't going to be any winners, everyone involved would lose.

I lost Joharra, and what I had in store for Niña, she was going to lose her dignity and possibly her life. Once again, I told myself this was business as usual, but I knew it was wrong, but as the saying goes, life is hard, but it's fair. I started rattling off what was needed.

"I'm thinkin' we gon' rent a car or a van to grab that bitch as she's walkin' home and take her to a stash crib,"

Pap interjected, "Wait, hold up. I on't know about renting a car cus' you have to use an ID, and that shit can be traced back to us. As for takin' that bitch to our stash house, that ain't gon' happen either. We need to git' a hotel room on the down low. Some real hood shit where we know motherfuckas' don't care about nothin' but a dollar, no ID, no cameras, nothin'," he said.

Stan added on, "I know a cat down in Millbrook who steals whips. We can use him."

I thought about what they were saying. The hotel idea was a good, but I didn't want to ride around in a stolen car with some bitch lying on the floor.

"Aight' here we go. We gon' use the Andrea Motel off of the New England by Co-op City. That shit is as low as it gits'. As far as the whip, I'ma go O.T. and rent one. As long as we clean it up before we return it, we should be good. Besides, I don't foresee us gittin' any blood in it unless she put up a fight which I doubt.

When Monday came, I called Spencer and told him to come git' me. It was 1:30 in the afternoon and I wanted to go and get the rental car before rush hour traffic. When he got to my house, I asked him how much it was gon' cost to head out to Newark, New Jersey to Enterprise car rental.

"Whatever," Spencer said. "I mean whatever you think is fair."

That's why the organization fucked with Spencer. There would be times he would take us places, and we wouldn't have to pay him until we had it.

"I got one hundred and fifty dollars on me, but I don't think it's gon' take us long. I'm probably gon' need you for no more than three hours. I want you to drop me off and I'ma drive the rental back to the Bronx. The rest is for the other night homie. I appreciate it," I said reaching into my pocket for the money.

I distinctly recall that day. It was clear and breezy. As we rode I had the windows rolled down and my seat was reclined back as far as it could go as I listened to the radio. The day was picture perfect. In my experience, that's the way it usually is. Everything is great, going as planned, things couldn't be better, and out of nowhere, life throws you a curve. An hour later we pulled up to the rental car office. I went inside gave the rental agent a three hundred dollar deposit and drove off of the lot with a Dodge mini-van. Something big enough to fit the whole crew inside, yet inconspicuous enough that it wouldn't get a second look from New York's Finest. As Spencer and I drove off, he beeped his horn to let me know he was out as he hit the gas. I pulled off easily. I wasn't going to do any speeding, or break any traffic laws. The last thing I wanted was to end up in some officer's logbook for a traffic stop.

When I got back to the Bronx it was getting close to 4 p.m. I parked the van a few blocks away from my house. My landlord's wife was nosey as hell. She was always watching what women came in and out of my house. Sometimes I thought she wanted to fuck me. I sat in the house eating and exercising. If anything did happen, at least I wouldn't be hungry if I landed in jail. I meditated and prayed. Yes, I prayed to God to help me be as merciful as possible. I prayed to keep me and my crew safe and free. And lastly, I prayed for forgiveness for the sins I was about to commit. I called Elisa to make sure we were still on for that night, which we were. While getting dressed I called the love of my life, Messiah. It was good to hear my baby's voice. He was the only thing that kept me anchored to sanity in an insane world.

The first words out of his mouth were, "Daddy when are you coming to git' me from mommy's house?"

I told him as soon as daddy finished his business trip. I always had a fictitious job or business trip to go on. That's how I shielded him. I never had any drugs around him or exposed him to anything that might corrupt his innocent young mind.

I walked down the quiet tree-lined block that Messiah and I lived on and wondered if I would ever see my home or my son again. I quickly pushed those thoughts out of my mind. I had to get focused on the task at hand. I couldn't have any thoughts of doubt or weakness. I started up the van and headed towards the Bruckner Expressway. First stop, the, Andrea Motel. As I pulled into the parking lot, I thought to myself, "This is a place you take your side chick. This definitely ain't a place you take your wifey."

I walked up to the front desk and gave the clerk some lame story about a friend getting married and how we wanted to rent a room for two days for a bachelor party. I told him it was an extra fifty in it for him if he could get me a corner room. He was glad to oblige me. For two nights it was one hundred and eighty dollars. Peanuts! I gave him two hundred and fifty dollars and told him we didn't want to be disturbed by the maids until the party was over. I winked at him and said, "If you know what I mean." He handed me the key to room number 307. I walked up the stairs, opened up the door and looked in. It was dingy looking, but that was cool. The important thing is that it was on the third floor and it was secluded. I went downstairs hopped into the van and took off.

On the way back to Franklin Ave. I called Elisa, "What's good mama, you ready to git' up tonight?" She was set.

"I been waitin' for your call all day nigga'. Of course I'm ready! Where you want me to meet you at?"
I was glad to see that she hadn't changed her mind.

"I'ma pick you up a block away from Joharra's house at eight o'clock sharp. Make sure you're there on time, and oh yeah, even though I told you before, make sure you don't say nothin' to nobody okay?"

I had to reiterate that point. There was too much on the line.

"I know that. I ain't stupid Llord," she said.

"Alright, I'll call you when I'm on my way."

I parked the van three blocks from Franklin Ave., close to Forest Projects. Rule number 204, never park your car anywhere near to where you hustle. Unfortunately, I sometimes broke that rule, but it is still a safeguard against the haters and the police, who just so happen to be some of the biggest haters out there. As I made my way to Franklin, I could see Pap, Ya-ya, Roc, Stan, and Trouble standing there.

"Y'all niggas ready?" I asked.

"Let's do it," Pap said.

Trouble said he was going to stay and run the block and meet up with us later that night.

"Sounds good to me pa'," I said. "Jus' stay on point for the boys."

I turned my attention to the rest of the crew.

"Aight' fellas, we gon' meet up with Joharra's cousin, then we gon' head up to Monroe College and wait for Disco's girl to come out. I on't want to grab her in front of nobody so let's wait for the right moment. If it don't happen tonight, then we'll do it another night."

Pap stopped me, "Look, man, we all grown here. We on't need you to walk us through shit. We gon' make it happen nigga jus' be easy."

I heard what Pap was saying but how the fuck could I relax when I had everyone's freedom in my hands.

"Pap I ain't tryin' to nitpick, but this shit is as real as it gits'. We can't afford no mistakes. Now like I was sayin' if it don't git' done tonight, then we'll do it some other time."

Pap gave a little sigh in frustration, "Yeah, boss we understand," he said putting his hand on the top of my head playing with me.

"Les' go then. It's that time of day," I said making my way up the block.

When we got to University Ave., Elisa was standing outside ready and waiting. Roc slid the cargo door open for her to get into the middle seat. I didn't introduce her to anyone. She didn't need to know anyone's name in the event something went wrong.

"Dime nena," I said holding my hand out for her to give me a pound.

"Hola Papi," she said giving my hand a squeeze. "Yo, I can't front, I'm nervous as hell nigga," she said.

"Don't worry mama, as soon as you point her out, you gon' git' out of the car aight'? You on't have anything to worry about," I said reassuring her.

I find it strange, how every other nationality will imitate our culture, our fashion, and our slang. Even go as far as using the word nigga like it's okay, but will rarely do business with us on an even playing field. What's even more unbelievable than that is we allow multiple races, African, Dominican, Puerto Rican, Jamaican and even the Arabs to throw the word nigger around like it's nothing. Like that word gives them instant street cred. Make no mistake, many of those same races believe they're better than the Black American, but when a White person uses the word, we're ready to fight and protest.

Anyway, we drove underneath the EL, made a U-turn and parked directly across the street from Monroe College. There were a lot of other cars waiting to pick students up from class, so we blended right in. Fifteen minutes later, out walks this beautiful dark skinned Dominican thing. My God, she was lovely. Elisa's eyes opened wide.

"Llord there she goes!" she squealed in a high pitched voice. It was the beautiful creature that I was scoping out.

"Damn Disco, I ain't mad at you nigga, mommy is fine."

"Elisa, here goes twenty dollars, take a cab and go home. We'll talk later."

It was crowded, so we let her walk a block and a half to a deserted stretch of street. I made another U-turn and pulled directly in front of her.

"Hello, Niña," I said extending out my hand for her to shake. "I'm a friend of Disco. He got arrested again, and he told me to come pick you up."

Now as dumb as she was for running her mouth to her girlfriends about Joharra's murder, she had more than enough sense not to get in a car with someone she didn't know.

"Let me call his phone first," she said looking unsure, but not quite scared.

She took me by surprise with her response. Fuck it; I was going to have to do it the hard way. As I was about to pull the gun out of my coat pocket, Pap came around the passenger side of the van and smacked her off of her feet.

"Git' in the car bitch," he said as he snatched her up by her jacket collar.

Her feet were dragging on the concrete as she was pushed into the van.

Pap looked at me and smiled, "I told you, you worry too much nigga,"

I drove off looking in the rearview mirror to see if anyone had noticed anything. We arrived at the hotel and parked in a corner spot next to the stairs to the room. We entered the room and turned the radio up loud enough to muffle our voices, but low enough so that anyone in the adjacent rooms wouldn't complain. We all had on hoodies when we grabbed her, but to be sure she couldn't identify us we blindfolded her. I did my thing and played the nice guy.

"You ok? Can I git' you something to eat or drink?" I asked trying to put her at ease.

She didn't answer me, so I cut to the chase.

"Here's what it is Niña, that is your name right? If you do exactly what we tell you, you're gon' make it out of here alive. If you don't, you gon' die. No ifs, ands, or buts. You gon' die tonight," she was crying hysterically.

Her make-up began to run down her cheeks. In between sobs, she asked why we had kidnapped her. The word kidnapped flipped a switch on in my mind. That was the first time I realized that was what we were doing to her. In the streets, we just snatch someone. Kidnapping sounds too dramatic, but in any event, kidnapping was the least of what we were going to do her.

"We want Disco to pay us twenty thousand dollars for your pretty ass. If he do, you can go home. If he don't, shit is gon' git' ugly, but we gon' think positive ma."

Pap walked up to me and whispered in my ear, "Llord, I'ma' go git' some crillz and a bag of diesel. Gimme' the keys and I'll go git' some food and pick Trouble up."

"One more thing, bring Tyson wit' you," I said reaching into my pockets for the keys to the van.

Roc and Stan were smoking weed and watching the Sopranos on HBO. Ya-ya didn't drink or use drugs. He was a strict observer of the Muslim religion.

"Why y'all watchin' this fake shit?" Ya-ya asked disparagingly to Stan and Roc.

"This is the fuckin' Sopranos," Stan said. "This is some of the realest shit on TV right now," he said giving Ya-ya the finger.

Ya-ya laughed, "Fuck them Italians. Let them come to the hood wit' that mob shit. We gon' run they ass back to Jersey or wherever they come from." Ya-ya was right, almost.

We don't have enough unity, money, or political connections to run the mob off, but we would die trying.

An hour later there was a knock on the room door. The room got quiet. I crept over to the peephole and looked out. It was Pap and Trouble.

"Right on time homie," I said bending down to pet Tyson our crew's pit bull.

"It's time to git' this party started. Let me git' that Pap," I said holding out my hand.

Pap passed me the drugs. I took an empty Pepsi can, poked holes in it and put weed, crack, and heroin on the top of it. I put the can to Niña's lips.

"Remember when I said if you want to make it out of here alive you do everything I tell you to do? Well, this is that time. I'ma light this weed up and I want you to inhale. If you scream or do anything but inhale you dead."

With that said I flicked the lighter and told her to smoke. Like most motherfuckas' I'm sure she smoked weed. That wasn't any biggie, but when she tasted the heroin and crack, she started to gag.

I told her to relax and to smoke a little more. I had her smoke enough of the cocktail hoping she would get a jones. Now it was time to call the nigga Disco.

"Roc pass me her cell phone."

I asked her what name she had Disco listed under.

"Lozario," she said with a whimper.

I scrolled through the phone until I came across his name.

"This is all you have to do baby. Tell Disco we have you and we gon' kill you if he don't pay up alright?" she nodded her head yes.

I dialed the phone number and put it on speaker. Disco picked up on the first ring.

"Where the fuck you been bitch? I been callin' your ass off the fuckin' hook."

Ya-ya started snickering. "This nigga' stressin'," he said.

"Lozario, somebody kidnapped me," she said crying inconsolably. "They made me smoke crack baby. Help me," she pleaded in between sobs. "They want money baby. Please pay them, baby, please," she said begging.

I took the phone from her.

"This ain't a fuckin' joke nigga. Meet me uptown at the Woodlawn Cemetery with twenty thousand dollars partna'. Be there in 3 hours. Come alone. If you call the cops or show up with anybody, this bitch is dead."

I hung up the phone. There wasn't anything to haggle about. Either he showed up with the money, or he didn't. I didn't care one way or the other. I turned my attention to Tyson. He was a perfect specimen. Strong and solid. "Come here boy, that's it come on." He was a big puppy. He started wagging his tail and pissing on the floor while running over to me.

"One of y'all put a rag in her mouth."

I had given some thought to what I would do when I had her. I flashed back to a novel that I had stumbled upon in my Aunt Pat's home when I was a child. "Jodie's bedroom master." It was a book on sadomasochism and bestiality. I took some french fries and stuffed them inside Niña's vagina. I grabbed Tyson by the collar and put his nose to her pussy lips. I'm not sure if it was the scent of her vagina or the french fries, but Tyson began lapping at her vagina in a frenzy. It was sick and sexual at the same time. My crew found it comical. Pap was laughing so hard he was drooling on himself. Then on cue, as if he knew what he was doing, Tyson mounted Niña. His pink doggy dick pumping in and out of her vagina. Motherfuckas' lost it. Yelling and smacking Tyson on the ass. As for Niña, she was broken. She didn't make a sound. Minutes later, Tyson began to jerk, his movement slowed, and we could see the semen running out of Niña's vagina. It had a thin watery consistency. I couldn't stomach it anymore.

I pulled Tyson off and let Niña lay there.

I waved my hand for Stan and Pap to come over and talk to me.

"I'ma go up to the cemetery ahead of this nigga just in case he wanna try some funny shit, I'd like to git' there early ahead of him. Pap, I want you to stay here and make sure nothin' else happens to shorty. I'ma take Stan wit' me to drive the van."

Pap told me to go handle up and call him when I was on my way back.

"One more thing," he said, "If I don't hear from you in two hours, this bitch is dead and we gon' clear outta' here."

Stan gave Pap a pound and said, "You already know."

We drove around for a while making sure there was nothing out of the ordinary. I dozed off for some much needed, although uneasy sleep. I woke up to Stan nudging me.

"Llord git' up," I jumped up and looked around. It was raining outside now. "What happened?"

Stan pointed to Disco standing twenty feet away. He had a book bag sitting on top of a parked car. He had his back turned to us. I pulled the gun out of my pocket and cocked it back. I cracked the passenger door open and slowly slunk up behind him. As I got closer, all I could think about was how my helpless baby must have begged for her life as he poured the gasoline over her and set her on fire. *Pow!* One shot was all it took to kill a man who had killed so many. One shot to vanquish a monster.

Disco hit the ground. He died so quickly he had no time to react. Both of his hands were still in his pockets. I grabbed the bag off of the roof of the car and looked down at his body. His right leg was twitching. Car alarms were going off.

Stan yelled out the window, "C'mon nigga les' go."

Before I jumped into the van, I did what I promised myself I would do. I pulled my dick out and pissed all over his face. I climbed into the van and opened up the book bag. Inside were stacks of cash folded with rubber bands. Stan glanced over and started punching the roof of the van.

"Yeah boy! That's what I'm talkin' about." He said driving off.

I called Pap and told him we were on our way across town. Make sure chick was dressed and ready to be dropped off. When Stan and I got back to the hotel, it was close to 3:00 in the morning. I picked up her purse and looked through it to see if she had ID with her address on it. We piled into the van putting the still blindfolded Niña in the front seat and took off. Thirty-five minutes later we pulled up to her building. It was empty outside. I gave her a final warning before we pushed her out of the van.

"Niña, we know where you live at. If you tell anybody what happened tonight, your family is dead." she didn't respond, but it was of no consequence, I couldn't see her telling anyone that she had been raped by a dog.

We dropped Stan off in Millbrook. I told him everyone would meet up on Franklin later in the evening and divvy up the cash.

That afternoon, Spencer and I went to return the van back to Enterprise. After that, I made a stop at my house to pick up the money and head to Franklin. I asked the crew if I could take five thousand dollars to Joharra's family, and they split the rest. They didn't have a problem with that. I called Elisa and told her to meet me over at Joharra's parent's house. I stopped over at a flower shop to pick up some roses for my baby's room. I got to the house and rang the doorbell.

"Quièn es?" It was Elisa.

"It's me Llord," I said.

She opened up the door and gave me a hug. She was glad to see me.

"What up nena? I told you it was gon' be alright," I said hugging her back.

"Where's Joharra's mother? I got something for her." I said holding the bag up.

"They're in there," she said gesturing toward the living room.

When I walked into the living room, Joharra's mother was sitting there looking gaunt. I could see she had lost some weight. She looked near death.

"Hola Señora. Còmo estàs?" I asked politely, but I knew the answer. "Elisa please tell her that I brought her money for Joharra's funeral and for anything that Jamila might need. Also, please ask her if I could put the flowers that I brought on Joharra's bed?"

Elisa translated, and Mrs. Castillo nodded her head ok. I walked into her room and laid the flowers on her bed and ran my hand across her covers. As I did, I inhaled the scent of her off of her pillow and cried. When I looked up, her stepfather was standing in the doorway watching me. He said nothing, he simply turned and walked away.

I never saw Joharra's parents or Jamila again, and I only spoke to Elisa once after that. She called to tell me that Joharra's body was being flown home to the Dominican Republic for her funeral. She also told me that the family had to take stones and dent her coffin before the burial to keep it from being stolen out of the ground after she was buried. Finally, my baby would have some peace in death, the peace that she hadn't found in life. As for me, after everything, after all of the violence and vengeance, I still hadn't found peace.

Chapter 14
Fast Forward

After the death of Joharra, I was mentally exhausted. I needed a break from the streets. That combined with my probation, the realization that selling drugs wasn't going to last forever and when shit hit the fan, I didn't want to be left holding the bag. As I've said before, I didn't want to be one of the brothers who would spend the rest of their lives reminiscing about how good things used to be. Like most cats in the hood, I had tried my hand at the rap game, and I had spent tens of thousands of dollars chasing that dream trying to make it big. But as I've stated, basketball, football, hitting the fucking lottery and making it big in the music industry was a one in a million shot. I decided to refocus on the real estate game. I ran my plan by Pap. He told me it sounded like a good idea, and I should give it a go. With his moral support and the thousand dollars a week he was still giving me, I had time to make it work.

With that thought in mind, I literally walked off the block and into an office job. My strategy was to go where the money was. So I went on interviews in midtown Manhattan because everyone knows that's where the money is. It had been quite some time since I had been exposed to the average working class White American. So, unfortunately, I was about to be reacquainted with subversive racism. You see in New York, the difference between the police officers who treat minorities with disdain and order us to shut the fuck up and lay on the ground and the Whites who employ us, is that unspoken racism. In corporate America, racism is a glass ceiling. That realization of no matter how hard you work or how much education you have, you are only allowed to move up but so far in your field. I believe I may have said this before, so at the risk of being repetitive, one of the many things that separated Pap and myself from the average hustler on the street was intellect and our resolve to succeed.

I had four interviews set up on that following Monday. I walked into an interview on 61st and York and did what came naturally to me, sell myself. I had bought a suit over the weekend and went in there and knocked them dead. I went on three more interviews that day, but I never got a return call from them. It didn't matter, I had gotten my foot in the door, and that was all I needed. What was astounding to me was not only the rent that people paid to live in Manhattan but also the qualifications that you had to have to get into the apartment. If a fifth-floor studio walkup cost one thousand dollars a month, the applicant seeking to rent that studio would have to earn fifty times the monthly rent. If the applicant didn't qualify, then they would need a co-signor who made anywhere from seventy to one hundred times that. These applicants would jump through hoops to qualify for the Manhattan rentals.

I learned that a Manhattan address was a status symbol to our White counterparts, much like jewelry, or cars are to minorities. I also became aware that their salaries were substantially higher than people in my community. Many of these applicants were stockbrokers whose salaries started at one hundred and fifty thousand dollars entry level. In the hood, if someone was making forthy thousand dollars a year legally, they were balling! Something else I found astonishing was the women of Caribbean and Hispanic descent walking with and pushing around young White children in strollers. Quite honestly, I was in awe! These well to do and upper-middle-class Whites had nannies by the boatloads, ergo maids, ergo slaves. The difference being, they weren't Black Americans, and they were modestly paid.

In retrospect, I don't know if Black Americans collectively had moved away from the role of domestics because of our history in these roles in America, or simply the pay was just too minuscule.

Another line of thought is maybe White America had come to believe what many in society and the world feels, and that is that Black Americans are unreliable and unemployable. Again, we as Blacks help perpetuate this myth as much as any other race.

Historically when there is a revolution of any kind, the insurgent forces kill or imprison government officials, law enforcement personnel, religious leaders, artist and scholars who don't support their political agenda. It's my opinion that the greatest weapon in any war is not bombs or bullets, but literature. When you can manipulate the thought process of an individual, or a race of people, then the tide of battle will be turned if not won. I feel America has been very successful in using literature to miseducate and indoctrinate Blacks. This indoctrination begins as early as elementary school. The first lesson we learn is that we were nothing more than a submissive, and helpless people, who were enslaved during the formative years of America. Second, the Reverend Martin Luther King is the most admired Black man in American history because of his beliefs in nonviolence and civil disobedience in the face of hatred and discrimination. Lastly, our scholars, scientist, and inventors are all grouped together. I personally don't recall any lessons on Black entrepreneurs in American history. While we are taught about Harriet Tubman, Frederick Douglass, Charles Drew and few others, there is no mention of Nat Turner, John Horse or of the countless slave revolts during the antebellum period.

When other contemporary revolutionary leaders like Malcolm-X, Huey Newton, and Bobby Seale are discussed, if mentioned at all, they are described as radicals and racist demagogues. In saying all of that, while New York is viewed as ultraliberal, I was the only Black man in my office which was run by two partners, Greg Barnes and Andrew Hakim. Greg was the stereotypical all-American Irish boy who oversaw the daily office operations. While Andrew, who was Middle Eastern, would bring all of the documents to the landlords of the properties that were being rented. He had the honor since he was the senior partner being that his family owned the majority of the buildings that were being rented.

It was from him that I learned, that although Donald Trump is one of the most noted developers if you will, he is not necessarily the wealthiest. At that time Trump owned approximately seventy properties in New York, while the Hakims owned close to four hundred. Looking back, I loved going to work in a suit and tie and touring astronomically expensive and beautiful apartments and closing the deal. On the other hand, there were these ridiculously small and overpriced apartments around Manhattan, and I loved them all. I would have and could have made it if not for the fact that real estate is a commissioned based business. Most times, I would go to work six days a week, ten hours a day and not rent an apartment for weeks at a time. To be honest, I only gave it six months. Yes, I should have given it more, but I was actually getting nosebleeds from the stress of not paying my bills. That twelve thousand dollar saving went fast, and unfortunately, Pap hadn't been able to keep paying me the one thousand dollars a week. So I quit the real estate business and went back to the streets.

Before I quit, I made a decision that I regret to this day. I called Linda and asked her to take Messiah until I got on my feet. It was an agonizing decision. Messiah was my life. He was the reason that I made it home at night. The reason I made home cooked meals. The reason I was alive and free. Before I did something reckless, I would think of what would happen to my baby without me there, but all that was about to change. It was time to eat again. I had to pay bills, and I had to get things back in order. I came home that evening and made dinner as usual. Over dinner, I broke the news to my baby.

"Messiah," I called to him fixing him a plate of his favorite foods, macaroni and cheese, fried shrimp, and corn on the cob. "When school is finished for the year, and you go on summer break-daddy is going to send you to live with mommy for a little while, okay," I said trying to sound cheerful as I broke the news to him.

The look on his face was answer enough. For the past few years, it had been us, him and me. Women had come and gone in that time, but he knew his daddy would always be there. While that would never change, our relationship wouldn't be the same. That difference would be distance and his mother.

In the years past, although Linda had been there from time to time, there were other times when I would have to beg her to call Messiah. Somehow in her mind, she thought that she was hurting me by not having a relationship with our child. That along with her moving to Pennsylvania, their relationship had almost become nonexistent. In my conversations with Linda, she had told me she would be fine with Messiah coming to live with her, but I could tell he wasn't happy about leaving me.

"It'll only be for a little while son. Just until daddy git's back on his feet. No more than a year. I promise."

He said what any child would say. "Okay, daddy."

The rest of the year flew by as it always does. I had taken the reins on Franklin Ave., and the organization was beginning to see a profit again. Pap was loyal, but he didn't have the discipline or work ethic without me being there to maintain a profitable business. To sum it up, the block had fallen apart in my absence. With me working long hours, I often had to ask Linda's youngest sister to come over and babysit for me, but even with such a chaotic schedule I still I wanted to make the most of myself and Messiah's last few months together. He and I went to Madison Square Garden to see the World Wrestling Federation, aka the WWF. He had plenty of sleepovers, outings with his friends, and the best nine months of our lives. Then, inevitably, it came time to pack his things up for the move. It felt as though my heart had been ripped out of my chest again. The only comfort I could find was that a lot of his mother's family now lived in Pennsylvania, so he would have plenty of cousins his age to play with.

When the day came, it was gut-wrenching.

"Messiah, you be a good boy you hear me?" I said squeezing him tightly. "Daddy's gon' come see you every other weekend, and I'm gon' call you everyday boy. You hear me?" I asked with half of a smile on my face trying to be strong enough for the both of us.

"Yes, daddy I'll be good," he said looking up at me with those same eyes that had looked up at me the day he was born.

Later that evening, Linda picked him up and took him and a major part of my life with her to Pennsylvania.

I was in a funk. I may have been depressed. I wasn't sure. Depression wasn't something my friends and I ever talked about. In my entire life, I had never met any Black man, from the streets that is, who would admit they were depressed. While we can accept a range of mental illnesses, a man suffering from depression isn't one of them. I never gave myself more than a week to mourn, if that. I would always throw myself into work, and now with Messiah gone, I would do just that.

Giuliani and the NYPD had become formidable foes. Every month we would turn on the television, and there would be a new drug initiative taking place. Initiatives with names like "Operation Impact" and the like and to be honest, it was the right thing to do, no question about it, but at the same time, he drastically cut social programs. Programs like Section 8, food stamps, and public assistance in general. Again not totally a bad thing, but he didn't stop there. He also put brothers and sisters who had been selling clothes and other items on the streets, albeit without a license, out of business, but what the mayor didn't understand was that the streets would implode. We have a saying in the streets, and that saying is, pressure bus' pipes. Simply put, with all of the pressure he was putting on drug dealers, cats would turn to other means. Motherfuckers were feeling the effects all over. Our crew included.

In the past year, even Pap's apartment had gotten robbed. Someone had cut a hole through the incinerator room and into his apartment which was right next door and cleaned him out. His daughter's mother had also gotten robbed in the lobby of his building. Things were getting out of hand. It had to be someone from his building or a motherfucka' from his building was feeding someone information about him and his family, but the worst was yet to come. We were still one of the few crews eating in the streets, so that made us a target. To combat the police crackdowns and the loss of income we decided to expand our hours. We resolved to work twenty-four hours a day, six days a week. If everyone played their part and did what they were supposed to, we would be getting, mo' money, mo' money, mo' money! A little plagiarism from the show "In Living Color," but as we know, (say it with me) things don't go as planned.

Ya-ya, Marcus, and Trouble were going to run the night shift and give Pap and me ten percent of their profits. In turn, we would tell all of our clientele that they were still associated with us, and they had the same product as us. It took a bit of the responsibility off of Pap and my shoulders. There were now three fewer mouths to feed. It sounded great in theory, except it made them susceptible to stick-up kids, and it gave them the freedom to run their operation as they saw fit. Which as it turned out wasn't a good thing. Customers were coming and telling me that these dudes were sitting on the steps in the building bottling up and serving the customers right off of the plate they were bottling on. Fucking dickheads! Rule number 369. On the streets, if you have a one thousand dollars it looks like ten thousand dollars, so following that train of thought; if you have an ounce of crack on a plate, it might as well be ten ounces.

No matter how many times I tried to explain the consequences of doing shit like that, they would have to learn on their own. I would often compare selling drugs to operating a circular saw and having to cut a toothpick into thirty pieces. The difference between the two is this, if you make a mistake when using a circular saw, you may lose a finger or two, but when hustling, you may cost someone years in jail, or worse, you may cost them their life. Like so many of my lieutenants, they felt as though I was trying to micro-manage their operation. To a certain degree, I was. I was trying to make sure everyone made money and went home safe. On occasions, they would tell me that I acted as if I was their father. It didn't help when a customer would come to me with a problem that they had with one of them, and I would override one of their decisions.

The call that I knew would come came between 12:00 and 1 am. I answered the phone. It was Marcus. I asked him was everything alright? Now that's a stupid question if I've ever heard one, because at one in the morning if it ain't a chick calling you trying to fuck, it ain't never alright.

"Nah Llord, you gotta' come to the block," he said sounding despondent.

"What happened now?" I asked. The butterflies began to stir in the pit of my stomach.

"It's bad," he said.

"Aw man." I thought to myself, but the words that came out of my mouth were, "Aight', I'm on my way."

I parked my car five blocks away and made my way towards 166th street. As I got closer, I saw the familiar sight of flashing lights and police cars. Ya-ya and Marcus were standing across the street from the building. As I walked over to them, I distinctly remember how dark the street was. I mean, in the evening, it's always dark in the hood, but tonight it was eerily dark. There were two police officers standing in front of the building, or the crime scene as it was. One of the officers turned and whispered something to the other who then turned and stared at me.

"Where's Trouble?" I asked. Ya-ya didn't respond. He stood there crying.

"Come on y'all, let's take a walk." We walked a few blocks to the 24-hour chicken spot.

"What happened?" I asked.

Ya-ya was quiet. Marcus started telling me the story.

It was simple, and it was typical. A stick–up that escalated into a homicide. Some niggas entered the building, saw Trouble serving fiends in the lobby, robbed him and shot him once in the stomach. Any customer that was in the building ran out. When Marcus made it downstairs after hearing the shot, Trouble was already dead, slumped against the wall. Ya-ya was upstairs bagging up when he heard the shot. He was crushed. Trouble was his right-hand man. Now to those of you who say, live by the gun, die by the gun, I say, you're right. I call a spade a spade. It is what it is, but once again I feel the same pain that I would feel if I cut someone down in the prime of their life. Trouble was just twenty years old with a one-year-old daughter. His murder, like most murders in the ghetto at that time, would go unsolved. People who haven't grown up in this environment probably find this endless cycle of violence and death farfetched, but it's true, and it never ends.

After I left the block, I called Pap and told him what happened. He was upset that I hadn't called him when I got the call and went to Franklin, but I explained to him that he didn't need to show his face at the sight of a murder scene. He understood.

Not long after that, motherfuckers had the audacity to hit us again. This time, the nigga that robbed us couldn't keep his mouth shut. He was going around the neighborhood bragging about how he made Marcus and Ya-ya pull their pants down around their ankles. To him, it was real funny. To us, it was the straw that broke the camel's back. To make matters worse, it was the same dude that Pap suspected of robbing his house and his baby mother. Man, shit was about to get real! Days had passed and still no sign of homeboy. His name was Eugene, but niggas on the streets called him Geno. Then out of nowhere, bingo!

One day Marcus and Ya-ya were walking on Boston Road, and they spotted him, but instead of running up on him and stomping a mudhole in his ass, they followed him like they were fucking private eyes or something. They came down the block and told us that they had seen Geno, but they lost him.

Pap started laughing, "Y'all lost him? He asked sarcastically. "Who the fuck are y'all? The FBI?"

I joined in the laughter.

"Why y'all ain't just run up on duke and git' in his ass?" I asked, but I knew the answer.

It was the possibility that Geno had a gun on him, the thought of getting arrested, or they were scared. Don't get it twisted, Ya-ya and Marcus were straight soldiers, but sometimes, in the heat of battle, even soldiers freeze up.

Patience is a virtue, that's one of life's necessities, and vengeance takes patience. Pap and I were chilling on the block when Stan came back from doing a perimeter check.

"I just saw that nigga Geno on 164th street chillin' like everything is gravy," he said resting the bike up against the fence in front of the building.

I ran upstairs to the stash house and grabbed a baseball bat.

"Come on les' move before that nigga bounce," I said to Stan.

"Hold up," Pap said, "I want some of that nigga, too."

We walked up the block to Boston road and made a right toward 164th street. As we neared, Pap pointed him out.

"There that nigga go right there."

With that said as Red Man put it, "It was time for some action." I ran up on him and broke the bat over his motherfuckin' head. He ran inside the corner bodega to get away from us, but we were right on his ass. As soon as we got inside the store, we all pulled out knives and began stabbing him. The three of us were on him with total disregard for the store's surveillance cameras. He was screaming for us to wait, trying to tell us that it wasn't him.

It was too late. He had violated a rudimentary rule. A rule that is followed by policemen, businessmen, Politicians, and criminals alike. I forget the number of that rule, although you may recall it. That rule, never speak on anything you don't want known. It only took seconds for us to stab him up to fifteen times in his ass and legs. We weren't trying to kill him, just make an example out of him. When it was over, I picked up the pieces of the broken bat, and we calmly walked out of the store and headed back to Franklin Ave.

Approximately a half an hour later, an unmarked car pulls up in front of our spot, and we see a bloody hand pointing out of the back of the police car window. It was Geno. That's right a fucking stick-up kid bringing the cops to our block telling them that we had assaulted him. So much for not snitching. Now that I think about it, how insane is it that they drive you around in a cop car before taking you to a hospital. *Hahaha.* I love the NYPD. A few days later the police went to my mother's house looking for me since that was my last known address, but I hadn't lived there for ten years.

It was my old friend Robocop. He was now a detective. He came to pay me a personal visit. Well, not exactly personal. He showed up at my mother's house with two other detectives. Robo was always courteous to my mother. He told her that he was coming to speak to with me off the record. While he spoke with her, the two detectives that were with him were searching my mother's apartment, opening dresser drawers and looking through her kitchen cabinets. Her Toy Poodle was running back and forth barking frantically. That's when one of the detectives pulled out his gun and told my mother if she didn't put her dog away he would shoot it.

Robo told the officer to holster his gun and calm down.

He apologized to my mother and said, "If Llord did something to this guy then he probably had it coming."

I mean come on, the police knew this dude was a stick-up kid, and sooner or later if you rob criminals you're going to get what's coming to you. I'm not sure if it was because the detectives threatened my mother's poodle, or simply Robocop letting me slide on this one, but the police never came back looking for me again. As for Geno, we never saw him in the neighborhood again. The last we heard was that his mother packed up and moved his family down south. She probably saved his life.

You know the saying, what doesn't break you will make you, and what doesn't kill you will make you stronger? Well, thanks to Mayor Giuliani, we were forced to reevaluate the way we did business, and it did indeed make us stronger, and better, or worse, depending on what side of the fence you were on. If he wanted to step up his crime initiatives, then we would step up our criminal activities. First, we needed to gather up all of our associates past and present. It was time to expand. Expand locations, business ventures, and personnel. For the next few days, Pap and I bounced shit back and forth contemplating the most effective course of action. Pap always wanted to buy and sell weight. As for me, I was always worried about security, so it made me hesitant to sell weight because it made you more susceptible to robberies, or God forbid the feds. When it was over, we had a dummies guide to crime. A 101 on building a criminal empire.

When we all got together, Pap spoke first.

"Aight', I know niggas is wonderin' what this shit is about. We gotta' step our game up," he said clasping his hands together scanning the room. "Me and Llord know shit is gittin' hot as hell out here and truthfully, it's gon' git' hotter. So we came up with a plan to make sure everybody git's a piece of the pie," he glanced at me asked, "Llord you wanna' take over?"

I stood up in the middle of the room.

"Yeah, I got it partna'."

Another one of Pap's man's from his building named Raymond showed up with our old lieutenant L.A. Of course, Marcus, Action, Ya-ya, Sleepy, Malik, Stan and Roc were there, plus a few other cats from the neighborhood that hadn't worked with us before.

"Here it is fellas'. Instead of us sellin' nicks' we gon' start sellin' twenties. That's gon' make it easier for the niggas who gotta' bottle up, and it's gon' cut down on the foot traffic."

Before I could continue, the skeptics began mumbling throughout the room.

Ya-ya was the first to speak up, "I know you on't think a fuckin' fiend gon' pay twenty dollars when they be comin' up short on deuces and nickels," he said shaking his head.

I wasn't surprised. I expected some resistance and doubt.

"Look, it's gon' be a slow grind, but in the end, it's gon' pay off. We have to change the way we operate. From an observation standpoint, one of the cop's main weapons is watching our clientele run back and forth like roaches. Wit' the twenties, all that traffic is gon' come to a halt. True we ain't gon' move as much product as before, but it's gon' give us a different type of customer. The heads that pick up bottles and cans, along wit' the homeless, gon' have to run to the nickel and dime spots, heatin' they shit up, while we gon' git' the workin' class and functional addicts. The ones who are gon' to come and spend money in one lump sum and be done wit' it. Now as you look around the room you probably thinkin,' 'If he wanna slow shit down why he bringin' in more people?' Glad you asked. We goin' into some new avenues of business, but before we discuss those new endeavors, I want to bring up a few things."

"First, y'all know my main concern is safety. I want to set up a whole new security team to patrol a ten block radius. They'll operate on the outside perimeters of our spots. They'll still ride bikes, but instead of usin' Walkie Talkies, they'll be usin' chirp phones to keep in contact with our lookouts at each spot.

Now the room was quiet. I had everyone's full attention.

"Once the money starts rollin' in, we gon' git' apartments outside of our perimeter and install cameras so we can monitor the police's every move from one safe house. Just like the police scanner, only now we able to see when they set up and send undercovers to our spots. A nigga don't even haf' to be in New York to monitor what's goin' on, no less standin' outside in the cold lookin' out. Those days are done. Also, along the lines of security, we have another major problem. That problem is snitchin'. You got niggas who wanna be thugs, drug dealers, and stick-up kids, but when the shit hit the fan, they can't do the time. I got a plan to combat this police cooperation epidemic. We gon' put a stop to this shit quick.

Anybody that ain't done jail time, or been wit' us in the heat of battle, is gon' have to take the head of security to where you stay at, so if shit go down, we'll know exactly where to find you. If anybody has a problem wit' that, then you can leave right now. No hard feelins'."

Another cat from Pap's building named Ant raised his hand like we were in school.

"So what you sayin'? You wanna know where a nigga live at in case they cooperate with the police and do what?"

It was hard to tell if he was being sarcastic or not. I answered as concisely as possible.

"We wann' know where a nigga live so we can go to his house and cut his fuckin' tongue out. And while we on the subject of violence, if any fiend brings somebody to cop from us that we don't know, and they don't know, one hundred percent without a doubt, we beat them bloody on the spot."

In my mind, I knew the path that I was about to embark on was wrong, but what makes me any different than the slave owners who believed slavery to be unjust, but refused to grant their slaves freedom because of the potential lost revenue? The answer is, I'm no different. Money trumps scruples every time. Shit, your average blue-blooded Americans are descendants of criminals and religious dissidents who upon landing in America, not able to survive on their own, would establish peace treaties lasting fifty years with the natives. That is until their true nature was revealed, greed. Once self-sufficient, their need for dominance and power would supersede honor, humanity, and gratitude, using brutality and deception to accomplish their goals, giving the American Indians blankets infected with smallpox and wiping out whole tribes to procure their lands. When the Indians fought back for their lands and people, the United States government labeled them savages and all but hunted them to extinction. All of this after the Native Americans saved their founding fathers from starvation. It's that same government that today profits from the sale of cigarettes and firearms that combined, kill close to five hundred thousand in the U.S annually. So why should I give a fuck about laws and morality?

"I'll say it again, if you want to leave, now is the time."

Everyone sat waiting to hear what I had to say next.

"Okay, now that we got the preliminaries out the way, les' git' down to business. We gon' expand into the sellin' weed, loan sharkin', coke, pills, guns, and lastly, but certainly not least, extortion."

Little did I know after all of the years of selling drugs that it would be extortion that would change the course of my life.

"We gon' make everybody pay, criminals and business owners alike."

That's when the room grew loud.

"Yeah, I know the shit sound crazy, but if we gon' do this then we gon' do it all the way. What the fuck we got to lose? If we git' caught sellin' crack, we gon' do the same amount of time for a direct sale as murder, if not more, so why not ride it to the wheels fall off? I say les' roll the dice homies. When we gon' wake up. The Italians started out in crime, the Irish and the Jews made they bones the same way. What we got? We ain't got shit that's what. Nothin' except the highest rate of HIV cases, the highest rate of unemployment, the highest rate of high school dropouts, the highest rate of incarceration, and the most children in the foster care system. Fuck that! It's time for a change and whoever ain't wit' that change is gon' pay one way or another. To be more precise, we gon' lead these black horses to the water and if they don't drink it, we gon' drown em' in it! The only way we gon' make a change is if we unite and organize."

I held up my hand with fingers spread.

"You see my fingers?" I asked. "When separate, you can break each finger one by one. But when joined together they make a fist powerful enough to knock a motherfucka' out. That same fist is the universal symbol of struggle, liberation, revolution, and Black power."

I had them eating out of the palm of my hand. While I had no formal training, studying human behavior came naturally to me. I knew no matter what your agenda, no matter how insidious, if you can articulate that belief to your audience, they will follow. Prime examples, Charles Manson, Jim Jones, or Adolf Hitler. If you build it, they will come!

"I know y'all wanna' git' outta' here, so I just got two more points to bring up and then we out- camouflage and invisibility."

I looked around the room at cats wearing gold chains and expensive clothes, and I was one of em'. While I didn't wear a lot of flashy jewelry, I loved beautiful cars and the latest fashion. If we wanted to be successful, these things had to change. At the very least while we were out on the block hustling.

"When I say camouflage I mean we gon' have to tone it down on the streets. We wanna give off the impression that we starvin'. When you come outside put on the oldest and dirtiest shit, you got. Wit' the slow down of the flow of traffic that should throw the boys off our trail. The second phase is invisibility."

None of my old crew were gang members, but some of the new prospects were, so I had to sell them on this theory of invisibility.

"When you out in your hood stop flaggin', no rockin' all red, or all blue, and stop throwin' up gang signs niggas. I know some of the homies gon' have a problem wit' what I'm sayin', but think about it. Every week you see thirty or forty cats in one set gittin' snatched up by the police and gittin' hit wit' football numbers. Niggas shouldn't even be talkin' outside, no less throwin' up gang signs. The shit I'm talkin' bout' is the only way we gon' beat the police and the feds. We have to be smarter, diversify, expand, and in the same breath, it has to seem like we don't even exist. It's different then what we're used to, but not only is it gon' make us rich, it's gon' give us longevity. The days of niggas on the streets bein' flamboyant are over. Ain't no more Teflon Dons. It's time to git' low and stay low!"

Their faces said it all. They were ready.

"If nobody got nothin' to add to that, I'm done. Me and Pap are gon' git' back at y'all wit' who's gon' run what as soon as we git' everything mapped out."

Pap told Sleepy, Malik, and Action to hold on.

"What up kid?" Sleepy asked.

He was smooth. He walked and spoke with a swagger. A swagger that came from earning his stripes in the streets as well as in prison. He was the definition of a thug and the women who like bad boys loved him. His baby's mother was one of those women, but like his brothers and cousins and most bad boys, he had a hand problem. He thought nothing of giving her a black eye and knocking her teeth out.

"Check it out Sleep. We got a special assignment for you, Action, and Malik. Y'all cats are gon' be our hit squad."

Sleepy smirked, "Hit squad? Y'all niggas is wild for the night," he said cynically.

Pap stopped him.

"Hold on, yeah I said hit squad. If we serious about gittin' money and expandin', then this is what it's gon' take. Now let me finish before you speak your piece. We don't want y'all on the block. Y'all ain't gotta' handle no drugs, no baggin' up, no hittin' the pitcher off- no doin' nothin' but waitin' till it's time to make moves on cats who ain't tryin' to git' down wit' us, or pay us to operate on their own. Y'all gon' git paid five hundred dollars a week to basically do nothin' until we got beef, and as we grow and make more money, y'all gon' make more money. The only question is, are you in or out?"

Before they could answer, I spoke up, "I'ma be wit' y'all when it's time to make moves. It ain't that I don't trust y'all, I jus' wanna stay sharp. You know let niggas know that I still put that work in."

Pap gave me a dirty look, but he didn't say anything.

He asked again, "Like I was sayin', y'all in or out?"

Action was the first answer, "Hell motherfuckin' yeah I'm in! Five hunnit' a week to lay-lo, shit why not?"

Malik was hesitant.

"Who you talkin' bout' makin' moves on? I ain't wit' killin' innocent people. I'm Muslim; I ain't wit that."

I understood exactly where Malik was coming from, but I also felt that this was bigger than hustling and extortion. I saw this as the beginning of a revolution. With the speech that I had just given, Malik still didn't see the big picture. "Look bro'. I study Islam, I read the bible, and I know right from wrong, but in the end, we as a people gotta' be willin' to fight, die, and kill for somethin' brotha'. This ain't about the streets no more. This is the beginning of a movement. And in every movement, there's gon' be some casualties. It's an inescapable cost of war akh'. I'll give you my word as a Muslim that we ain't gon' hurt nobody wit' out justification."

I was looking directly at him to get a read on his thoughts. He reluctantly agreed giving me a pound.

"Aight' bro' I'm in."

I respected the fact that Malik wanted to stand by his principles, but again, he would also whip a bitch out without a second thought.

Pap turned to Sleepy.

"What about you Sleep?" he asked.

"Nigga show me the money and I'ma show you what the fuck I'ma do," he said putting out his hand as if to say, 'Fuck you, pay me.'

I laughed, "Don't worry nigga' y'all gon' git' paid on Saturday like everybody else," I said.

Pap asked Action once more to be sure, "You in or out?"

Action smiled, "You know what I'ma about."

With that said, we had put together a hit squad that would kill on a moment's notice.

Pap and I left them to begin working out strategy deciding on who would be best for what position. We knew we were going to have to rotate who went into the local businesses to extort the proprietors. That way, the store owners wouldn't be able to finger any one of our people. They would never know who would show up for that week's payment. We decided that we wouldn't spare anyone from paying us except the Black business owners. To reiterate it has nothing to do with race, just basic economics. In our neighborhoods, which are split down the racial lines between Blacks and Hispanics, the main Hispanic demographic is Dominican, Puerto Rican, and Mexican. And while our brothers from the Caribbean and Africa have black skin, even some of them feel they are better than the Black American and have a condescending attitude towards us. Just as alarming are the attitudes of the European immigrants, who came here from some of the worst conditions imaginable. Unbelievably when they arrive in America, they too, have an air of superiority when it comes to dealing with Black Americans. That same attitude exudes from those who come from the Middle East and Asia as well. The only ethical ambiguity that I wrestled with was when dealing with the Jewish, Arab, and Mexican community.

My empathy for the Jews I believe is self-explanatory. They have been persecuted for thousands of years. The only race, I believe that has been oppressed more than the Black man, but with that being said, they have become, with help from the United States, self-reliant. As for the Mexican community, they are America's new slaves, overworked, underpaid, and not wanted here. Immigration laws are passed enabling law enforcement to stop and question immigrants for no other reason except the color of their skin and their ethnicity. Those from Central America and South America are assumed to be from Mexico and lumped into one category unless they are dark skinned immigrants from Honduras or Panama, due to the average American's prejudices and ignorance. As for the Arabs, granted, while they come here and open up businesses in our neighborhoods and say, "What up my nigga'?" like they're one of us, they still don't employ us in their stores, but their conviction to their cause is unwavering. As much as I empathize with and admire the Jews, the Mexicans, and the Arabs, they would still have to pay to do business in our neighborhoods. Any business that didn't pay would be burned to the ground, and we wouldn't stop there. Any of our landlords who had offices downtown would be burned to the ground also. That's right; we would take the fight to where they lived and did business. No more destroying the communities that we lived in out of frustration.

I was almost done with probation. I only had two years left. For the last three years, I had been reporting to my probation officer faithfully every month while simultaneously building a criminal empire right under her nose. I had established somewhat of a personal relationship with her, and I manipulated that relationship to further my cause which was to get off of probation early. Her name was Ms. Garner. She was an overweight Black woman who was also a lesbian. She had confided in me about a number of personal issues that she was dealing with. While I lied to her about my criminal activities, I felt a genuine connection to her. She identified with and recognized the crisis facing Black America, Black men in particular.

"Hey, Ms. Garner," I greeted her enthusiastically.

"Hello, Lloyd. What you been up to?" she responded gleefully as well.

I expressed to her that I was thinking about going to Apex Technical School for welding.

"That's fantastic, how long is the course?" she asked.

"Well, it's about seven months if I'm not mistaken. The good thing about that is, they have job placement so when I'm finished it's a strong possibility that right out of school I'll land a job," I said.

She had been thumbing through my files occasionally nodding her head in approval. She closed my file and looked up.

"I'll make a deal with you Lloyd. You finish school; find yourself a job, and you're off probation."

"Ok, Ms. Garner, I'ma hold you to that," I told her smiling.

Leaving her office, I felt rejuvenated. Albeit I suggested school as a scam, I felt as if I had a chance to do something positive. I hadn't felt that since getting my GED.

Back in the neighborhood, Pap had the block jumping. There was a new sense of purpose. The lookouts were on the corners dressed down and blending in with the crowd. No one had on jewelry, and everyone had on the oldest clothes they could find in their closet. I loved it.

"Pap, what up big homie?" I asked giving him a pound.

"I on't know Llord, shit is kinda' slow, "he said shrugging his shoulders.

"It's gon' be like that for a while til' the word gits' out that the price went up to twenties. Relax big boy," I said.

I'll admit, I was a little worried that my plan would backfire, but I had to display a countenance of confidence.

"Don't stress it, nigga. Before you know it, we gon' be makin' money hand over foot. Jus' be easy."

He breathed a sigh of relief when I said that. Even though we were partners, he still needed me to take the helm during crunch time.

"We better homie! Anyway, I got shit laid out. Stan is gon' to run the loansharking business which we gon' call, the Banking Division, and Marcus and your cousin Doggie is gon' run the extortion game which we gon' call, the Donation Fund. What you think?" he asked.

To me, it sounded great. It put a nice spin on something nefarious.

"I like it homie. It makes shit sound a lot less treacherous. The only thing I on't know about is if Marcus and Doggie are strong enough to handle the extortion business," I said doubtfully.

"They ain't gotta' be strong. All they gotta' do is keep track of who pays and who don't. That's it. As things fall into place, we gon' eventually send different niggas in to collect the payments just like we discussed. I got it partna'."

He was right; he did have it. He had thought things out pretty well. I guess he just wanted my input to give him some assurance.

"Ok, you right, you got it. The main thing is to stay on top of niggas, and if anything comes up, me and you'll figure shit out."

With business out of the way, I told him how things went at probation.

"I told my PO that I'm goin' to Apex Tech. She seemed to think it's a good idea. I can't front boy; I'm excited to be goin' back to school," I said as we walked across the street to get a little privacy.

"Why wouldn't you be? That's whassup' nigga. We already know education is the key," he said.

"Yeah, no doubt, but I was also thinkin' that once we git' everything in order as far as the new ventures, we try to git' everybody back in school or at least git' a job on the side. That way, everybody got somethin' to fall back on if it don't work out." I said.

I hoped I didn't sound self–righteous. I hated motherfuckas' like that. Once they stop smoking, drinking, or start eating healthy, they had the answers for everyone else's life.

"I on't see a problem wit' that," Pap said. "Jus' keep in mind everybody ain't cut out for school or that legal lifestyle. Until then, you handle your business, and I got shit out here."

In hindsight, his statement was close-minded as hell, but that's where we were at as a generation and culture in the 90's. At that time, drug dealing was a way of life, and the only way many of us saw as an opportunity to make more than minimum wage.

"Oh one more thing," he said. "I forgot to speak to you about it before. Why the fuck you tellin' niggas you gon' go on hits wit' em'? You supposed to be a leader. Shut the fuck up and lead."

Before I could reply, he cut me off.

"I got shit to do. I'll holla' at you later."

Pap never pulled punches with me. He always kept it one hundred. That's what made him my closest friend and brother.

WARRIORS OF THE WASTELAND

Chapter 15
9/11

Looking back, Apex Tech saved my life. Now not everyone will have the same experience because despite taking out student loans and federal grants, you still have cats that come to school, smoke weed in the restrooms and miss days at a time. It was a quick course. We were taught entry-level skills. Enough for you to land a job and get on the job training. I attended school between the hours of 8:30 am and 3:00 pm. Afterward, I would head to Franklin with my textbooks, study theory and do my homework on the block. I devoted just enough energy to pass my classes, but still, I passed effortlessly. In the month of November, around Thanksgiving, I got to the neighborhood and I saw a crowd of people standing outside a bodega on 166th and Forest Ave. watching as it burned. The firefighters were doing their best to keep it from spreading to the adjacent building. In the middle of the crowd, I spotted Pap watching while sipping on a bottle of Blackberry Brandy. I walked over to him.

"What up nigga? What happened? The Dominican niggas' had some religious candles or some shit burnin?" I asked looking at the people standing out in front of their building shivering.

It was starting to get cold and dark, and there were still remnants of the snowfall on the ground from two days ago.

Pap took another sip of his brandy and whispered in my ear, "Nah nigga we happened," he said putting his arm around my shoulder. "C'mon," he said gesturing down the block.

As we walked together, he began to tell me what happened.

"Marcus and Doggie went into the bodega and told papi behind the counter about our little donation fund. Before they could finish their sales pitch so to speak, he started wit' the 'putas' and 'cabrons' and all that other disrespectful Spanish shit. They walked out, made the call to Sleepy, Action, and Malik, and the rest is history."

I felt sick.

"These niggas couldn't do nothing else besides burnin' motherfuckas' out they buildin' right before Thanksgiving? Damn nigga," I said throwing my hands up in disgust.

The look Pap gave me said it all.

"Listen Llord, me and you, mostly you, came up wit' this shit and niggas carry it out. Ain't no turnin' back, and it definitely ain't no time to be second guessin' or gittin' no fuckin' conscience. What's done is done. You said it yourself, we gon' ride or die. If these niggas don't pay, they gon' be outta' business. Besides, this is gon' send a clear message to any other motherfucka' that don't wanna pay."

He was right. It wasn't any turning back, but I knew it wouldn't be long before the feds would be on the scene. We had officially entered the realm of racketeering. We were definitely goin' to have to step up security.

Our plate was full. With the extortion and loansharking, our organization was becoming more violent than ever. Regrettably, it was a necessary evil as a prerequisite for growth. So, in the midst of going to school, I would have to deal with the security issues as well. I headed back to Spy-Tec, a store that I had purchased a more reliable police scanner from. It was located down by the Westside Highway. When I walked in the sales clerk remembered me.

"Hey, Jason! Long time no see."

I always gave a different alias when doing business.

"What brings you back around these parts?" he asked wringing his hands together.

It had been some time since I had been to his store; I was surprised to see how much technology had advanced, Nanny-cams in children's toys, shoe mounted cameras, I guess that was for the perverts. What really caught my eye were the cameras that looked like satellite dishes for cable TV. Now I was the one rubbing his hands together.

"Walter how much for those cameras there?" I asked pointing at the display.

"For you Jason, I'll do six hundred apiece, and they come with the installation manual on CD-ROM. It'll walk you through setting up your cameras for remote offsite viewing."

I did the math. I could have a man in one location watching two cameras and still have a man on the ground patrolling the neighborhood. Twice as much security for the same price. I loved it.

"I'll take two, but you give me a nice discount, and I'll be back for more if things work out."

It didn't hurt to ask.

"Alright, give me a one thousand dollars for the two units, but make sure you bring me some more business."

Before I left, he explained that there were no wires to install, I just had to mount it on the wall outside of an apartment window, put the CD-ROM in the hard drive and follow the instructions on syncing up the cameras with the computer. It was a relatively new technology called, Bluetooth.

Since technology was Pap and Marcus's thing, I let the two of them work on installing the cameras. With the security, or the first stage of an advanced security system being set up, I could concentrate on the books, and from the looks of it, things were going well. The twenties had picked up as did the loansharking. The only thing that was doing poorly was the donation fund. I now understood the reason for the crew burning down the bodega. There was no getting around it; we would have to step up our level of violence.

I walked over to Pap, "Look man, I know you don't wanna' hear it, but the next donation fund job that cats go on, I'm goin' wit' 'em."

Pap shrugged his shoulders.

"Aight, you on't never listen. Jus' remember I told you to stay on the sidelines."

I hated when he said shit like that. It's always a jinx. It's the same as when someone tells you to be safe, without fail, something usually happens.

The first stop on our next job was an Arab deli. The thing that struck me as it always did when I walked into a deli were the pictures of young children, some as young as Messiah holding AK-47's. It was 7 pm, mid-December and it was freezing. The store was empty except for the two Arab men standing behind the counter. Me, Marcus, and Doggie all had on sweat hoods. I greeted one of the men behind the counter.

"As-salamu alaykum."

He greeted me back, although hesitantly. "Walaikum salam," he said eyeing the three of us suspiciously.

"What do you need?" he asked in a heavy Arabic accent.

It wasn't any use pussyfooting around. I got right down to business.

"I don't know if you heard, but we have a community donation fund and we been goin' around to the businesses in the neighborhood asking for contributions."

Before I had a chance to finish, he interrupted me.

"Listen, listen," he said waving his hand. "I was hoping you and your people would come into my store. I have heard about your donation fund, and I have something better than money to offer you."

Doggie laughed and asked him, "Oh yeah, what's better than money motherfucka'?"

"Knowledge!" he exclaimed in a condescending tone. "Please come back tonight at 11:00 when we are closing the store, and we will talk further."

I was skeptical. Rule number 19, trust half of what you see and even less of what you hear.

"How do I know when I come back you won't have police or the FBI waitin' for us?"

He paused for a moment, "Do you remember when a group of Middle Eastern men were arrested for selling arms out of their chicken restaurant on 174th and Boston Road? Those men were associated with our organization and besides my brother; I am taking more of a risk meeting you here tonight than you are meeting with me. I have much more to lose than money."

What he said made sense, but it would be little consolation if it was a set-up.

"Ok, I'll be back tonight, but if anything goes wrong, I promise you, this will be your last night doin' business in this neighborhood." With that said, I turned to leave. "As-salamu alaykum."

As soon as we turned the corner, Marcus exploded.

"What the fuck yo'. Why you always gotta' come around and throw a monkey wrench in shit? Me and Doggie had a nice system worked out. It was simple, either they pay, or they don't. Ain't no tradin' this for that! Can I suck yo' dick or can you take my daughter? They either pay up or suffer the fuckin' consequences, but here you go! Now we gotta' take a fuckin' chance comin' back here tonight."

I didn't say anything; I let him vent.

"What we gon' do when we come back, and this Arab nigga got the hot boys waitin' for us? Or worse, him and those other Arab niggas got AK's waitin' to spray us?" he asked visibly upset.

"I hear where you comin' from pa', but I'm jus' tryin' to think outside the box. I understand tho'. If you feel like that, you on't have to come wit' me tonight," I said. "I'll come back solo. I'll come back wit' the toast. But I'll come solo. Trust me when I tell you, it ain't no hard feelins'."

When Pap heard what happened, he didn't say anything. He just gave me that "I told you so" look which was worse in my opinion. Fortunately for me, I wouldn't have to go alone. Ya-ya and Malik said they would come with me to deal with their Muslim brothers. When we walked up to the deli, we could see people moving about inside.

Malik was the first to go in, followed by me. Ya-ya waited outside to watch our backs in case he saw any police activity or masked Arabs with guns coming in behind us. Malik and the deli owners exchanged salutations. He had worn his Kufi, and he also had grown his beard to the length that most Muslim men wear their beards. When they saw him, the expression on their faces began to radiate with fondness. I immediately sensed the tension that I had experienced earlier that evening subsiding.

"As-salamu alaykum, brother. My name is Mumin, and this is brother Kasir." Malik introduced me, and with that, the niceties were done.

"Okay, Mumin I don't have time for the long hellos. What you got for us?" I asked.

He looked annoyed with me, but I didn't give a fuck. Yes, I empathize with the Arabs in their struggle against Israeli and American imperialism, and I'll concede that some of the Arabs that worked in the smoke shops selling us baggies and scales were humble, but a lot of the Arabs who worked in the delis would put our money down on the counter like they didn't want to touch our hands. Some of them wouldn't even respond back to you when you greeted them in Arabic.

Mumin spoke up, "Llord is your name? Well Llord, we in the Arab nations have watched the injustices your people have suffered at the hands of America and we have often wondered when your people would come to the realization that the key to overcoming oppression, while protests are great for television, American democracy is a joke, but history has shown that armed confrontation is the only real answer. Yes, in an ideal world your peaceful protest would be enough, but speaking pragmatically, oppression must be met with terror, and that brings us to why I have asked you here tonight."

I was interested in what he was saying, but it wasn't going to stop me from burning his store to the ground if I couldn't profit from it.

"Git' to the point akhi," I said growing impatient with all of the talk. (You'll notice that I have a short attention span.)

"I'll let Kasir explain it to you," he said.

Kasir looked young, but oddly, he also looked worn, as if he had seen too much, too soon in his young life. I knew that look. I had seen it all of my life growing up in my neighborhood on the faces of disenfranchised men and women.

He spoke softly, "Please follow me."

He led us down into the basement of the store through a small passageway that opened up into a large padded room. I assumed that they had constructed a firing range, but I was wrong. There was an odor that I couldn't quite put my finger on, but it quickly came to me. It smelled like manure. Cow manure to be exact. They had bags and bags of fertilizer stacked six feet on pallets lined against a back wall. My God, what had we stumbled across? I remembered some years ago a terrorist drove a vehicle into the garage of the World Trade Center and detonating it killing six and injuring more than a thousand. In my neighborhood, we were unaffected by this act of terrorism. We were more concerned with AIDS, crack, and poverty at the time. Not to mention, America was more concerned with its drug war and giving us draconian sentences, while the extremist were making bombs and simultaneously plotting to bring down the government.

"Turn your attention to the small cylinder in the center of the room and hold your ears."

No sooner than he said that, there was a loud boom. It left a small crater in the floor.

"What the fuck! Y'all niggas crazy?" I yelled pulling out my gun, waving it at Mumin and Kasir.

My ears were ringing.

Mumin smiled smugly and said, "And that my friend, is what is better than money."

They were out of their fucking minds. Malik was elated. He and the Arabs were hugging and saying things in Arabic which I didn't understand. You would have thought he died and met the Prophet, Muhammad.

"Alright, Mumin you were right, but how do I make money from this information? It's only valuable to me and my associates if we know how to use it."

"It is very simple to make these devices brother," Kasir replied. "But it is also extremely dangerous and as equally as hard to obtain the components without raising suspicions. Please bear with us, and in time you will have everything you need."

Malik did something that he never did which was to make a decision for our organization.

"No problem akhi. We'll be in touch."

We shook hands and were on our way. When we came back outside, Ya-ya was pacing back and forth.

"What the fuck? Y'all was in there forever. I ain't hear no gunshots, so I figured y'all was good, but I wasn't a hunnit' percent sure; I was ready to come in blazin'. What the fuck happened?"

Malik grabbed his younger brother. "Yo, our brothers is deep in the Jihad Ya'. If they woulda' killed us down in the basement, you woulda' never heard a sound. These niggas set off a fuckin' bomb down there. Ya-ya stopped dead in his tracks.

"Git the fuck outta' here," he said in disbelief.

"Nah nigga, it's true," I said affirming Malik's statement. "Now les' git' back to the block and put the toast up before y'all two niggas' be makin' Salàt up north," I said anxiously.

We were all excited; we were about to ramp things up.

The next day Pap was all ears. He listened as Ya-ya, Malik, and I filled him in on what happened at the deli the night before. He couldn't believe that the Arabs had the gall to set off an explosion. We decided to let Malik handle all the negotiations with Kasir and Mumin. It would also be his job when the time came, to learn, and teach a select few of us how to make explosives.

As our organization grew, we linked up with more sets of gang members. One of those sets were the Vampire Bloods out of Edenwald Houses from the Northeast section of the Bronx. The big homie in their set was a cat named Dracula who was a criminally ingenious. He introduced robberies into our business model. That is, jewelry stores, check cashing establishments, and banks. Nothing petty like snatching chains or purses. He was the one who also introduced a proposal, which was that any member who is stopped by law enforcement and they're armed, they have the option of shooting it out with the police. We took a vote on the issue, and it was decided that it would be left up to the individual. Dracula reasoned that it would make law enforcement hesitant about speeding to a crime scene when gunshots were reported. Like I said he was ingenious.

One of the Crip sets in the Bronx were the Hellbound Crips out of the Mitchell Houses in the South Bronx. The leader of their set was a brother named Doughboy. He was in a league of his own. He presented white collar crimes to us, credit card schemes, fraudulent checks, and identity theft, and that was just the tip of the iceberg.

Meanwhile, I had graduated from Apex and found a job. Not long after that, I was released from probation, but before I was let go, I had to give a DNA sample. It was humiliating. I stood there in a room with thirty other men and women of color with my mouth opened wide while a probation officer swabbed the inside of my mouth and underneath my tongue with something that resembled a large Q-tip. I felt like a slave. When we were done, the officer put each swab into a plastic tube and we were given a final fuck you, or warning as it were that Big Brother, the FBI would have our DNA on file to reference against any crimes committed in the past or future. With that said, I was finished. Off of probation. My first job in thirteen years was with a non-union contractor paying me fifteen dollars an hour to weld and use an oxy-acetylene torch. It was good money for me. The most I had made in life legally up to that point. For the men I worked with it was a different story. They were Mexican immigrants. The boss who happened to be Greek was a slave driving son of a bitch. He was paying these men five dollars an hour. They worked fifty hours a week, no overtime pay, no health benefits, and perilously unsafe working conditions.

It boggles the mind how the average American feels that Mexicans have no right to come to this country and work when

America is a nation of Immigrants. What's more irrational is that some Black Americans subscribe to this nonsense not realizing that some fifty to sixty years ago we were America's unwanted workforce. While working, I met an Italian guy named Frankie Vella. He reminded me of the character Starsky from that TV show in the seventies, "Starsky and Hutch." I affectionately called him Starsky, and he called me Huggy Bear. A Black character on the show who happened to be a pimp. As he and I worked together for a while, I found out that he belonged to one of those anti-government, free American organizations. Organizations like the one Timothy McVeigh, the notorious Oklahoma City bomber belonged to. Starsky's organization had a compound somewhere out in the Midwest where they stockpiled food and guns in the event of Armageddon or a race war.

One day I asked, "Starsky, in the event Armageddon or whatever does happen, can I bring my family and live on the compound with you and your organization?"

He never even paused to think about it before he answered me, "No Huggy Bear. The most I can do is throw some food outside the gate for you."

Hahaha. That's what I' talking about. You cannot be mad at honesty. Even when it's racist!

While I can laugh at his unabashed retort, the sad truth is there are groups out there with similar agendas. Groups like the Aryan Brotherhood, Aryan Nation, Neo-Nazis, Skinheads, and lest we forget, great- grandpa's Ku Klux Klan. They are buying weapons, going to firing ranges, and taking their young children with them. They are preparing for war, and the enemy is us! As for Black America, too many of our young men have been criminalized, therefore denied the right to bear arms. While we still buy guns, albeit illegally, we are stopped, frisked, and jailed while White America buys arms indiscriminately and just as indiscriminately, goes about killing their peers, children in schools, the workplace, and anywhere the public amasses at astounding rates. I don't advocate senseless violence, Black or White. I merely ask why laws are made to benefit one demographic and oppress another, but America's day of recompense was near. That day was September 11th, 2001, or "9-11" as it is more commonly referred to.

My first response was one of shock, followed by empathy for those I saw jumping out of the tower windows and off of the rooftops, but if I may, America is a nation that has been involved in more wars, with more countries in modern history, than any other nation. Should we remain unscathed while the people of other nation suffer at our hands? Americans were told that we were attacked by Iraq on the orders of Saddam Hussein, a brutal dictator who allegedly had weapons of mass destruction. We later found out that the latter was untrue, which led some Americans to believe that we were at war for oil, and others to speculate that we were at war to settle a score that President Bush had with Saddam Hussein over an alleged assassination plot on the elder Bush. Others came to a conclusion that it was a combination of the two.

Saddam might have still been the ruler of Iraq today, or at the very least until his own people deposed him if he had not tried to placate America. Whatever the outcome, for a brief period, White America was glad to treat us as fellow Americans as they always are when they need us to fight their wars. Frankly speaking, I could care less about 9-11. Not long after, America's contemptuous views and treatment of Blacks returned as it always does. Not to mention, America has made and continues to make money hand over foot in the oil industry and on defense contracts, all on top of the bloody bodies of Iraqi men, women, and children.

Chapter 16
Live by the Gun

On the streets, there was an air of opportunity. Not only was the federal government in a frenzy gathering information on terrorist organizations abroad, but they were also preoccupied with the surveillance of the Arab immigrants here in the United States. This took the heat off of the drug organizations. The NYPD had their hands full securing the city, and the icing on the cake was that Mayor Giuliani was at the end of his second term. If I didn't know any better, I would think that my lucky rabbit's foot, four-leaf clover, and constant penance was finally paying off. We called a meeting immediately to plan the best course of action.

We decided to take advantage of the diversion that the terrorist had given us. Dracula suggested that with the NYPD focusing on securing the bridges, tunnels, and subways, it gave us free rein to step up our crime wave. He observed that the need for a gun during bank robberies was unnecessary. All anyone had to do was present the bank teller with a note and prestò, the charge of armed robbery magically disappeared. But we came to the conclusion that the bank tellers kept very little funds in their teller drawers so robbing a bank was just a quick fix for minimal amounts of money.

What's a little known fact is that just as quickly as we called a meeting which was days after 9-11, it's alleged that the unions and its contractors with ties to organized crime made calls as to what locals would get what contracts, to do what jobs during the cleanup of Ground Zero the day after the attacks. In other words, all of the hoopla about patriotism, all boiled down to money. The media made a point of showing the outpouring of support from Americans, but what it didn't show were the amounts of goods stolen from businesses in the Wall Street vicinity. There were even rumors of the

FDNY and the NYPD looting jewelry stores and other establishments in the midst of the chaos. It was also rumored that the union contractors that were paid excessive amounts of money in overtime for the cleanup, assisting in the rescue efforts, recovery of bodies, and subsequent demolition, turned away non-union companies who volunteered.

What my people and I didn't foresee, or didn't foresee happening so quickly, was the crack epidemic coming to an abrupt end in New York. It was a year after 9-11 and business began to decline. Our newly elected mayor, Mayor Bloomberg, stayed the path of his predecessor Mayor Giuliani. That along with the federal government tying drug trafficking and the proceeds thereof to the Taliban, the ruling party in Afghanistan, whom the U.S. identified as a supporter of the terrorist group Al-Qaeda, who it was discovered were the real parties responsible for the 9-11 terrorist attacks, began to cripple the drug trade in New York. With that information, they galvanized a renewed commitment to the war on drugs. That, along with the downsizing of the welfare rolls in New York and the continuing arrest and imprisonment of our clientele, the drug trade as we knew it was crushed.

This had a two-pronged effect. While it did slow our business down tremendously, our brothers and sisters were slowly getting their lives together. The crackhead was becoming a thing of the past, and although rehabilitation was bad for business, it was great for our community. Fortunately, we had income from our other ventures. But I knew that a life of crime would become a thing of the past like the crackheads we served. Knowing that, I turned my attention to getting into the union. I knew what millions of Americans know, getting into a union is like finding a pot of gold. You have no idea how many Black men and women would love to be one of those people you see waving a flag on the street at construction sites. So when I heard that the Iron Workers Union was holding a test for apprenticeships, I did what hundreds of others did. I slept on the street overnight to get an application to take that test.

I was one of the lucky two hundred out of close to a thousand men and women who received an application to take the test. I filled out the application, mailed it in, and received a date on which myself and two hundred other hopefuls were to show up. When it was said and done, I and thirty-nine other people passed. Yes! I finally made it, or so I thought. It turned out to get into the Iron Workers Union it did take winning the lottery.

When I called to see about getting into the apprenticeship program, the secretary informed me that I would have to call every six months to see if my name was on the list of those chosen out of the lottery, and if I wasn't chosen in a two-year period, which I wasn't, I would have to repeat the process all over again. Meaning I would have to sleep out on the sidewalk again hoping to get an application to take the test again. Fuck that! I had enough. During that two year period, while I was waiting to get picked in the lottery, I took an exam for the MTA and passed that. Some months later I was sent a letter informing me that I was denied employment because of my past felonies and credit history. Ok, I understood the felonies, but what did my credit history have to do with me obtaining a job? How was I expected to repair my credit and become a law abiding citizen if I couldn't find gainful employment?

It was Jim Crow all over again. You know when they would ask Blacks how many bubbles in a bar of soap in order to vote. America keeps finding ways to keep Blacks underemployed or unemployed. I'm reasonable, if I was seeking to work in an office where I would be in direct contact with large sums of cash, I could understand, but the MTA not wanting to employ me as a track worker? We could argue the point of credit being in direct correlation to one's character, but then we should also use that same gauge to judge, Wall Street, the Banking industry, and the Auto industry. All of whom America's taxpayers have had to bail out. When does someone serving time in prison, completing probation or parole, warrant them a second chance? A chance to take care of themselves and their families? During the time that the drug trade was diminishing our communities were changing, places like Harlem and communities in Brooklyn, New York, that had always been predominately Black were now being inundated with Whites. Our communities were changing right before our eyes. It happened gradually. It began with the war on crime and drugs. It continued with the lowering of the welfare rolls, and finally, the city closed down tenements in our neighborhoods displacing people that lived in a community their whole lives and moving them to another.

In the midst of all of this, our economy collapsed. Wall Street was in ruins, literally and financially. While we had begun an aggressive crime campaign, our White counterparts were committing white collar crimes with reckless abandon and callousness. Companies like Enron, WorldCom, and Tyco to name a few, plundered their stockholder's 401k plans and retirement accounts leaving tens of thousands nearly destitute. While a man many considered a buffoon, President Bush, made out like a bandit in the oil industry. The Vice President and his cronies fared well in the defense sector as well working with defense contractors. The most renowned, the "Blackwater Security Agency." They allegedly made billions in no-bid defense contracts.

The need for a shift in our priorities was becoming evident. It wasn't enough that I had a job, our organization had to delve into legal businesses. Not just extortion, but actually opening up legitimate businesses of our own. I asked Pap to call Dracula and Doughboy to set up a get together between the four of us. We met up in

Greenwich Village at a Jamaican restaurant called, Negril Village. It was an informal meeting. The homies Drac' and Doughboy were glad to see me.

"Llord, what it do boy?" Drac' asked embracing me.

"What's good pa'? What up Doughboy?" I said giving my newfound brothers a pound.

Here we were four Black men doing something that hadn't been done in decades. We were unified although different. Dracula was Blood, Doughboy a Crip, and Pap and I both studied Islam and Christianity, but we had one thing in common that unified us all along, our struggle. We had no flag of our own, no language, or even a country that would accept us as their progeny, but each of us, powerful in our own right, recognized that our economic and social ills were more than enough to bond us together.

"I guess y'all are wonderin' why I asked everybody here tonight," I said. "I don't know where to start."

Before I could continue the waitress walked over to our table, she was gorgeous. She spoke with a sultry Jamaican accent. She had her hair in locks which were pinned up in a bun. She handed each of us a menu.

"Can I get you, gentlemen, something to drink while you look over the menu?" she asked. Pap ordered a shot of Hennessy straight. Drac' ordered Grey Goose and cranberry. Doughboy ordered Belvedere and orange juice, while I ordered something that wasn't the trendy in drink.

"I'll have a Black Russian sweetie."

As the waitress walked away, I ran what I had on my mind by my brothers.

"I been workin' in the construction field for a couple of years now, and I've had the opportunity to work side by side wit' these union cats. I found out that these motherfuckas' is makin' double, triple, and in some cases quadruple what a non-union worker makes. We need to git' a piece of that action," I said looking around the table.

"Sounds good to me Llord, but how do we git' our hands in the cookie jar?" Doughboy asked.

"Good question bro'. When I was a kid I used to go around wit' the coalition from site to site tryin' to git' guys jobs. I say we start up our own coalitions and git' our people some of this union money."

They were quiet.

"Llord, right now we got a lot of things goin' on. Who's gon' head this thing up?" Pap asked.

"I will. I'm already in the field workin' for pennies. Shit, I might as well git' paid and help niggas git' jobs in the process," I said sipping on my drink.

The waitress came back to our table and took our orders.

"It shouldn't be hard, we jus' gotta' file some paperwork at the courthouse wit' the county clerk's office, find us a storefront for people to meet up at in the mornin', and just like that, we have a coalition. The only problem we might have is if there's violence. I heard the feds came in and broke up a lot of the coalitions for that reason."

"How they gon' break up the fuckin' coalitions when the fuckin' Irish and Italians built the unions on violence?" Dracula asked shaking his head in disgust.

"You already know," Doughboy said. "When them crackers do shit, it's all gravy, but when a Black man go and do the same thing to feed his family, now the shit is illegal."

"I mean, yeah, you right, but the shit is deeper than that," I said. "You have millions of Black people payin' taxes to the city, state, and the federal government. Which in turn, uses those tax dollars to fund highway, school, and numerous construction projects, but minority companies' git' less than 1% of those contracts. If memory serves me correctly, that's was one of the main reasons the colonies revolted against England. 'No taxation without representation.' All I'm sayin' is that if we don't start gittin' our fair share, well, y'all know what I'm sayin'."

"How much you need to git' started?" Doughboy asked.

"I'll git' back to you wit' the specifics once I have all of the numbers crunched. Now let's eat. Shit, I could eat a horse," I said savoring the jerk chicken.

The conversation turned to sports, women, and of course, money. Renting the property was easy. We had many properties that had for sale or for rent signs on them in our neighborhood. I had a phone line and a desk put in, along with several folding chairs and a coffee maker for anyone who wanted to sit and have coffee before we went out in the morning.

I had business cards printed up and handed them out throughout the neighborhood. It wasn't long before the phone started ringing. A lot of men in the area were out of work. When we would go to different construction sites petitioning for work, I began to notice that many of the menial jobs were filled by Blacks, that is when we weren't overlooked for Islanders, Mexicans, or European immigrants, Portuguese, Irish and Italians more specifically. Irish fresh off the boat, the only ones who understood much of what they were saying were those from Jamaica or other Caribbean islands. Let me make it clear, I have no qualms with any immigrant that comes to America and makes an honest living, but through no fault of the immigrant, America will give them jobs that a Black American would give our right hand to obtain. Many of those immigrants come to this country with a clean slate no matter what crimes they may have committed in their homeland, while our indiscretions follow us for life. No matter though, I got my people in at the bottom rung as laborers which was a step up making thirty dollars an hour, which is more than the average Black man makes working two jobs.

When we would go to these sites, I would see the heavy equipment being operated by White men. In fact, the vast majority, roughly ninety-eight percent of these operators were white. They would sit in these machines in the summer time with the air conditioner blowing, and in the wintertime, while we were outside shoveling, flag waving and doing the mule work for thirty dollars an hour, they were sitting in their machines with no coats on, making fifty dollars an hour to basically operate a giant video game. That was an occupation I wanted to get my people into.

When I asked the operators, the ones who would speak to me, how could I get my guys into the Engineer's Union, their answer was always the same. "You gotta' know somebody." Okay, who do I know from Long Island or other predominately white areas where most of these guys came from? No one, that's who, but I was determined. I started going around to union halls talking to delegates. For the most part, they were cordial, but usually condescending, as if to say "Good luck, but it ain't gon' happen." With such a cavalier attitude I knew we would have to apply more pressure on these unions. Besides, there was a multitude of complaints of racial discrimination on these sites when my guys would come into the office to pay their dues. One of the men said his boss asked him, "Is it true that all Black women's pussy stink?" or, "What's the one thing you don't want to call a Black man that begins with N and ends with R? The answer, neighbor!" I'll admit that's funny, but I had to convince many of these men who come from the streets not to punch their employers or co-workers in the face.

There were things that I had personally seen, like tattoos of "SS" insignias, tattoos of spider webs that represented the Aryan

Brotherhood, and one tattoo that I saw that this worker was particularly proud of, a tattoo of Jesus Christ being crucified on the cross by a Jew resembling a supervillain kneeling down on one knee driving a stake through Jesus' feet. How did I know the villain was a Jew? The supervillain's helmet had the Star of David emblazoned on it. The final straw for me was when I walked onto a job site and saw a shop steward named Bob Carney, who was also a delegate for the Carpenter's Union walking around with a necklace that had a noose dangling on the end of it. I approached him, introduced myself, and stated that I found his necklace offensive. His response was, "Yeah, and?" I lost it. I had enough. I let him know that good ol' days were over. I let him know that we wanted a piece of the American dream, and if we didn't get a piece, no one would have peace, period. I said holding up my fingers in air quotes. By then a crowd had gathered. I'll give it to Mr. Carney he didn't flinch.

"I'll tell you what Mr. Atkins, make sure that dream of yours don't turn into a nightmare," he said holding his fingers up in air quotes mimicking me.

One of the guys that were with me started to make a move towards him, but I put out my hand and stopped him.

"Come on, let's go," I said calmly defusing the situation.

As we piled into the van, one of the guys asked me, "Lloyd why you ain't let us fuck that redneck up?" he asked punching his fist into the palm of his hand.

"It's simple brother. One, if you assault him our name is tarnished in the construction industry. Two, we make it harder for any other coalitions to get their people jobs. Lastly, and more importantly, a lot of you guys are still on parole. I'll handle it."

You see what Mr. Bob Carney didn't understand is this. We as Black Americans, many of us literally have nothing to lose. That's why we don't panic when there's a recession or depression. As Black

Americans, we live our entire lives in a state of recession or depression. There used to be a saying that when America has a cold, Black America has the flu. Well in the new millennium that saying has been upgraded to reflect the times. It's now said, that when America has a cold, Black America has walking pneumonia.

When I told Pap what happened, he was furious.

"So what you tellin' me is that in 2005 this devil walkin' round' wit a fuckin' noose pendant on his necklace," he asked chuckling. "These Whiteys' is off the fuckin' hook!"

"I couldn't believe it myself homie. I had to git' a closer look at the shit before I said anything," I said.

"So what you wanna' do?" Pap asked.

"I wanna' go down to the job site and torch their machines. Those fuckin' machines cost hundreds of thousands of dollars, if not millions," I said.

"Don't they have security guards on those construction sites?" he asked

"Yeah but it's usually some underpaid immigrant gittin' nine dollars an hour. We go to the job site wit' hardhats and vest, tell the security guard that we there for the night shift, once he opens up the gate, we tie him up and torch shit. In and out. Finito!" I said.

Pap, who never wanted to go along, was the first to say he was coming. I guess that noose thing struck a nerve.

The construction site was located in the most convenient place possible. In Flushing Queens directly across the street from a housing project. Pap, Ya-ya, and I went in through the front gate. Along with our hard hats and vest, we had on dark safety glasses to hide our faces from the security cameras. When the security guard opened up the gate to let us in, Pap pulled out a gun and told him to turn around and put his hands behind his back. The guard who happened to be African wanted to be a hero and start yelling.

"What? What do you want here?"

I don't understand some people. They're getting paid eight to ten dollars an hour, and they're willing to die for someone else's property. Pap hit him in the head with the gun, and he crumpled to the floor. Problem solved. We tied him up, and duct taped his mouth shut.

Malik was sitting in front of the housing project on a bench with a cell phone to let us know if the police drove up. Once inside, I went to the two most expensive pieces of equipment on the lot. An ABI hammer and a Bauer drilling rig. The ABI was easily a million or more. The Bauer rig was close to three hundred thousand. As I unscrewed the cap on the gas canister, it hit me. I didn't have to burn the machines, all I had to do was put dirt in the gas tank and the hydraulic lines. It would be the same as putting sugar in the gas tank of a car. It would set them back months in expenses and lost production time. Not only would the results be the same, but it wouldn't draw any immediate attention from the police or fire department. By the time the crews showed for work the next morning and untied the security guard, we would be long gone.

Things went smoothly. Not only did we cause over a million dollars in damage, but the incident also made the news, the papers, and television. To top it all off, the police didn't have a clue who was responsible for the sabotage. By mere happenstance, economic terrorism would become another weapon in our arsenal.

What I've come to believe is this. Revolution with guns and violence is not enough. Here in America, we need more. While groups like the PLO, IRA, and Hamas have gained political power throughout the world, here in America organizations like the Black Panthers, have been decimated and rendered politically and economically ineffective. So now, we as the new generation of revolutionaries have learned to succeed, we must combine the tactics of Martin Luther King, Malcolm X, and the Black Panthers. Simply put, power to the people, and we shall overcome by any means necessary!

Meanwhile, as I focused on the streets, and other businesses, time marched on. I made time for my baby as much as possible, but he wasn't a baby anymore. The one year that he was supposed to go to live with his mother turned into seven, but it seemed as though we were never separated. We spoke on the phone almost every day, and I continued to do my best to travel up to Pennsylvania every other weekend. I also did the best I could to make sure Messiah had everything he needed financially. I made all of his football games on Sundays, but my guilt was eating me alive. I can remember when he was younger and he first went to live with Linda; he would call me crying telling me that his mother had left him in the house with her aunt while she went to the local bar. I also recall how he was hit in the mouth with a bat, an injury so severe that his teeth went through his upper lip and that stupid bitch didn't even take him to the hospital.

Over the years, Linda's and my relationship had deteriorated. Mainly because of my womanizing and her lack of parenting skills. I think she was secretly envious of me and Messiah's relationship. When we got into arguments, she would often call me, "Super Dad". I should have gotten him back years ago. I don't know why I hadn't, but I overcompensated because of it, but tonight was our night. A father and son's night out. Something that we did when he would come down to the city.

"So what's goin' on big boy? You been workin' out?" I teased grabbing his bicep.

He said what he always said, "Git' off me old man!"

"Come on, don't you love your father? Give your daddy a kiss on the mouth." I said puckering up my lips.

To which he would reply, "Stop man, what is wrong with you."

I loved every minute of it, and so did he. That was our ritual. That's how we broke the ice if we hadn't seen each other in a while.

The banter would always end with me telling him that he was going to be my baby forever, and even when he was married, I would still kiss him on the mouth in front of his wife and kids.

"Where we goin' dad?" he asked plugging his iPod into the car's auxiliary port.

"We gon' head up to Red Lobster for the All you can eat Shrimp Fest and maybe catch a movie after that man, but didn't I tell you not to mess with a Black man's radio," I said smacking his hand while doing my best Chris Tucker impression.

While Messiah was busy shuffling through his playlist, I noticed a car seemed to be following us. I made a right on Tremont and Lawrence Ave. The car made the same right. Okay, I thought to myself, it might be the police, feds, or maybe some stick- up kids.

"Messiah, you got your seatbelt on?" I asked calmly as not to alarm him.

"Yes, dad. I'm not a baby." he answered me in that voice that teenagers use when they're annoyed with us.

I kept looking in the rearview mirror. I saw that the car was still tailing us.

"Son, I don't want you to git' nervous, but I think the cops are behind us."

Like the product of his father that he was, he asked, "You don't have nothin' in the car do you, dad?"

What a sign of the times. Here was my teenage son asking me if I had anything illegal in the car.

"No, boy. You know I don't move like that. Especially not with you in the car with me. But I'ma run this red light, if they don't hit the sirens, then it ain't the boys."

I went through the red light and no sirens, but they ran the light too.

"Messiah hold on," I said as I floored it.

I was driving like a madman, driving in the wrong direction down a one-way street. Whoever it was, was right on my ass. I couldn't shake them. Where were the cops when you needed them? I drove on the wrong side of the street towards oncoming traffic. They shadowed my every move. Messiah was scared.

"Dad jus' pull over and see what they want!" he yelled terrified more of my driving than anything else.

"Shut the fuck up and hold on," I shouted as I cut the corner sharply, tires squealing.

As I turned the corner, I ran into the back of another car sitting at the light. I could hear the car chasing us screech to a halt. *Blam! Blam!*

"Messiah git' down!"

Blam! I felt a bullet tear through my neck, and then, I woke up handcuffed to a hospital bed. At first, I wasn't sure where I was. Then it all came back to me. Messiah! Sitting at my bedside was Zenobia. She was always there through thick and thin, through the ups and the downs. She would always be there. Ultimately, she was still my mother.

"Ma' where's Messiah?"

I could move, just barely. My neck was bandaged, and although I was in pain, I could wiggle my fingers and toes. Thank God.

I asked again, "Ma 'where's Messiah?"

She dipped a rag in a glass of water and wiped my face.

"He's alright baby, Messiah's fine."

But something was wrong I could tell, she wasn't looking me in the eyes. At that moment a detective walked up to a cop stationed outside of my room. He said something to the officer, took out a notepad and walked into my room.

"Lloyd glad to see you up. I'm Detective Lansky from homicide. I have to tell you; you're lucky to be alive. The bullet went straight through without hitting your spine or any major arteries," he said writing something in his pad.

His statement fell on deaf ears.

"What do you mean homicide? Ain't nobody dead. Ma', where's Messiah? Ma', where's Messiah? Ma', where's my baby? Mommy, where's Messiah?"

I was crying uncontrollably as Zenobia sat in the chair sobbing quietly. Messiah was dead. My life was gone.

"Lloyd I'm sorry for your loss, but I need to know why witnesses said that you were driving like a bat out of hell fleeing from the men who opened fire on your vehicle?" he asked.

Zenobia jumped up from her seat.

"That's enough detective. My son is lying here in a hospital bed with a bullet wound in his neck, and he's just found out his son, my grandson is dead. He's not answering any questions right now. And why do you have him handcuffed to the bed when he's the victim?"

"Fair enough. Officer Blakely come in and take the cuffs off."

He handed Zenobia his card.

"Have your son call me when he gets out of the hospital," he said, putting his notepad in his inside jacket pocket.

"No problem," Zenobia said putting his card in her purse.

I closed my eyes and replayed that night in my head over and over again. What could I have done differently? More importantly, who was to blame? I had way too much time to think while I lay in the hospital for the next two weeks. Thinking of Messiah being buried with me unable to attend his funeral. God knows I wanted to die too. Why hadn't I been killed along with him? The only thing that got me through it all was my family coming to console me and pay their respects. Everyone except Linda. I could only imagine what she must be going through. Our son was dead. I had no idea who killed him, but I knew it was because of me.

Chapter 17
The Revelation

No one from the organization came to visit me in the hospital, which I expected since the police were all over me. When Pap finally came by my house a month after I got out of the hospital, he was curiously silent.

"Whassup' brotha'? How you been doin?" he asked.

I saw the concern on his face. I looked terrible. I was walking with a cane, and I had lost nearly twenty pounds in a month. Some of it attributed to my injury, and some of it was because of my not eating properly, but that wasn't the only vibe that I was getting from him.

"Why you lookin' at me like that?" I asked trying to get up off of the couch.

Pap was the only person in our crew who knew where I lived at. No one else who had been to my new home since I had moved from Quimby Ave. years ago.

He gently put his hand on my shoulder, "Sit down homie. I got something to tell you."

I had no idea what was coming, but I knew it couldn't be good.

"I don't have to tell you; you know more than anybody else how the streets talk. Niggas can't keep their mouth shut too, well, save their lives," he said, his words trailing off.

"You know Raymond? The cat from my building? The one L.A. brought to the meeting? Well, he approached me a couple of days ago wit' some information about what happened to you and Messiah. When he told me the story, I didn't believe it at first. So I checked it out for myself, and, it was true."

In all of the years that I had known Pap, he was never one to mince words. Now he here he was barely able to speak.

"Pap please man. If you know somethin' just spit it out!"

I listened as he told me how Raymond, who was one of our bottlers, was talking to L.A., who had once been our head bottler. I fired him years ago because I suspected him of stealing, but after we started expanding, since I never had proof of his stealing, we brought him back into the fold working for me in the coalition office locating construction sites for us to find work for our people.

L.A. told Raymond that while he was out searching for construction sites, some White boys approached him and offered him twenty five thousand dollars to tell them where I lived at. He went on to tell Raymond that he would have given them my address for less than that, but he had no idea where I lived. I mulled over what I had heard.

"So how you know it's true homie?" I asked him.

"Cuz' nigga, L.A. is spendin' money like it's water," he said.

"That fucking snake," I mumbled to myself.

Pap wasn't through.

He went on to tell me, L.A. gave my sister Champagne (Charmane) ten thousand dollars for my address. I was speechless. Oh my God, Champagne, why? We had our differences in the past. I remember smacking her in the face once when she was talking about killing herself over a boyfriend, but I thought we had gotten over that. I had also given her a job answering the phones. I felt light-headed.

"Pap I need to lay down," I said walking slowly to my bedroom.

I could understand why L.A. did it. He was the type of nigga to walk over a dollar for a dime. I recall when we were on a bus once escorting the mules, I asked him what he was in the game for. I said to him that I thought he wanted his own legal business and a better life for his family. That ignorant motherfucker's response was, "That's what you git' for thinkin'. I never told you I wanted those things." I should have fired him on the spot.

I had egregiously violated two rules at the same time. Rule number 111 and number 152, rule number 111, never fuck wit' a stupid motherfucka and rule number 152, never give a thief a second chance. Stupid motherfuckas don't know any better, and thieves have no loyalty. Rules are made and put in place for good reason. I had broken both of those rules, and now I was paying for it. As for my sister, I could only come to one conclusion, and it was sad, but true, greed! She was Zenobia's daughter as much as I was her son. It had taken me a lifetime to break the cycle of amoral behavior, but Champagne was still a young snakeling.

"Pap who else knows what you told me homie?" I asked.

Nobody partner. Jus' you, me, and Raymond," he answered.

I thought about what I was about to say, "I want Sleepy and them to pay Champagne a visit. I don't care what they do to her." I paused for a second, "But I want her to suffer."

Pap looked at me, "Llord you sure? Think about what you sayin' man, thas' your sista'." I nodded my head. "Yeah you right, but Messiah was my son."

As Pap got up to leave, he asked almost as an afterthought. "What about that nigga L.A.?"

I got up off of the bed and walked him to the door, "Come git' me tonight. I wanna' personally make sure he got his money's worth."

We went to L.A.'s house around 10:00 that evening, Pap, Stan, Ya-ya, Marcus, and Roc. All of the original crew were there with me. Pap knocked on the door.

"Who is it?" It was L.A.'s wife Christina.

"It's me Pap."

Christina opened the door.

"Pap what you doin' here so late boy?" he didn't answer her.

"Chris' where's L.A.?" he asked her.

"He's in the shower. What's the matter wit' you? Why you actin' like that?"

She could sense that something was wrong. I could hear it in her voice.

Again Pap ignored her.

She called out to L.A., "L, Pap and the guys are here."

We heard him turning the water off in the shower.

"Tell them I'll be out in a minute ma'," he yelled back.

Christina turned to me, "Llord how you doin' boo? I'm so sorry to hear about Messiah."

Her sympathy was genuine.

"Thanks, babe," I said.

I had known her close to sixteen years. I had taken Messiah to their daughter's fifth birthday party. She was a sweetheart, but unfortunately for her, she had hitched her wagon to a falling star. I've said before that I was a sociopath, but I was wrong. As I pulled the ball peen hammer out of my back pocket and hit her in the face with it, I couldn't help but feel remorseful. Her blood splattered on my face as she fell to the living room floor. Her nose was spewing blood.

"Tie her up and sit her on the couch fellas'," I said.

When L.A. came out of the bathroom, Stan hit him the face with the gun.

"Don't say a fuckin' word, sit your ass down at the table."

We duct taped him to the chair and stuffed a dishrag in his mouth and taped it shut.

"I don't understand nigga. I gave you a chance to git' money wit' me time and time again, and this is how you repay me, nigga? I told you this shit was bigger than me. Bigger than us; I hope it was worth it!" I said as I began to beat Christina about the face and head until I heard her skull crack.

I was covered in blood. I went to the sink and rinsed off my face and hands. Through the gag in L.A.'s mouth, you could hear him pleading in a high pitch guttural moan, but I wasn't finished. I went under the kitchen sink and grabbed the bleach. I walked over to his sixty-gallon fish tank filled with exotic saltwater fish. L.A.'s pride and joy. I began to empty the bleach into it. We watched in amusement as the fish struggled for air in the bleach-filled water until they floated to the surface of the tank one by one.

Ya-ya and Roc had already taped and tied up their daughter Crystal. It took every bit of callous in my body, but it had to be done. I took a sheet off of her bed and knotted it around her neck. Once I had it tight, Ya-ya and Roc pulled it over the top of her bedroom door and attached it to the doorknob. Her hands were tied behind her back, so all she could do was flail her legs and kick at the door. She shit and pissed on herself as they hoisted her tiny eleven-year-old frame up off of the floor. I watched as the blood vessels in her eyes burst, and the flailing subsided. Until finally, nothing. May God forgive us.

There was no expression on L.A.'s face, just a blank stare. He watched as I poured bleach down the drain to wash away any DNA evidence. We poured gas throughout his apartment, over Crystal, Christina, and then him. I can only imagine that he had no reason to resist. He sat there without making a sound.

"Aight' fellas, it's time to go," Pap said, pouring gasoline on the blood-covered jacket I had now taken off. He lit the jacket on fire and tossed it into the apartment and closed the door.

The next morning's headlines would read, "Three bodies found in an apartment building burned beyond recognition." On page twelve in the Daily News, there would be a small article about the body of a "Young Hispanic or African-American woman found decapitated and dismembered in a plastic bag on a Harlem street."

Some days later, I got a call from Detective Lansky asking me to come to the 43rd precinct and answer some questions. I hadn't spoken to him since the death of Messiah. I told him I would come in early the next morning. That morning as I got dressed I thought of Messiah again. I could see him plugging in his iPod. I put on my coat and headed out the door. When I arrived at the precinct, I told the officer at the front desk I was there to see Detective Lansky. He pointed in the direction of the stairs.

"Hello Lloyd, come in."

As we walked back to the interrogation room, I saw a banner hanging over the desk of a detective that read, "Remember you are hunting a dangerous animal." It was extremely offensive, but status quo for "New York's Finest."

"What can I do for you detective?" I asked irritated. Already put off by the banner.

"Well, let's see Lloyd. Where do I start? Your mother filed a missing person's report on your sister who worked for you. Another one of your employees, Douglass Curry, also known as L.A., and his entire family were murdered. Not to mention, less than two months ago your son was killed riding in the car with you. It seems to me that everyone that comes in contact with you ends up dead. So you tell me, what can you do for me?"

I knew he didn't have anything on me. If he did, I would have been in cuffs already.

"I really don't know detective. I'm torn up over what's goin' on. As far as I know, I don't have any enemies. I mean, the only thing that comes to mind is maybe some other coalition is tryin' to muscle me out of the business. Besides that, I don't have a clue," I said.

He asked me a few more questions before letting me go, the last one being, you know, that TV shit "Where were you two nights ago?"

To which I replied, "I was in the house with a bottle of vodka which I find myself drinking more of since the death of my son."

What I said was partially true. I was starting to drink every night to fall asleep. As distraught as I was with the death of Joharra this was much worse. The pain was incomparable.

As I left the precinct, Detective Lansky told me he'd be in touch. I called Spencer. I wanted to go to Messiah's grave and place flowers on his tombstone. Linda still wasn't accepting any of my calls. I understood, but I was hoping that we could have been there for each other.

It was an hour's drive to the cemetery in Jersey. I couldn't help but notice the birds flying overhead. It was a beautiful October day. It took me some time to find his grave. When I did, I cleared a place in front of his tombstone to place the roses. I said the Lord's Prayer and began to wonder and ask myself the same question that I had asked L.A., was it worth it? I contemplated where I had come from, from drug abuser to drug dealer, to businessman, to eventually evolving into, for lack of a better word, a militant, but what were the circumstances that brought me to this point?

I began to realize that racism is but a small part of what ails Black America. For me, the Skinheads or other racist organizations are not our problems. For me, it's the Banks, insurance companies, and car dealerships that participate in the practice of redlining. The companies that pay me less for doing the same job as my White counterparts or pass me over for promotions, but we have to accept responsibility for our shortcomings as well. Who should we blame for the fifty pairs of sneakers, thousands of dollars' worth of jewelry, and no health insurance, a sixty thousand dollar car and no home? Who should we blame for Black men not being fathers to our children? Who should we blame for our sons emulating thugs and pimps? Who should we blame for our daughters gauging the value of a man by the material things he possesses over his education? The answer to all of the above questions is us!

Listen, if we're to keep placing blame at the feet of White America for our problems, then perhaps we should bestow the title of father, master, or God on them as well. If we're not ready to do that, then we must begin to hold ourselves accountable for the state that we're in. We have enough money in our communities to open up our own banking institutions, schools, pharmaceutical companies, automobile factories and so on.

The esteemed Dr. Dennis Kimbro has noted that Black America, with an annual income of over a trillion dollars, is the sixteenth wealthiest nation in the world, but our dollars stay in our community for less than six hours, and less than forty percent of us have bank accounts. Meanwhile, our entertainers and athletes are in the clubs spending thousands on alcohol and making it rain, but by no means am I suggesting that America should be let off the hook. I'm aware of the fact that no matter how successful our entrepreneurs, their businesses will have to pay taxes to a system that doesn't have our economic wellbeing in mind. To those of you who disagree, I ask that you look up a class action lawsuit brought against The USDA. In that lawsuit, Black farmers documented how the U.S. Department of Agriculture methodically denied Black farmers aid, while giving aid to White farmers.

It wasn't until 1999 that some 20,000 of these farmers were awarded monies that had been denied for decades. In 2008, that bill was amended to include another 70,000 of these Black farms, but before 1999, and in between 1999-2008, tens of thousands of Black farmers were forced to file for bankruptcy losing their land and their livelihood. In the end, again, I'm not a racist, I'm a capitalist. Unfortunately, there will always be prejudice in some form or fashion around the world, that's not my concern. My focus at this juncture is self-empowerment. As for those athletes, entertainers, businessmen, and millionaires who feel they don't have to give back or be role models to our children, guess what? You don't, but we're watching you.

So is it worth it? It has to be. There will always be casualties and collateral damage in war, and yes, Black America, we are at war, and bloodshed is the price of victory. The other question I continuously ask myself, why has God spared my life, time and time again? A God, who is merciful, but just. Surely, I'm not doing the Lord's work? Or am I? I'll have to wait and see.

Spencer walked up behind me and handed me a burner phone. On the other end was Pap. "Llord, Malik said that Mumin and Kasir wanna meet wit' you at 8:00 tonight. You know the spot."

Yeah, I knew where it was at.

"Aight' man. Tell em' I'll be there."

I stood up, "Take care baby. Daddy will see you soon. I love you." I said kissing Messiah's tombstone.

I.Y. WADE

Are African Americans Being Recruited by ISIS?

Protesters in a street showed defiance of a midnight curfew meant to stem ongoing demonstrations in reaction to the shooting of Michael Brown in Ferguson, Missouri (August 2014)

Considering the social conflict between cops and protesters in Ferguson, Missouri, the terrorist group commonly known as the Islamic State of Iraq and Syria (ISIS) is using the strategic moment in American history to recruit African-Americans to join the Islamic State's jihadist movement.

Those fighting alongside ISIS, a globally growing terrorist group in which U.S. Secretary of Defense Chuck Hagel said was "as sophisticated and well-funded as any terrorist we have ever seen", have made no secret that they have vowed to bring turmoil to America. ISIS members promised to "divide America in two", while their spokesman Abu Mosa promised to raise the flag of Allah over the White House.

In the aftermath of the clash between militant police forces and protesters in the St. Louis suburb, the <u>Washington Post</u> reports that many ISIS members see the Michael Brown shooting and confrontation between Black citizens and government forces as confirmation that the terrorist group's ideas of oppression and racism in America are completely accurate.

In attempts to reach out to the black community, supporters of ISIS have started the social network hashtag movement #FergusonUnderIS and #ISISHERO. An organization that tracks online terrorist activity said that most of those tweets and post on social sites are targeted directly toward Black Americans.

Chapter 18
Armageddon

It was 8:01 in the evening and Kasir and Mumin were running late. It was only a minute after 8:00, but I was pacing back and forth looking at my watch.

"Malik I hope these cats don't have us waitin' all fuckin' night," I said.

Malik checked the time on his cellphone.

"Llord relax, give em' ten more minutes. If they ain't here by then, I'ma give Mumin a call."

No sooner than he said that, a late model Lexus pulled up. Kasir was sitting in the passenger seat, Mumin was driving, and there was a third man sitting in the back seat.

I couldn't make out his face, but his skin was so black, his complexion looked blue. As the car pulled up in front of Malik and me, it came to a stop. Mumin got out and opened up the door for this Willie looking African dude. The three of them walked over to us.

"As-salamu alaykum," Malik said to our Arab comrades kissing the two of them on the cheek.

"Walaikum salam brothers. This is brother Amadou Mohammed Sideeku." Mumin said with his hand on the African brother's back.

The African had a briefcase in his left hand as he walked over to greet the two of us.

"Brother Llord, Mumin and Kasir have told me a lot of good things about you and your people, and while our causes are different, our goals are the same."

I can't say if I knew exactly what his cause was, but it didn't matter. My goal at the moment was money.

"Are you ready to proceed?" Amadou asked.

"Brotha', my people and I have been ready for this since you and my ancestors were brought here in chains. The more important question is are you ready to pay?" I asked shivering.

It was getting cold. I could see my breath when I spoke.

"Where you from brotha'?" I asked Amadou.

I wanted to feel him out before we got down to business. You can never be too cautious or suspicious. The feds get to everyone, but it was of no consequence, even if Malik was ready to give up without a fight, I wasn't. I didn't have anything to live for. Messiah was dead. I didn't care if I lived, died, or had to kill.

Amadou said he was from Mogadishu, Somalia. I knew very little about it except that Somalia is involved in piracy and has been a war zone for the last twenty years. I guess you could say it's the South Bronx of Africa. It wasn't a detailed resume, but it would have to do.

"Let's git' down to business brotha," I said cutting to the chase. "My people and I are willin' to place explosives on buses, trains, and bridges for a small fee."

He said nothing.

I continued, "We're ready to place explosives on buses for $100,000, on a train, for $250,000, and on any bridge for a mere $1,000,000.

Before I could finish, he let out a sigh and interrupted me.

"Brother Llord, for that amount of money my people could place the explosives ourselves," he spoke with a conviction that could be mistaken for arrogance.

I hate to feed into stereotypes, but Africans are known to be frugal. Here we were talking about not only changing history, but making it as well, and he wanted to haggle over prices.

I could have walked away right then and there, but I put my hand on his shoulder and explained as plainly as I could how the profiling of Muslims would make it nearly impossible for his organization to carry it out.

"Yes, brotha', you're right, except for one detail, the federal government is all over the African and Arab community," I said, speaking to him with just as much conviction if not more.

"My people and I are homegrown terrorists. Our numbers are too many to monitor. If we carry out just one bombing, the effect that it will have on the American economy will be in the millions. The effect that it will have on the American psyche will be priceless. America ain't Israel. If a bus or train blows up, Americans ain't gittin' back on one no time soon. So you in or out?" I asked extending my hand to shake on the deal.

"You are truly wise beyond your years Llord. You have missed your calling. You should be a general fighting a war somewhere."

I smiled, looked him in his eyes and said, "I am."

He smiled back, "What guarantee do I have that you will not cross me once you have my money?" he asked.

I took no offense to his question; it was completely reasonable.

"What I can tell you is this, while I'm no boy scout, I live, and I die for my honor, which means more to me than any amount of money. Besides, like you said, our cause is one and the same.

Amadou looked at Malik and me, turned and sat the briefcase on the hood of the Lexus. He removed five $10,000 stacks of money and handed the briefcase to Malik.

"There is $250,000 in this case. I expect to hear from you soon with a date as to when you will be moving forward."

Malik took the money out of the briefcase, put in it a black garbage bag, and handed the briefcase back to Amadou. Again you can never be too careful, who knows if there was a tracking device in the briefcase.

"Brotha' Amadou, you won't be gittin' a call from us. Watch the news like the rest of America."

We shook hands, said our Salaams, and they were on their way.

As they left Ya-ya called Malik on his cell phone, "It's all clear. Marcus and Doggie are watchin' the Ave."

Malik called Pap and told him we would be meeting him at our stash house in the Webster Houses. As we pulled out from under the Third Avenue Bridge, Malik looked at me, "We did it, bro'! We did it," he said.

I could have said, "This is just the beginning. We still have a lot of work to do. We have to get our message out to our brothers in the South, the Midwest, the West Coast, the Southeast, and all throughout the North. We need guns, land, and businesses. We have to teach our people that the world is bigger than America. Explain to them that technology is making it possible to do business all over the world. We have to start with the children. We have to instill a pride in being Black in them. We have to teach them that they are more than ballplayers, rappers, booty shakers, and thugs. Teach them that they are the future mothers and fathers of our race. Teach them that they're our future educators, engineers, captains of industry, lawyers, doctors, judges, Secretaries of State, and yes even the future Presidents and First Ladies of this country." Instead, I let Malik savor the moment.

"Yeah man, we did it," I said, turning on the radio.

259

Credits for Contributing Articles and Inserts

Institute for Children, Poverty& Homelessness, Feb. 2012

National Public Radio/www.NPR.org, July 5, 2012

Janell Ross/ Nancy DiTomaso, Mar. 29, 2013

Wikipedia, Dec. 2009, 2013-2014

Samuel Smith/ Reporter for the Christian Post, Aug. 24, 2014

All scripture quotations are taken from the King James Version of the Bible

261